THE DEVIL'S MUSIC

THE COMPANY FILES: 3

THE DEVIL'S MUSIC

THE COMPANY FILES: 3

GABRIEL VALJAN

Praise for The Devil's Music

"A tour de force."—Rhys Bowen, international bestselling author of *The Venice Sketchbook*, The Royal Spyness and Molly Murphy series

"Valjan's sharp-as-a-stiletto, vintage-flavored prose and deft hand with suspense and intrigue earns *The Devil's Music* a place on the shelf with classic mystery authors like Chandler and Macdonald."—Ellen Byron, Agatha Award winner and *USA Today* bestselling author

"Compelling and memorable characters."—Tina deBellegarde, Agatha Award-nominated author of *Winter Witness*, a Batavia-on-Hudson Mystery

Characters

- **Jack Marshall**: Company man.
- **Betty Marshall**: Jack Marshall's wife.
- **Elizabeth Marshall**: Jack Marshall's daughter.
- **Walter Bedell Smith**: Jack Marshall's former boss.
- **Walker**: Company operative. Alias: Walter Thompson.
- **Irwin Adler**: Writer for radio and screen.
- **Judith née Kaplan Nussbaum**: Mr. Adler's sister-in-law.
- **Roy Cohn**: Lawyer with Senator Joseph McCarthy.
- **Robert Kennedy**: Assistant counsel to Senator Joseph McCarthy.
- **Leslie**: Company operative. Alias: Margaret Gardner.
- **Vera Williams**: Actress.
- **Frank "The Prime Minister" Costello**: Crime boss.
- **Steps**: Associate of Frank Costello.
- **Vito "Don Vitone" Genovese**: Crime Boss.
- **Carmine "Lilo" Galante**: Associate of Vito Genovese.
- **Sheldon**: Company ally.
- **Tania**: Former refugee and Sheldon's "niece."
- **Albert Anastasia**: Associate of Frank Costello and enforcer of Murder Incorporated.
- **Johnny "Mercury" Mercuro**: Associate of Frank Costello.
- **John Ford**: Director.
- **Jack "JL" Warner**: Studio executive.

Chapter One

It was hot in Virginia that night, and the cicadas hummed like electric wires in the evening air. There was the occasional glow of a lightning bug. This was the waiting game. Two phones were on the desk.

They waited, Jack Marshall and his wife Betty.

Seated, her fingers knitted something invisible. He leaned back, contemplating the sky outside the open window, as his chair pulled music up from the floorboards with its rocking back and forth. Two fingers of whiskey gone, a short glass rested on the blotter when the white phone rang.

The front legs of his chair slammed down. He picked up the receiver. Her fingers stopped. A man's garbled monotone worked his ear. She stared when he said, "I understand. That's unfortunate. Thank you for calling."

"It's done, isn't it?"

"Yes. He went first, around eight. She took longer, about five tries, but it was all over by eight sixteen."

Betty shook her head. "You said all they had to do was talk, and none of this would've happened. How will I explain this to the children tomorrow after they see the morning papers?"

Jack went to say something, but the other phone rang, the beige one. She knew what that meant. He told her, "Go and check in on them, please. I'll be with you in a moment."

The phone was still ringing, his hand on top of the receiver. Secure line.

"I will." Betty closed the door behind her.

Jack picked up the phone mid-ring.

"Hello. Yeah, I heard, Beetle. Our man on the inside told me everything."

The insect music outside had stopped while he listened to his old army friend, Walter Bedell Smith. The nickname Beetle was a twist on his middle name. Beetle spoke with a Hoosier accent. The Rs dominated in words like Truman, reprieve, Eisenhower, Reds, and J. Edgar Hoover.

Jack hung up the phone. Beetle had done all the talking. He listened.

Betty was correct. All they had to do was talk.

Beetle called it three years ago when he said that the statute from 1940 would've sufficed for the prosecution. 18 United States Code § 2381 was clear about "aid and comfort within…or elsewhere." The prosecutor, Irving Saypol, and his assistant, Roy Cohn, decided otherwise and chose a law from 1917 for their legal strategy instead.

Beetle argued that prison time would've softened the edges and everybody could've saved face; could've had a nice conversation around a table, gotten some names, and everybody would've walked away with something.

It didn't end up that way.

The Company had a man inside Sing Sing watching Hoover's men in their makeshift offices stacked with supplies, waiting to take down the next Tolstoy novel, their typewriters and tape recorders ready and waiting for the signal that never came.

All they needed was one word from the rabbi that they'd wanted to talk. One word.

Anything and everything would've come to a stop. A simple word from either one of them would have ended it all. It didn't even have to be "I confess." Even with Eisenhower denying clemency it would've stopped had Hoover's boys gotten the word.

That didn't happen.

Julius and Ethel Rosenberg died this night, June 19, 1953.

And like Beetle said, "She called his bluff, Jack. Hoover and his boys got nothing. Ditto for us. We went to the county fair and have nothing to show for it. Nothing but acres of corn as far as the eye can see. It's back to the game of proportionate responses. The Soviets do one thing. We respond like a reflection in the mirror. You know what's coming next, don't you?"

The cicadas returned for an encore. The sun had set, a quarter moon started to rise. Jack Marshall didn't answer his former boss about what came next. They both knew.

A lightning bug lifted outside Jack's window, a soft yellow glow before it disappeared into the dark, and there was that sound again, electricity in the wires, the music of martyrs.

Chapter Two

Click. Click. Clickety-click.

There were the thumps of the space bar, the hand to the lever on the left side of the typewriter to slide the carriage over after the bell. Another line, another step toward the bottom of the page. The sound of Walker's writing competed with a visitor outside his Malibu home. A woodpecker.

The redhead had introduced himself a few days earlier while Walker sat outside on his porch. The bird landed on the railing and assessed Walker with one beady eye, flew off, and then returned moments later, this time on the other side of the patio, to render his approval with the other eye.

They'd come to an agreement, between the bird's music and his writing. The bird would drum its beat, and Walker would peck at the keys on the Remington typewriter Terry Doyle had stolen from Warner Brothers in Burbank as a farewell present after Walker finished his stint at the studio as Walter Thompson for the Company.

Terry assumed he could score the five-finger discount without Jack Warner knowing about it. Wrong. Warner sent Terry a set of replacement ribbons with a handwritten note.

Mr. Doyle,

These ribbons could work wonders around your feet, like chains did for Bo Weinberg. Likewise, the typewriter you stole from me would make a fine anchor for your swim off any pier. Give WT my regards.

JL

The typewriter was a mark of respect between writers since this particular model was given to senior writers. Novices received black Remington Noiseless Model Sevens, often decrepit and with cracked paint. Walker's model was a block of green steel. The inside covers of the carrying case were lined with felt. The green keys were silky. The tab and trim were tight. The color suited Walker since he was an army man.

His Friday ritual at the desk was to include a cold bottle of Adohr milk within reach while he wrote. Adohr Milk Farms dispatched the same man his way for deliveries. Walker waited for the blue truck out of Tarzana with Adohr-able Milk, the farm's slogan, painted on the sides. Drivers wore starched white uniforms, dark bow ties, and caps.

Elmo was Walker's man. In addition to fresh cheese and eggs, Walker paid Elmo extra to bring a variety of newspapers from Los Angeles. Elmo was a sad-eyed vet, a working stiff with a gimp leg and the worst case of nerves around sudden sounds. A navy veteran, Elmo had served in the Pacific theatre. Walker understood the man's sorrows, even if he had served on the other side of the world.

Walker poured off the cream into a glass for the icebox and placed it next to the bottles of Bull Dog beer. He returned with the milk to his desk. His mother would have disapproved, but time in the infantry in France, Germany, and Italy did away with the courtesy of a glass from the cupboard. Walker saw himself as a grown man, and he could do as he pleased. He'd earned numerous combat decorations and deserved his milk straight from the bottle. After the war, he joined Jack Marshall in Vienna and went to work for the Company. They interviewed and recruited former Nazis. When someone wasn't killing them first.

Mother passed years ago. No woman was around to civilize him, not even Leslie. She'd made that decision for the both of them in Vienna and finalized it in Los Angeles. Walker wondered what Mother would've thought of Leslie.

After Vienna, the next big job for Jack was to work at Warner Bros. A script doctor and intermediary between studios and blacklisted writers had been murdered and a clue suggested Hoover was up to something. That operation ended two years ago. He left the studio on good terms, which was a remarkable feat since Jack Warner turned into a cobra with anyone who poached talent from his studio. Warner, to his credit, extended an open invitation to Walker to work freelance on projects.

Hours later, he rose from his desk, the pages stacked. A day's work finished. At five forty-five in the afternoon, the phone rang. Walker answered it and heard Jack Marshall's voice. "The Rosenbergs were executed."

Walker glanced at his wristwatch. Three-hour difference. "What do you need?"

"I need to bring you in. In addition to Jay Edgar and his pet senator from Wisconsin, we have a problem, and its initials are RC."

"Roy Cohn."

Walker heard Jack sigh. Rare. The first time Walker heard that exhalation was when they had been relieved in Alsace, only to receive orders to march into Germany. Neither of them had known that Dachau was waiting for them, or that men in their unit would execute Nazis on the spot.

"You there?" Jack asked.

"I'm here. An unpleasant thought came over me."

"Roy Cohn has that effect on people, but it gets worse."

"Worse?"

"Now that Roy has made his reputation with the Rosenbergs, he has the fire in his belly, and he'll want to settle old scores. He's bringing ammunition."

"Ammo? What more does he need? McCarthy and Hoover back him." Walker rubbed his forehead, the onset of a headache because of a name. Roy Cohn was the one mortal who'd dare to breach the gates of hell, just so he could throw Old Scratch off his throne. "What's he thinking?"

"Cohn plans to deliver on McCarthy's accusation that Reds have infiltrated the military, and Cohn will target government contractors, and there's more."

Walker understood the implications. The Company had recruited Nazis and some Soviets in Vienna. These engineers, scientists, and technicians were then rehabilitated and embedded in various companies around the country to beat the Russians in the arms race. Cohn's sweep for Communists meant exposure, a liability in the Company's rivalry with Hoover's FBI.

"You said there's more, Jack. Who or what does he have?"

"An ambitious twenty-seven-year-old from Boston."

"Anybody we know?"

Pause.

"Kennedy," Jack said.

"The leash is off the dog, and the lawn just got bigger."

The name Kennedy irritated people in DC like a cheap wool sweater. Washed up in politics after Churchill threw him off the Cliffs of Dover because he had alienated everyone as an isolationist, courted Hitler, and, like Charles Lindberg, disliked Jews, former Ambassador Joseph Kennedy was at it again. Everybody knew the old man wanted a son behind the desk in the highest office of the land. His oldest boy, Joe Jr., had died in an accident during the war. His next-oldest son was now the US Senator from Massachusetts.

"John Kennedy," Walker said. "He wants to climb the ladder for daddy?"

"It's what I was thinking, but not him."

Walker did the math again and wondered what he'd added up wrong, and then imagined Hoover's hand in the matter. John Kennedy had worked in Naval Intelligence until Hoover relocated him to the Pacific and started a file on him. Ensign John F. Kennedy cut a romantic figure in his navy whites, despite the unfortunate habit of leaving his fly unzipped. Hoover documented every wrinkle in the bedsheets and recorded every groan in numerous bedrooms. John must've suspected because he resorted to using closets for his conquests. That Hoover hated the Kennedys was an understatement; he loathed the entire family.

Hoover's love for leverage hit the jackpot when Jack Kennedy bedded a blonde number who had interviewed Adolph Hitler. It didn't matter to J. Edgar the woman despised der Führer. All that mattered to him was he had pictures of her on Hitler's arm at the Olympics and Uncle Adolph was fond of her. Even called her a "Nordic beauty."

"If not Jack Kennedy, who then?" Walker asked.

"His brother Robert. He's co-counsel with Cohn."

Walker swallowed hard. "I did not see that coming."

"Nobody did."

"Add him to Cohn and McCarthy, and we have a trinity."

"Correct," Jack said. "And with Hoover dancing on top of his desk in the dark, if they could help him bury the Company."

Jack was right. Roy Cohn and Robert Kennedy would act as McCarthy's bloodhounds, and J. Edgar Hoover would jump at the chance to rip out Allen Dulles's throat. Allen bore the distinction of being the Company's first civilian director and having Eisenhower's ear about policy against the Soviets, which left Hoover passive and at a tactical disadvantage. His agency played defense and the Company, offense. Add one last indignity: Hoover had no say when Truman formalized the existence of the Company on September 18, 1947. Nothing Hoover hated more than not having power. Nothing.

It was clear as the cursive on the blackboard. Go Commie hunting with two feral lawyers, find former Nazis and Soviet émigrés hard at work within the government's defense industry, and the Company was kaput. Hoover didn't care that the recruits kept the Stars and Stripes ahead of the Russian bear.

"I would've put my money on Jack Kennedy," Walker said.

"John's not the picture of health. Bad back from the war and all. His father moved on to the next healthiest. Robert Francis Kennedy is our man."

"For the presidency?"

"Doubt it," Jack answered. "Big Company America would never allow it. They'll outspend Joe Kennedy, and the last time the country considered a Catholic for the office was when Al Smith ran. Not sure if you remember this, Walker, but the Ku Klux Klan marched on the Capitol because they thought Catholics were un-American."

Walker remembered. The Klan attacked Catholics in his Midwest before, during, and after Prohibition. He recalled their "America First" rallies and parade marches. As for Al Smith, he had been tainted by his association with the corruption of Tammany Hall and his opposition to Prohibition. Al lost, and Hoover carried forty states and won.

Walker had another concern. "Kennedy can't be naïve. Roy Cohn and Hoover will have him run point and then throw him to the curb while the car is moving. What's your plan?"

"Come east before Roy Cohn sets fire to Hollywood with a new book of matches. He tried once, and he'll take another run at you and Jack Warner."

Jack had a point. He and Cohn had clashed during a clearance meeting with Warner's man, Leonard Moore. The skirmish left Cohn humiliated and with an appetite for revenge that rivaled Jack Warner's but lacked the mogul's refined methods.

"I'll get on the next bird out of Burbank."

"Excellent. That leaves me with just one more thing to do."

"What's that?"

"I need to bring Leslie in also."

Walker hung up the receiver. His friend, the woodpecker, drummed his tree. Walker looked at his typewriter. The green Remington could take a round of shrapnel. The Adohr milk bottle next to it looked like a glass grenade, only now it was either Roy Cohn, this young Kennedy kid, or both, who were about to pull the pin and lob the next explosive.

Chapter Three

Jack needed to reel Leslie in because as Margaret Gardener, secretary to the late Phillip Ernest, therapist to the stars, she'd thwarted J. Edgar Hoover's network of psychoanalysts and Hollywood informants. One of the best agents the British had during the war, Leslie had fooled Jack once when MI6 embedded her in his office in Vienna, and she fooled him and Walker yet again when she took to the hills above LA with a girlfriend, the actress Vera Williams.

Gone it seemed were her days of daring and disguises, of infiltrating Hitler's inner circle and killing enemies with her good looks, or with a Radom, a Polish-made pistol. Jack understood the experiment in domesticity, though he suspected that Leslie, or Maggie, as Vera called her, would soon swap the apron strings for a garrote when the novelty wore off. Leslie was too hot in the blood to stay tamed. Nonetheless, with Roy let loose, he had to rein her in for her own safety and do it with the skill of a pianist at the keys, soft and subtle.

Leslie lived with Vera Williams on Mulholland Drive, in a house on a hill with two bedrooms, two bathrooms, and attached bungalows. What Vera Williams enjoyed most about her home was the place in the evening when there were constellations, above and around her. Everybody who was someone in the picture industry came to her house on Fridays. Her Los Angeles at night glittered to the horizon, aglow with stardust, lights, and crushed dreams.

The midnight soirée at Vera's place had the usual cast. Ronald Reagan was there in the corner with his friend Bill Holden. Reagan wore grey slacks and a white shirt open at the collar, not for showing off that broad chest of his, but to give his Adam's apple some space since he was loquacious and lush tonight, more so than usual. Next to him, Bill Holden was holding court with a potted palm and a vodka scepter.

"It was a warning to any spies out there," Reagan said. "Betray your country and you'll end up in the hot seat like the Rosenbergs in Sing Sing. Law-abiding Americans can sleep tight and white tonight."

Ronnie's next speech would be about how to stop those "godless Soviets."

Groups of writers were split between two davenports, while Ron continued his oration. Hired help offered canapés on silver trays. Some of these writers were blacklisted and wrote under pseudonyms or "fronts." Everybody knew this and called them by their aliases.

Studio spies attended Vera's shindig, but few talked to the screenwriters, blacklisted or not. Nobody wanted to hear or read themselves quoted in either a Hooper or Parson column, or in some hush-hush magazine the next day—or worse, find themselves called before the House Un-American Activities Committee.

Vera wore a dramatic black gown of silk and crepe with mesh panels that revealed a hint of flesh from the side. She was a star with an orbit of warm admirers, and trailing behind her was Margaret Gardner, her companion.

Maggie didn't mind playing backup to Vera. Her starlet dress was a blue-bias cut number in velvet with a silk bodice. Velvet might have seemed rich for June, but it was late in the evening and the wind off the Hollywood Hills ran with some ice.

A pair of headlights raked the main window. No one thought much of it, although some of the Europeans in the room, Maggie included, had that reflex from the war to look up and listen for planes. It was just a car, possibly another late-arriving guest. At the last party Harry Hay showed up with a hired van, lights on, and a portable piano strapped in the back. The piano was a cheap number with a few good octaves left on its wires. Harry exhibited some flair on the ivories in a Noël Coward sort of way, but he'd lost most of his audience later when he discussed politics and Hopi mysticism. Ronny couldn't stand the man, ridiculing Harry for his lavender tie and gold-twist cufflinks.

This car belonged to Lenny Moore, Jack Warner's clearance man. The car doors clapped shut twice because Lenny traveled with a bodyguard. Moore had taken his hat off, out of respect for Vera. The muscle with Lenny was a squat man, in a two-piece suit that was as fashionable as the '46 Town & Country two-door convertible behind him. Leslie followed Vera to greet Lenny.

"Pardon my intrusion, Miss Williams."

"Must we be so formal? You and your friend should come inside for a drink."

"No, thank you. I'm here with a message from Mr. Warner."

That Moore had ventured out in the middle of the night, that he'd gone up into the hills to bring the word of Warner meant something was important. Moore acted as the studio head's prophet and warned Jack Warner of any legal issues before they became liabilities.

"What is Mr. Warner's message?"

"JL is preoccupied and worried."

"Worried about what? I can take it." Vera clasped her hands behind her back. Maggie put her hand over hers. Vera gave it a solid squeeze.

Moore's own hand worked the brim of his hat while he talked. "The Rosenbergs were executed, and Mr. Warner believes Roy Cohn and HUAC will run more names through the gauntlet, and he thinks yours will come up."

"And I take it that you agree with him."

"Given your support of blacklisted writers, yes. JL thinks it'll get nastier than usual."

"You came here with a plan, didn't you?"

Moore's fedora rotated like a roulette wheel, and it was time to choose a color. Red was for Communist, or black, as in out of a job.

"I suggested to JL that you take an extended trip before HUAC revoked your passport. I said to him that the studio can say 'health reasons,' or 'in need of R&R,' or some other nonsense, but JL had a better idea. His idea is a good one, Vera."

Vera's hand tightened around Maggie's. "Out with it, then."

"He wants you to go to New York and work the stage."

"More like kick me to queer street and become invisible is more like it."

"I beg to differ," Moore said. "JL's idea is genius, if you'll let me explain."

"Then explain," Vera said, her grip strong.

"HUAC has to find you to serve their subpoena. Keep a low profile and you'll be safe in New York. HUAC hasn't had any success in serving a subpoena to anyone who works theatre, on or off Broadway."

"Did you forget that the Rosenbergs were executed in New York?"

"You'll be in your element, Vera, only on a different coast."

Moore appealed to Vera's sense of community. Writers who didn't jump in the car for Mexico or board a plane or a ship for Europe found work on Broadway.

"Not for nothing, Lenny, but Broadway doesn't pay."

"JL said he'll honor your contract until the weather clears."

That was proof God existed. Jack Warner was willing to shell out dough.

"Been a long time since I've worked the stage. I don't have much choice, do I?"

Moore shook his head. The chauffeur stood there stone-faced.

"You won't be alone, Vera," Moore said.

"I know that, Lenny. I've got Maggie."

"Of course you do, but what I meant is JL is sending someone else back east with you."

"Who?" Maggie asked.

"A fellow I stole once from one of your parties. Walter Thompson."

The couple watched Moore's car pull away. Pebbles kicked up and chattered against the underside of the vehicle. Maggie didn't mind hearing the name Walter Thompson, but she knew that Jack Warner wasn't behind the idea. Only one person could pull the lights off a Hollywood set and swing them over to the New York stage that fast. Only Jack Marshall.

Chapter Four

Walker shared the cabin of the Lockheed Connie with two businessmen. An eight-hour flight, give or take, for the red-eye from southern California to LaGuardia Airport was more than enough time to review the thick envelope from Jack, handed to him by a courier before boarding.

Two Ivy Leaguers sat opposite him. Government contractors. Both men looked fresh off Boeing's corporate press, with briefcases, hair Brylcreemed and parted to the side, skinny dark ties, shirts white and starched and tucked into gray slacks. Their mother had sent her Bobbsey Twins into the world with matching gray jackets and white Cagney pocket squares. When Walker said he'd take the next bird out of Burbank, he meant a military flight. The only thing military on this Lockheed were the two vets flying the plane and himself.

Walker tried not to think of his days and nights inside of a Douglas C-47 Skytrain over Europe where he waited for the signal from the sergeant ahead of him. Walker confirmed today's sky. There were no clouds of metal flak or lightning coming up from gunners on the ground, no line, no single file, and no "Geronimo" out the open door into the cold and bottomless air.

As soon as they achieved altitude, Walker undid the clasp and extracted a fat stack of typed-up intelligence and a dog-eared manuscript. He read the latest on the happy couple, Leslie and Vera, and did his best to remain objective. He wondered what the surveillance Jack ran on him said. He imagined it all on the page, the weekday noted and the time military, and the ink, purple.

- *Subject writes several hours a day. [Remington Quiet Riter, 1951 model]*
- *Subject consumes one bottle of [Adohr] milk while writing. Friday habit.*
- *Milk deliveryman. [Negro veteran. Pacific theater. Purple Heart, Okinawa]*
- *No visitors except for one pileated woodpecker [male]. [No female companionship]*
- *Non-smoker. Low alcohol consumption [3 bottles of Bull Dog beer weekly].*

And so on and so forth. Every bracketed bit of information was a potential pressure point, a soft spot for blackmail. His life in Malibu was about as exciting as a monk during Lent. Walker's eyes arrived at a new name on the page in his lap.

Irwin Adler, except Adler wasn't Adler. His real last name was unpronounceable. Too Jewish for the entertainment crowd, so he changed it. Legally. Walker skimmed the bibliography. The man was no hack, but Irwin was a little stale to be doing theatre, unless he'd taken a crash course in playwriting with Professor Kenneth Thorpe Rowe or his star student, Arthur Miller.

Irwin Adler was on a self-imposed sabbatical from radio, from CBS in Midtown Manhattan, thanks to Senator McCarthy from Wisconsin. Irwin upped and left because the clearance company CBS used to monitor employees had located a speck of dust. Networks kept lists and exchanged them with private security firms for more names. Jack and Walker referred to the lot of them as The Rat Train. Everyone around the boardroom table was paranoid about subversives in their midst and the morality leagues boycotting their station.

CBS was working hard to shake off the joke within the industry that CBS stood for the Communist Broadcasting Company. Irwin Adler hit the pavement before he received the pink slip. He relocated to off-Broadway to wrangle a cast of misfits for meager pay with his script and limited budget.

Walker read the man's personal details. Adler sat atop the tip of the perfect triangle of catastrophe called the mid-life crisis. His wife was AWOL, off with another man. Mortgage payments were past due. Then there was something Walker hadn't expected: medical bills for a kid. Adler had refused to institutionalize the child. Walker thumbed through the rest of the dossier.

Jack had copped a draft of Adler's manuscript. Walker fanned the pages, read the title page and suppressed a groan. Jack had sent him a musical. Walker couldn't hold a note as a choirboy, but Jack seemed to think Walker could pull the con off. Jack had clipped something behind the title page of the manuscript. Typed **ROSEMARY KENNEDY, 1941** on front, Walker unsealed the envelope and unfolded the document. He winced at what he read in the medical report. Jack had provided the personal and painful material to either drive Kennedy away or remind him that family secrets don't live in attics forever. He inserted the item on Rosemary back into its envelope and set it and the manuscript aside to skim one last report.

Robert Kennedy.

Walker knew the family name, but not much about "Bobby." He suspected big brother John, the good senator from New England, would protect little brother Robert on the playground of life, whether it was from Roy Cohn or Republicans. Jack read Robert Francis Kennedy as an opportunist, a man who saw a seat at the table of the House Un-American Activities Committee as his path to power.

Assistant Counsel Robert F. Kennedy.

The title might not seem much to the eye or have legs, especially with Cohn and McCarthy at the microphones, but J. Edgar Hoover himself started out as subaltern to Attorney General Palmer and was responsible for a brutal campaign of massive deportations of immigrants in 1920. Three decades later, Hoover was the top lawman in the nation with presidents afraid of him. Power was power, and this Kennedy wanted some.

The next section of the dossier pertained to organized crime. Family trees included leaves with names and aliases. Most of those named had lived and died short, brutal lives. Among the living, a Company analyst detailed all their criminal specialties, legal and illicit. A map illustrated territories and an organization chart detailed the executive structure of Cosa Nostra. Walker familiarized himself with the biographies of Albert Anastasia, Frank Costello, and Vito Genovese.

Walker read the last page, an address handwritten on it. Jack's writing.

There were numbers and streets and, in parentheses, the words "Hell's Kitchen" underlined. Walker wanted to smile. He'd been to Philly, but never to New York City, and wondered whether Hell's Kitchen was Jack's idea of humor, or some sort of code for this assignment.

The two boys across the way were snoring. Walker hungered for a cold Bull Dog from his refrigerator and to work the keys of his Remington typewriter. He missed Woody Woodpecker in his backyard. He looked down at the manuscript. He had a musical to read, and no parachute.

Vera and Leslie shared a Checker to the hotel. Another cab followed them. The second taxi in the caravan was for Vera's luggage. Several square, grooved aluminum cases contained her dresses, her jewelry, and casualwear. Leslie carried a modest soft leather travel bag.

The women were tired from their flight. The Manhattan skyline left them subdued and downbeat; so different were these buildings and lights from their horizon in Los Angeles, the San Gabriel Mountains, and skyscrapers against a desert backdrop.

The ride down Broadway was dull. A red marquee for Kirk Douglas in *Act of Love* was the neighbor to Phil Silvers in *Top Banana*. Jaywalkers timed their crossings, from one side of civilization to the other.

"A musical, can you believe it?" Vera said, as she gazed through her window.

"Think of this as a vacation."

"Don't go thinking JL is doing all this out of the kindness of his heart. MGM is working on musicals, and he wants first crack at the next big thing on Broadway before Louie B. Mayer gets wind of it."

Leslie remained quiet. Vera prattled on.

"MGM has *Seven Brides for Seven Brothers,* and Warner is still crying over the fact that he gave away his cartoons for a pittance, and his studio hasn't had major news since Busby Berkeley cracked his car up and killed three people. It's been nothing but swashbucklers with Flynn and hoodlums with Raft."

Their cab parked curbside, in front of a hotel on 7th Avenue. It wasn't

Mulholland Drive in the Hollywood Hills or Vera's downtown Los Angeles apartment with its marble vestibule, but the Park-Sheraton Hotel was across the street from Carnegie Hall, in Midtown. It cost five dollars a night, a price that must've pleased Jack Warner because he paid eighteen dollars a night at the Pink Palace, back when there was no Beverly Hills Hotel, let alone the city of Beverly Hills, and Sunset Boulevard was nothing more than fields of lima beans. The Park-Sheraton Hotel was cheap, a steal compared to the Chateau Marmont, and if there was one thing Jack Warner loved more than his mother Pearl's potato latkes with applesauce and sour cream, it was when his dollars moved as slow as Cecil Turtle in his Looney Tunes films.

Chapter Five

Saturday. Walker waited for his contact at the corner of 50th Street and Broadway. A cheap breakfast in his stomach, he searched the crowd. He held in his grip a few changes of clothes inside a Samsonite. The sidewalk smelled sour because it had rained overnight. The sun remained shy, hidden behind some clouds, and car exhaust competed with what was left of clean air.

He spotted his contact. Odd fellow for a Company man, since most of them came from the service or the universities. This guy looked like he had spent his night in a Turkish bath with a harem of martinis. He wore scuffed loafers, wrinkled slacks, and a white shirt, open at the collar. Walker could forgive the missing tie. He couldn't forgive the hair. He couldn't forgive the stubble, and he especially couldn't forgive the bloodshot eyes. Those eyes weren't red from the Tabasco on his morning eggs.

They shook hands and moved. They walked a whole two minutes together until they arrived at a nondescript entrance on West 50th Street.

"Adler is inside," the man said. Walker looked and then turned to ask his colleague a question, but the man had disappeared into the crowd. Now Walker understood why his nameless friend was a Company man. Like smoke, he had wafted in, made an impression, and vanished.

Walker opened the door. The place was cool, dark, and forbidding. He set his luggage down before he descended the stairs. The theatre seating was tiered and formed a semicircle around a stage. Sawdust haunted the air, and something questionable crinkled and crackled underfoot. Adler was alone and seated. A light overhead shone down on the man's head; a bald spot exposed. Adler was intent, hunched over and writing. Splayed on the seat next to him was a document. Walker recognized it. Adler heard him approach.

"I take it you're the hired gun from Jack Warner."

"Walter Thompson is the name."

Adler stepped up for the handshake, switching the pencil to his left hand.

"Are you union perchance?"

"Independent contractor," Walker said.

"About what I expected from Jack Warner. You get paid when you work. Good thing, because nothing is happening here for three days, on account of the union. They call it negotiations. I call it a shakedown." He waved his arm, to indicate his empire like an impotent Caesar. "Everything you see is union, including the light bulbs. Everything is on the meter, on the union's clock. Not a soul in the joint, and yet people are paid." He rubbed his fingers together. "Welcome to New York."

"C'mon, it's not new, Mr. Adler."

"How do you figure?"

"Ghosts are paid," Walker said. "It's the Hollywood way. You, of all people, know that."

"I see your point, nonetheless, I lost my set designer this morning. Do expect the union rep to find you, though. You can count on it. He is what I'd call…persuasive."

"I can look after myself, thank you. Might I ask how you and JL know each other?"

"Worked with him years ago. We got on well because I let JL win at chess. I let him win at tennis, too, and I saved myself from ruin by allowing him to win at golf as well."

"Ruin?"

"JL threw parties on Sundays, which often included a round of golf. His property had a nine-hole golf course and I beat him the first time I played him. I should've known better because the next weekend when I went up to Angelo Drive, he had a surprise for me."

"A surprise, how?" Walker said, to feed the story and establish rapport with Adler.

"JL's next door neighbor, Harold Lloyd, also had a nine-hole pitch-and-putt course. JL was so determined to redeem himself that he'd convinced Harold to build a walkway, and next thing I know, I'm playing eighteen holes. I learned, then and there, you let Jack Warner win at whatever the hell he wants. I wrote scripts for him until my wife wanted to come back east. She said our son needed specialists. Health issues."

"Sorry to hear that."

"Anyhow, JL tried to persuade me to stay, rallied white coats around me for the cause, but I left anyway. Biggest mistake of my existence, next to marriage. If you'll excuse me, I need to make an important phone call."

Adler rushed off, down a hallway, his hand in his pocket for change for the phone. So far, so good. What Adler said matched with what Walker had read on the plane. Walker thumbed through the script Adler left behind. There were annotations worth reading, insight into the man's thinking about this production. Walker skimmed a few pages.

A dog wouldn't eat the paper it was printed on. Pure indigestion for both man and his best friend. Walker considered the stage, the layout, and wondered how all that would work for this competitor of *Oklahoma*.

The empty theatre possessed excellent acoustics. Adler's side of the conversation carried emotion and frustration, and the unmistakable words of "New Jersey." Adler attempted the hushed tones of a man with a secret, but he couldn't sustain it. Within minutes, he was loud and angry before he slammed the receiver down.

Adler returned, face red, and he pointed to the manuscript in Walker's hands. "You read fast?"

"I do. More union problems?" Walker eyed the hallway.

"Oh, that. No. Sister-in-law in Jersey. She's taking care of my son, and she's frustrated with him. Sorry you had to hear that."

"Whereabouts in Jersey?" Walker asked.

"Edgewater, in Bergen County. She moved north from God's country."

"God's country?"

"South Jersey, as in Fort Monmouth. She worked there for a spell before she lost her job. Now she looks after my boy. I'm grateful for that, I am, but you know, stress can take the first coat of paint off in the morning."

Walker nodded. He recalled his boyhood fascination with the Revolutionary War. Bergen County was Loyalist territory, hostile to the rebellion against King George. Edgewater was near the Palisades Cliffs, which General Washington lost to the British and their Hessians in the Battle of Fort Lee.

"You said your sister-in-law worked at Fort Monmouth. Isn't that a military post?" Adler flinched. Walker sensed bad history and softened his approach. "Army man myself. New Jersey sure seems to have a lot of forts. Fort Dix, for example. Anyhow, it's mighty swell that she and her husband are helping out with your son."

"I'm afraid he's out of the picture, the weasel. I don't want to trouble you with the family drama." Adler moved the pencil from his back pocket to behind his ear. "You should settle in. We can discuss edits tomorrow, which reminds me...has Miss Williams arrived?"

"Sorry, Mr. Adler. I wouldn't know."

"I should put in a call into the Park-Shearon Hotel where she's staying. She is due to arrive soon with her companion."

"Companion?"

"Didn't JL tell you? She's Vera's assistant." Adler smirked. "A euphemism, if I've ever heard one."

"Does this assistant have a name?"

"Margaret Gardner. Know her?"

"We've crossed paths," Walker said. "Call her Maggie. She'll appreciate it."

"JL told me you've had some experience with unions."

Problems at work and problems at home, and Adler's mind ran on several tracks at once.

"An experience," Walker answered, uncertain whether Warner intended sarcasm, since the studio head had ribbed him for his close association with Terry Doyle, the studio's provocateur, and alleged labor agitator.

"Any help is appreciated," Adler said. "You ought to rest. Where are you staying?"

"Hell's Kitchen. Instead of meeting tomorrow, let's meet in, say, three days.

You said yourself the union has this place in a lockdown. Three days will give me sufficient time to read the script and your notes, and for me to see what I can do with the material."

"I suppose," Adler said, and looked around the place.

"Three days of rest for everyone. Now, if I can borrow the script?"

"Yes, of course. And what am I supposed to do in the meanwhile? Time is money."

"Didn't you know?"

"Know what?"

"Jack Warner is subsidizing this creative endeavor."

"He is?"

"He is." Walker put his hand on Adler's shoulder. "Go spend time with your son, take him off your sister-in-law's hands, and enjoy Asbury Park together."

"You know, that's a great idea, but I still need to find a set designer."

"I might know the right person for the job. See you here Tuesday morning, Mr. Adler."

Walker needed to update Jack, let him know he'd arrived, and get settled into the digs Jack had arranged for him in Hell's Kitchen. He also had committed Jack Warner to underwrite the play. He climbed up the stairs and out of the theatre to the street above. The mention of Fort Monmouth conjured up ghosts of the colonial past and the recent present. Disparate parts in Jack Marshall's report started to coalesce and form a narrative.

Julius Rosenberg was a radar inspector at Fort Monmouth. After his arrest, anybody with a Jewish name, anybody who lived in a radius around the army installation, and anybody who had a connection to electronics and schematics received the once-over from military investigators. Then came Hoover's men door-to-door, and they weren't selling perfume like the Avon Lady.

Adler's star at CBS crashed during the dragnet. Jack's dossier said Adler's wife skipped town, ditched her kid, and headed for Destination Unknown. Therein lay the "family drama" Adler had alluded to in passing. It was a peculiar spousal exchange. Adler's wife left him for her sister's husband, and her sister migrated north to tend to Adler's sick child. Whether the abandonments fomented a romance between the betrayed in-laws was unclear. What jumped off the page like red ink at Walker was the maiden name of the two sisters: Kaplan.

A Kaplan was accused of having Communist sympathies before the Rosenbergs were arrested and charged with espionage.

Walker whistled an army tune, but not the kind used at Fort Dix or Monmouth. He didn't have to like Jersey, but he knew enough to know that New Jersey was the Garden State, and it was all coming up Rosenbergs.

Chapter Six

Walker asked the soda jerk for nickels and placed a quarter on the counter. He noticed the kids on the steel stools. One young boy nursed a chocolate milkshake, while his buddy puckered his lips on a lime phosphate.

Walker accepted his change and walked into the booth. He pushed the accordion door shut, picked up the earpiece, and dropped his first nickel. He told the operator the exchange in DC. She told him the toll and he fed the phone more coins. The call went through.

"How is everything?" Jack asked.

"I've yet to check into the place you arranged for me. I'm tired from the flight and running on fumes." Walker turned inside the booth, his back to the stools and counter. "I've got an ask."

"This soon?"

"Reach out to Sheldon for me and tell him I need him."

"Sheldon is in Boston," Jack said.

"I don't care where he is. Have him here by Tuesday, the latest. You know the address for the theatre." Dead air. Jack needed to hear the reason. Walker told him. "I need a set designer and his skills with a needle and thread."

A pause about the size of a continent.

"You know he's good at more than needle and thread."

"I need him, Jack. See what you can do for me, okay? Pretty please."

"Seen Leslie or Vera?"

"Nope. Let me acclimate first before I walk into the ring, two against one."

"Leslie's on our team," Jack said.

"Let me be the judge of that; it's the combination, Jack. Vera only cares about Vera."

"That's not fair and you know it. Vera took care of the doctor in LA for us."

"That kind of proves my point."

"Fair enough," Jack said. "I'll make sure Sheldon shows."

Walker hung up and pivoted inside the booth. Door closed and behind glass, he reviewed the *Time Life* snapshot of Americana at the counter. Like a Rockwell, it looked innocent until you looked closer. The kid with the chocolate malted and holding his belly was the guy who knew better but still did the stupid thing. The kid with the lime phosphate was Vera as a tomboy, the child who stood out because everything he did had to make a statement, including choice of beverage.

The new girl at the counter, the one in the middle, was Leslie. She was the heartbreaker. The sad kid on the far left, whom he hadn't noticed until now, was him, the sap who couldn't catch an even break on an odd day, because someone behind the counter controlled everything. That someone was Jack Marshall.

Walker killed his pride and the last of the change in his pocket and called the Park-Sheraton Hotel. He kept courtesy to a sharpened pencil when he spoke with Vera. They'd agreed on a time later that night for dinner. He didn't ask after Leslie because he could hear her in the background. Vera was polite as ice.

Walker located the address Jack had arranged for him in Hell's Kitchen. Uncollected garbage behind him, the number above the doorframe in front of him, he surveyed the neighborhood. The locals were working-class, the hard life etched onto their faces, though drink and the pack-a-day of unfiltered smokes added a few more lines to the story of their lives.

The glass in the door to the vestibule was the cleanest part of the building. Walker searched for the apartment number of the property manager. He pressed the little black bug of a button. There was no buzz, so he pressed it again. A door on the first floor opened, and out came the poor man's version of Anthony Quinn. A bad leg gave him the limp and a sour attitude. "Whaddaya want?"

And like any good landholder, dark eyes appraised Walker, sized up his net worth, and estimated the amount of money he carried. Cash was king here.

"A room was rented out in my name: Walter Thompson."

The man's mood changed in an instant. The misanthrope found a long-lost smile in his archives of memories. The leather in his brogue softened to melted butter. He didn't ask for proof of identification either. Nothing.

"Aye, come right in, Mr. Thompson. A deliveryman showed up and paid a month's rent in your name. Your benefactor was kind enough to have the local butcher send over the best cuts of meats and other sundries, which put me in good with the wife. You tell him we appreciate his kindness."

"I shall. About that room?"

Terry Doyle had taught him that diction betrayed a man's view of the world and his place in it. "Benefactor" reeked of Dickens. The man started the procession deeper into the building and Walker listened to his guide.

"Furnished, and the wife stocked your icebox and left fresh linens."

"Kind of her, thank you."

"The messenger man verified the room himself, looked around he did."

"I'm sure it met with his satisfaction. Where is it?"

The man's finger pointed skyward, which meant stairs. He explained the room came with a view of the river. Most of the men in the Kitchen worked the waterfront, he said. He mentioned that bohemians and all sorts of artists were moving into the neighborhood "Lazy bums is what they are. Commies and anarchists, for all I know, but they pay the rent."

They climbed three flights. Walker didn't break a sweat with his baggage, but the ascent was a labor of Hercules for the property manager. He'd held the railing and used it for support every step of the way. The man slipped a skeleton key into the door, paused, and asked Walker, "You ain't Italian, are you?"

"No, why?"

"The wife brought in some flowers for you. Mums are bad luck to the dagos."

He unlocked the door and pushed it in. The first thing Walker saw was a Remington in its case and a bouquet of chrysanthemums next to it. Jack had supplied him with a typewriter.

The walls were plaster, slapped with fresh paint, and the floor swept clean. The bed looked like it would've killed Proust, while the desk near the window was as minimalistic as a Hemingway sentence. He scanned the room as a portrait for still life. There was a scratched walnut table for meals, and two chairs. The kitchen and the icebox were modest, perfect for a bachelor. There was a settee across from the bed, stained as if it had seen its share of spilt beer, stale perfume, and fast encounters of the sordid kind. A rug covered the middle of the floor, probably because the wood had gone bad there. The throw reminded him of the sisal carpet Leslie had in her apartment in Vienna.

"What are you?" the man asked him.

"Pardon?"

"You ain't Italian, and you don't look Irish to me. What are you?"

"Heinz," Walker answered. "Fifty-seven varieties. I'm a little bit of everything. You?"

"Greek and a splash of mick."

There was some truth to Walker's answer. He didn't look ethnic, nor did he pass for milquetoast either. His people hailed from Middle America, and yet he didn't look corn-fed, or built like a fullback. He was the enigma Jack Marshall and the Company wanted and needed. Walker spied two curious items in the room.

"What's with the pail and wrench?"

"You really aren't from around here, are you?" the landlord answered, somewhat tickled. "The pail is for your beer. There's a dozen watering holes on the street below. They'll fill your bucket with beer, but the law says you must leave the saloon with it covered." He pointed to the modest cupboard. "Dishes and glasses are inside. You'll find affordable eats on nearby Restaurant Row, and you'd best avoid Battle Row over yonder on West 39th Street after dark. Ain't a day go by that they don't find body parts there, but don't you worry much. Hard to believe but gangs keep Hell's Kitchen safe because the police couldn't be bothered. Pay no mind to the brawlers unless you're at the right place at the wrong time when they're settling a beef."

The beer pail wasn't what Walker had thought it was, which left him with one item.

"And the wrench there?"

"To clang the pipes for heat during the winter. Takes but a minute before Satan below spits and farts steam your way. With summer upon us, consider it a slapper, a wee heavier form of persuasion than the blackjacks the coppers carry, but it does the job just the same."

"I don't expect any trouble."

"Thought the same to myself." The man smiled and displayed a set of bad teeth. "You seem the type that ends trouble before it starts. Ain't none of my business, but my guess is you're here and then gone before the month's done."

"And what makes you say that?"

"Whenever the Italians have a mixer with the Irish over who should run the piers, a mechanic from out of town like yourself appears, and the next you know, the problem is solved. The spiff is paid, and it's back to payoffs and kickbacks." The landlord glanced at the block on the desk. "None of my biz, but why would you need that monstrosity?"

"It's a typewriter."

"Sure it is, and I'm Shakespeare."

Walker watched the man leave. He needed some shut-eye before dinner tonight. He set his bag down, undid his jacket, and rubbed the back of his neck as he approached the desk. He worked the latch, lifted the cover, and smiled. He hoisted the chunk of steel out of the bay and noticed the sheaf of paper underneath. Jack had been thoughtful and provided quality stationery. Eaton's Corrasable Bond.

He grabbed the case and sensed something, more weight. He shook the bottom half and, while it didn't rattle, there was something. He stuck his hand inside, tapped around with his fingers. A false bottom.

He worked the panel loose and grinned.
His M1911. His .45. His Grable.

Chapter Seven

Vera contemplated a reservation at the Stork Club but decided against it. She remembered Josephine Baker's infamous experience at Sherman Billingsley's establishment. First, she'd have to get past the club's Saint Peter. He'd allowed the famous chanteuse on the premises because she was the guest of another couple, otherwise Negros were not allowed. After a smash performance at the Roxy, Josephine came in for drinks and ordered a steak. The drinks arrived but the steak took an hour. Vera had read about the libel suit Baker lodged against Walter Winchell that night, heard about the nightclub's skirmishes with Mayor La Guardia over taxes, but, like any self-respecting New Dealer, Vera detested the owner's stance against unions. For years, guests had to cross a picket line to venture inside for a meal. In his own way, Sherman reminded her of Jack Warner and the moguls.

She decided on dinner and a show at the Copacabana instead. Vera had as much of an understanding of Lenny Moore's advice to "keep a low profile" as Elmer Fudd did about hunting. All that one of Cohn's men with a subpoena had to do was blow a duck call, and Vera would have stood up for the buckshot, thinking it was a photo op. Her choice in clothes didn't help.

A large shard of cut glass dangled from each ear. A silver scarf draped her shoulders. The black contoured dress hugged her curves, and the stiletto heels boosted the signal of sex and hormones. Leslie was the more sensible one of the pair. She wore a strapless white princess gown and white gloves.

Walker joined them. When their party neared the stand, they saw the Copa's evening manager slap a waiter for bringing out a dish with the carrots on the wrong side of the plate. Vera gave her name to the man at the podium. He ran his manicured finger down the reservation list, written in the style of penmanship that included flamboyant curlicues.

He led them to their table and then dealt out the menus and announced the specials. The culinary theme, he said, was international and experimental. One chef cooked French cuisine, while the other one did Chinese. He indicated where they'd find the traditional offerings on the menu.

Walker thought the Asian side of the cardstock was a step up from what he ate at the tiki bar he frequented in Hollywood, where his drinks came with little toothpick umbrellas and the food was limited to five choices, all of them done out back in the parking lot on a grill.

Vera ordered two rounds of Fines de Claires oysters and foie gras as appetizers for the table. She asked for the waiter's recommendation on champagne. He suggested a grand cru. Leslie chose the filet of lemon sole Breteuil for her entrée. Vera selected the pan-fried pheasant with garlic, marjoram, and grated truffle. Walker settled on something local and masculine, a roasted and stuffed tom turkey from Vermont.

They kicked off the evening with cocktails while they waited. Gin and Sin for Vera, a Rob Roy for Leslie, and since the warm weather reminded him of LA, Walker ordered a Sloe Gin Fizz. While they drank, they discussed their flights, the adjustment to the time difference, and other elements of culture shock that accompanied the passage from one coast to another.

"So, you met with the director this morning?" Vera asked Walker.

"Irwin Adler, and it's a musical."

"What's this horror called?" Vera asked, knowing the answer.

"Band Wagon."

"Now I know how a Roman felt when he heard the dreaded word *exile*."

"What did you expect for playing hostess to down-and-out writers with red shadows?"

"Aren't you going to defend me, Maggie?" Vera said to Leslie.

"Walter doesn't mean you any harm, Vera, and I'd hardly call this exile."

"What do you call it then? A hiccup?"

"Try and make the best of it," Leslie said.

"Next stop is the sauna with a dull razor."

The waiter arrived with the oysters and the foie gras. Another waiter set down fluted stemware, while his colleague presented the bottle to Vera. After the cork was popped, he poured the bubbly for Vera and Leslie. Walker asked for a beer. He figured if dinner was going to come with a side of misery, he'd enjoy a cold one, even if culinary decorum dictated that one does not drink suds with oysters or goose liver. The waiter iced the bottle and left for the bar with Walker's order.

Leslie doled out some bivalves to Vera. Her eyes met Walker's. Once the waiter returned with a draft and set it down, Leslie raised her flute and elbowed Vera to do the same. Crystal tinkled and tapped Walker's pint glass.

Walker limited himself to one beer while the bubbles carbonated Vera and Leslie between courses. It had been a long time since Walker heard Leslie giggle.

She lifted her snakeskin bag onto the table for some unknown reason. Her eyes watched Walker watching her. He had his GI-issued .45, Grable, under his arm in a shoulder holster. He wondered what she was carrying inside her purse. Leslie was lethal at close range.

Walker broached the inevitable. "I read the script and it's a howler."

"Which is why all the bad dogs find themselves off-Broadway," Vera said.

"More like off-off Broadway, but I think it's salvageable with a little rewriting. I have a few ideas of my own."

"Is the director…what was his name again?" Vera asked.

"Adler," Leslie said. Her recall proved she wasn't pickled.

"Is Mr. Adler open to revisions?" Vera asked.

"He is, and I should mention that the script belongs to Warner."

Walker didn't want to discuss his ideas for the rewrite. He'd strip the musical down to its chassis and rebuild the play as a drama, inspired by what he had read about the Kennedy family on the flight to New York.

The entrées appeared. No handprints were imprinted on the faces of the waitstaff. Walker dug into his turkey with his utensils. Leslie used the side of her fork to break off some fish, while Vera started in on her bird. After a few bites, Vera pressed Walker on what he had in mind for the revised play.

"Something contemporary, like a woman who takes a stand against her husband. There's family, drama, and a small touch of politics. You're perfect for the part, Vera."

"I'm flattered, really, but I'm afraid of how Jack Warner will react since you've absconded with the original intent of his work and replaced his western musical with your own creation. This all reminds me of a short story I read recently—a western called *The Man Who Shot Liberty Valence*, by Dorothy Johnson. After JL hears you've revised his property, you may find your name in the title instead. *The Man Who Shot Walter Thompson*."

"It's my understanding JL bends toward whatever makes him money."

Vera held her flute, the champagne inside of it, flat and dead. "So true, but never forget that in JL's world, writers do what they're told. You'll need to convince the man that your idea was his idea."

A hand appeared on Vera's shoulder. She turned her head and looked up at a handsome fellow in a dark suit, hair slicked back, and a hearing aid in one ear. It was the singer Johnnie Ray, Mr. Emotion himself. Johnnie was a nightclub legend, famous for dramatic performances, dreamy vocals, and a sound; not quite Sinatra but something else altogether.

"I knew it had to be you, Miss Williams. I've been a fan of yours for a long time."

"Why thank you, Mr. Ray. I love your song, 'Cry.'"

"Thank you. I've been working on a new song, and I'd be honored to sing it for you."

"I'd love that."

Half of Manhattan stopped eating and the white palm trees in the Copa stood still when Johnnie took the stage and sang "Cry." After the applause he told the audience about this new song he'd wanted to sing for Miss Vera Williams, the actress, out in the audience. A spotlight lit up the table like a flare over the darkened Atlantic. Vera's earrings sparkled, and both Leslie and Walker looked away, to avoid the unwanted attention of photographers. When the song finished, the satin voice moved into "Somebody Stole My Gal" and Walker glanced over at Leslie and watched her in profile.

He had tried to love her. She was his shattered wine glass. He picked up all the big pieces, the easiest to see and find, but it's the smallest fragment, the sliver stepped on weeks or months after the fact that hurt the most because it's so unexpected. Tonight, she had pierced him.

The key to their room clanged in the bowl. Vera steamed into the bedroom. She unfurled the silver scarf from around her shoulders and flung it in the air. After the latch had clicked, Leslie worked a stud earring loose with her fingers. She entered the room and said nothing. The second earring freed, Leslie placed the pair inside a jewelry box and looked into the mirror. In the reflection, Vera stood there, hands on her hips.

"You look at me as if I'd broken curfew," Leslie said into the glass.

"You ruined my night."

"I ruined your night?" Leslie reached for the brush and used it. Leslie's strategy was to use a boomerang, to redirect accusations back at the accuser. Oftentimes, when Vera heard how silly she sounded, she dropped the matter.

"You rushed me into a cab, moments after Johnnie sang the song, and we skipped the show."

"Vera, I'm tired. Please get undressed for bed."

Leslie slipped off her shoes. The carpeting under her toes soothed her. She wished she could light the fireplace in their room, but it was summer, and Vera provided the wrong kind of heat at that moment. A window they'd left cracked, a breeze disturbed the white drapes. Leslie decided against the voyage to the velvet chair on the other side of the room, where she could recline and peel off her nylons. Anything to avoid a collision with Vera. Leslie yawned, a ploy to discourage Vera from battle. She managed the zipper on her dress on her own. She hung up her clothes in the armoire She found her negligee, a copy of one Harlow loved, but decided against it. She preferred to be naked and wrapped a robe around herself.

"I thought we had a nice evening," Vera said.

"I thought we did."

Vera started undressing but she didn't start with the earrings. She kicked off her stilettos. Leslie said nothing. Vera shimmied out of her dress and let it drop on the floor.

"You're upset Walter left early, aren't you?"

"No, Vera. I'm not upset Walker left early."

"Walker? I said Walter and you said Walker."

Leslie clenched her eyes, cursed herself.

"We had cocktails and split a bottle of champagne, Vera. You know how the bubbles fizzle my brain. I was probably thinking of Johnnie Walker. Say, I could go for a scotch. Champagne was always too girly for me."

Leslie wasn't sure whether the distraction had worked. She tried another tactic.

"Want to know why I'm upset? I'll tell you. I'm mad we're here, on account of that tyrant Joe McCarthy and his little pipsqueak, Roy Cohn. You've swum long and hard to reach the surface at the studio. Work, work, work—all those years, and for what? We're here, and it's more of the same. Work, work, and more work. The one chance we had for a cracker of a night, and Walter has to cut out early to start work on the play."

"What are you saying, Maggie?"

"What I'm saying is if the man has to draft a script, you can imagine the amount of work you'll have to put into this project."

Vera slipped into her robe. She patted the bed, inviting Leslie to join her. "He's a writer and that's what writers do," Vera said. "JL wouldn't have sent him over if he thought he couldn't deliver. I'm sorry for the outburst. The truth is, I'm jealous."

"Of Walter?"

"I see the way he looks at you. I worry."

"Let him look all he wants," Leslie said. "The name Walter isn't exactly my idea of the siren call in the darkness, and let's not forget the shortened version: Wally."

Vera fell over, laughing. "I don't know why, but Wally makes me think of that cartoon penguin from Hoboken, who cried ice cubes."

Leslie turned over onto her stomach and cozied up to Vera. Her fingers played with the nubbed surface of the terrycloth robe. She seized her opportunity for diplomacy.

"We should be careful, Vera. We don't want word to get back to JL."

"Don't worry. I can handle Jack Warner. I paid tonight's bill with my own money, not his. JL is the only person I know who would charge you for the olive in a martini he made in his own house. What is it that you're really worried about, Maggie?"

"Johnnie sang you a song, and there were photographers tonight. There's the society pages tomorrow, Vera, and important people read them. People will speculate why a Hollywood actress is in town."

"For the play, of course."

"A play that's still unwritten, remember? We came here to avoid a subpoena. Cohn has McCarthy behind him."

"Roy Cohn is a little vile toad of a man. Look on the bright side."

"Bright side?" Leslie asked. "What bright side?"

"He targeted Walter and look what that got him. Egg all over his face."

"This is different, Vera."

Vera moved and pulled down the covers. The sheets were cold. "Different how?"

"Walter is a writer and, as you know from experience, he can disappear and write using a front, like the writers at your parties. You're a star, which makes it all the more fun for Cohn to try and shoot you out of the night sky."

"Let him try. Just let him try."

"Vera?"

"I'd like to see that reptile try."

"Vera?"

"What?"

"Take your earrings off and shut up."

Vera smiled. She placed her earrings on the nightstand, rolled onto her back and reached down and untied the sash and parted the robe. "You feel like making love."

"Is that a statement or a question?"

"You tell me, Maggie dear."

Leslie admired Vera's resolve. She'd slipped once, with Walker for Walter, but the other secret, the one she couldn't divulge, was that Vera's shrink, the dead Dr. Ernest, had fed names to J. Edgar Hoover, and Hoover was as patient as Job and as duplicitous as Moriarty.

Chapter Eight

As soon as he entered his apartment in Hell's Kitchen after leaving the Copa, Walker pulled off his tie and started in on the script. A skim of Adler's notes in the margin convinced him that Adler was not confident about a musical. Neither of them had a clue as to whether Vera could carry a tune or if she had two left feet. Vera Williams may have survived the studio system's crash courses in the arts, but she was decades away from her diploma. Walker relied on what Terry Doyle taught him at Warner's.

Write tight, leave lots of white space, and defer to experts, like Adler's ear for dialogue since he was a radio man.

Aristotle's *Poetics* said that a play required unity of action, unity of place, and unity of time. Walker had another trifecta in mind. Cohn, Hoover, and Kennedy. Both the army and the Company had taught him to attack the weakest point. Roy Cohn was too easy of a target and the man didn't care what was said about him in public. J. Edgar Hoover was too big of a mark. That left Robert Kennedy, and Walker was determined to split the trinity and force the Catholic to divorce himself from Cohn and Hoover.

When he thought of the Kennedys, he thought of the Bible and Catholicism, of Exodus, Deuteronomy, and Numbers. Fathers and sons. When he thought of the generations of success, he thought dynasty, the line from Boston mayors to bootleggers to money and all the sins on the path to wealth and prestige. He chewed on that phrase from the Good Book, "the sins of the father," except that they weren't visited on the sons. The envelope with **ROSEMARY KENNEDY, 1941**, the horror that he read within it, reminded him that the daughter could pay—and did.

At first, he brooded over the keys of his typewriter, uncertain where and how to start, the plight of every writer. His fingers fell into a natural tempo as he gathered his ideas and themes. Each carriage return reminded Walker of a church bell calling the faithful. He would find his melody in Rosemary's tragic story using his right hand and work out a rhythm for the family conflict with his left. Soft, sad, and quiet, the story rose with the stack of paper. He composed through Saturday night, looking up, on occasion, at the stars outside his window. When he finished, a new day had started.

A quick trip to the corner store the next morning introduced him to the shop owners. In small talk with the elderly couple, they said they'd never seen him before. He told them he was new to the neighborhood. The wife made him two sandwiches and her husband put together a Bachelor's Box, all the things a man alone in the city might need.

Toiletries. Coffee. Bottles of milk, soda, and orange juice.

Walker, touched by the thoughtfulness, did not remove the two packs of cigarettes. He didn't smoke. A Q&A in Vienna ended any glamour smoking offered.

The wife wrapped one roast beef sandwich and one pastrami in butcher's paper. At the register, the husband asked if he wanted to go "on the book." Confused, Walker asked what that meant. The grocer explained that it was their version of store credit. Many of the men, he said, had little left over from their paycheck because of the kickback to the crew boss, who picked them for the day's work. The shape up program, it was called. Then there was rent and utilities, another payoff to the ward boss, who guaranteed them peace if they weren't union. "We help each other out here," the old man said. "When they can pay what they can on the book, they pay. You don't work the docks, do you?"

The wife said something fast in Italian. "Pardon my manners," she said. "I was telling my husband you don't ask a man what he does for a living the first time you meet him. It's Sunday. You a Catlick?"

"Worse, a writer," Walker said. "I was hired to fix a script."

"You expect inspiration in this neighborhood?" she asked.

"Let's just say someone powerful is interested in seeing this play written and performed."

"Now that we understand." The man pulled the skin below his eye down.

Walker paid cash. On his way back to his apartment with provisions, he contemplated the Keynesian economics of Hell's Kitchen, the version not taught at Columbia or Harvard. The old pair, like the rest of the neighborhood, lived that phrase from the Book of Job, "by the skin of their teeth."

On Tuesday morning, he visited Adler, said a quick hello, and handed him two manuscripts, the annotated original, and his first cut of the play, tucked inside a cardboard box. Adler heard "play" and launched his protest. Walker offered no explanations. He excused himself, saying he needed breakfast. Adler shouted a recommendation and an address.

He thanked the director and bounded up the stairs, down a hallway, and through the door. He walked down the street, happy to inhale the fumes, the city smells of the steam from the hot dog vendor's cart, the cloud of salt and dough from a man selling hot pretzels. A car horn blared. Someone yelled a profanity. Walker felt among the living, delirious and enthusiastic as Walt Whitman was with Manhattan's "barbaric yawp."

Inside the establishment Adler recommended, he found booths near the front window and a jukebox against the back wall. The music machine played forty-fives instead of seventy-eights. He read the chalkboard and ordered waffles from the lady behind the counter and pointed to the empty booth he wanted. She scribbled his order down, nodded, and cracked gum.

He slid into the booth, looked at the street life outside his window. His fingertips drummed the Formica surface, and his thumb thumped the space bar that wasn't there. He thought of calling Jack, but it could wait. He'd forgotten they were both on the same coast now.

The tap of the ceramic mug on the table startled him. "Coffee?" He said yes, thanked her, and returned to the spectacle outside. Another sound and he turned with a smile, thinking it was the waitress again. It wasn't.

His contact. The man he'd met after he'd landed sat opposite him. He didn't have a name. He wasn't supposed to have one, so Walker thought of Robinson Crusoe. "It's my man, Friday."

"Here with news."

"Want some breakfast?"

"No, thanks."

Walker appraised his guest. Friday blended in with the locals. The wool cap pulled down to cover the tops of his ears made it impossible to know the color of his hair. A light coat, like any dozens of longshoremen or laborers on the street, the man was anonymous as Mr. Smith or Jones. Walker suspected dungarees below the table.

"The request you made went though, and you should see him later." He meant Sheldon. The waitress delivered the waffles and a caddy of syrups.

"While you eat, I'll draw you a picture of the labor situation at the theater."

The splash of maple syrup made the butter inside the squares of his waffles rise and spill over. Walker worked the heel of his fork to break his breakfast down into smaller pieces. He told Friday he was listening.

"Guy's name is Steps. He's called Steps because he's steps away from The Prime Minister or he's the steps you take to reach The Prime Minister. He controls the unions for the theatres, and he runs the local rackets."

"What can you tell me about this Prime Minister?" Walker worked his way through the waffles and slugs of coffee, while Friday talked.

"He's one of the old-timers, and he has serious pull."

"How serious is serious?" Walker asked.

"If he calls Mayor Impellitteri, the mayor takes his call. He owns most of the politicians and judges."

"Which means he owns a good part of the police force," Walker said. "What I don't get is why the labor racket off-Broadway? There's little money for the effort."

"The Prime Minister happens to like theater and he loves opera. Believe it or not, he's easy on the off-Broadway productions when it comes to protection money. He doesn't squeeze as hard."

"How benevolent of him. He's a hood and Steps is his man. Got it."

"That's where you're wrong and you're right. You're right, he's a gangster, but you're wrong if you think The Prime Minister is from the Sears catalog. He's set up his rackets like a company, where regional managers report to him. But he's had problems lately."

"Problems? What kind of problems?"

"Remember the Kefauver hearings?"

Walker nodded and then it hit him. "Are we talking about Frank Costello?"

"One and the same."

Estes Kefauver was a slow-talking senator from Tennessee, a strong New Dealer after FDR's own heart. Kefauver was a liberal and a determined trusts buster with a sense of humor. He made the cover of *Time* last year, sporting a toothy smile under a coonskin cap. The politician had already launched broadsides against what he called "organized crime." And then came the televised hearings. The nation met The Prime Minister, a man with a raspy voice who used his hands, like a seasoned actor. "Cosa Nostra" entered the lexicon, a phantom word, like Hoover's "Communists."

"If memory serves, The Prime Minister is in prison on account of Kefauver."

"Contempt of court for walking out of the hearings. Twice. Sentenced for that and then tax evasion." Friday shrugged. "Like that'll stop the man from running his company."

"Any advice on Steps?"

"I'd suggest you view Steps as Montjoy."

"You have time to read Shakespeare?"

"I'm not a barbarian."

"Fair enough. Steps is Costello's herald. I get it." Walker wiped his mouth with the napkin. "Curious as to how you found out all of this."

"From the maître d' at the Copa. I should go, and good luck."

Walker returned to the theater. Adler was as quiet as a kid in Bible class. He liked the script and said he had suggestions for some of the dialogue. "We need straight speech without all the commas. People came to see a play and not hear a novel."

Vera and her assistant arrived at ten am, invigorated, and with fresh coffee in their hands. Adler apologized for the single copy of the script but said he'd have his sister-in-law type up copies. Walker suggested to Adler that he bring his in-law and the kid into town. Adler thought it a bad idea, that his son was too excitable, and rehearsals might over-stimulate him.

Vera volunteered Maggie to type up copies. Walker watched how the suggestion landed. Without waiting for an answer, Vera handed Walker's creation to Leslie, who accepted it with the pastor's wife's practiced smile. Leslie mumbled about the need to find a typewriter, either to buy or lease. Leslie had been typecast as the secretary again. First, in Vienna, then Los Angeles, and now, New York.

Vera dressed simple, or what Hollywood considered working clothes. Her tulip dress was from Dior's Spring Collection, a white dress with tiers of dark and detailed scallops. On her feet, stilettos again, but white this time, and the heels with enough inches to make the average man feel not so average.

A starlet's personal assistant always dressed second-best. Leslie appeared in a geometric-print dress from Emilio Pucci, with black zigzag lines on white silk. Perfect for the studio lot and for the afternoon martini later.

Vera asked for a summary of the play. Adler looked to Walker for permission to give the synopsis. Walker nodded. Leslie tried to hide that hurt look he knew well. He had seen it in Vienna when Jack had sent her out of the office to fetch tea for an unexpected visitor. Adler talked.

"In the first act, we meet a married woman named Rose. She's a dutiful housewife and mother, struggling to maintain her home and marriage. That's your character, Vera. Her husband, Johnnie, is a hard worker, but not too bright. He feels compelled to prove he's a man because he was declared unfit for military service, 4-F during the war."

"Which war, World War II or Korea?" Vera asked. Adler turned to Walker for guidance.

"It's your call, Mr. Adler. Please continue."

"Johnnie had wanted college, but Rose became pregnant. Johnnie does the right thing. They marry and have their child. The kid, however, was born with complications." Adler stopped and looked to Walker. "I have a question. You never specified the health problem."

"How about polio?" Vera suggested.

"No polio," Walker said from his seat. "Too sentimental."

"He's right," Adler said.

"I'd like to make a change, Mr. Adler," Walker said. "How about changing the name of Johnnie? The wife's name is good. It's symbolic, but I doubt the audience will take Johnnie seriously if we give him an everyman's name. We have him with intellectual types later. How about something authoritative, something biblical? I was thinking of Joseph."

Joseph, it was. Joseph was patriarchal.

"I like it." Adler marked a page. "Husband Joe invites coworkers to the house. They're a mixed bunch of personalities, but all of them are college-educated. They discuss progressive ideas and politics. They form a secret social club."

"What kind of work do these men do?" Vera asked.

"Ad agency. Everything is going well for Rose and Joe, until their little girl's health worsens. There's marital tension, but that's not the main conflict."

"All that was subplot?" Vera asked, already thinking she'd lose the spotlight.

"The conflict is within the advertising firm," Adler said. "See, Joe has been questioning some of the ways his employer conducts business. He takes issue with the firm's account with Big Tobacco. Joe's father smoked and he died from a respiratory illness, which is why Joe doesn't smoke. His father's death haunts him. He dislikes smoking enough to hound Rose into quitting the habit, which she does while she's pregnant. When their child becomes ill, Rose blames herself."

"Mr. Adler," Walker interrupted. "Stick to calling him Joseph; the name has more gravitas than Joe."

Vera raised her hand. "Won't we lose sponsors if we criticize tobacco?"

Walker fielded the question. "Why? Nobody has proven smoking is unhealthy. Don't worry so much about tobacco since we know who our sponsor is."

"Then there's the twist," Adler said, his hand twisted in the air like a corkscrew. "The ad firm's executives learn about the social club, and they panic. Joseph comes to tolerate the tobacco account because it pays the bills, but these meetings, their discussions of politics and big ideas threaten the big men upstairs. They're worried about unionization. The execs hire investigators who interrogate each employee to learn who is a member of the secret club."

"Afraid of unions?" Vera said. She looked to Walter. She'd known about him, his friendship with Terry Doyle, and the man's flirtation with organizing writers. "You seriously want Jack Warner to read this?"

"I think we're getting ahead of ourselves," Adler said. "This is a draft. Think of triangles, shall we? Act One is Joseph and Rose and child. Act Two is friends, work, and loyalty—"

"This is a message piece," Vera said. "Didn't Arthur Miller do something similar?"

Adler responded to Vera, and Vera directed her anxiety to Walker. The walkthrough of the script degenerated into a cacophony of raised voices until there was a sharp, piercing whistle.

Leslie.

"Settle down, people. It's a draft, and let's not forget it. All I have to say here is that Act Three had better have a showdown and resolution, and not some *deus ex machina* bullshit. If we do this, then we do this right. In the real world, someone pays the price for taking a stand. If this play is to have legs with an audience in New York, it costs someone something. Now, if you'll excuse me, I have to rent a typewriter."

Her words left them quiet. Walker knew her cursing was proof that having to type the manuscript had gotten to her. Leslie was halfway out when a man entered and stood at the top of the stairs. The lighting was strong enough to reveal a silhouette in a dark suit, a blue tie on a lighter shade of blue shirt.

Leslie recognized him first. She glanced over her shoulder at Walker.

That was when he knew.

It was Sheldon.

Chapter Nine

It was the godawful heat Jack hated the most. Frigidaire air-conditioner on, and four thousand pounds of Cadillac steel still couldn't put a dent into the humidity.

He drove west from DC all night with a thermos of iced tea and a paper bag next to him. He'd devoured the sandwich that Betty had made hours ago, the crumbs and the last of the potato chips were gravel on the leather seating. Jack thought about the meeting he would soon have at the Federal Correctional Institution in Milan, Michigan.

Francesco Castiglia, born in Calabria, had little on him until the contempt of court charges at the Kefauver hearings in '51 and a conviction for tax evasion in '52. He was serving eighteen months on the earlier charge and faced five years on the second one. Prior to these two events, not a speck of lint had stuck to the man. Like most immigrant kids, he ran with a crew, the 104th Street Gang in East Harlem, and he'd had some petty crimes on his jacket. The heaviest charge had hit him before he turned thirty and that was for illegal possession of a firearm in 1918, after which he never carried a gun. In all the years since, including another world war and Korea, he'd been the Invisible Man, a shadow on the wall, a whisper in the dark.

The hearings, televised nationally, introduced audiences to tailored grey suits, wide lapels, an elegant handkerchief in the left breast pocket, and the pair of hands that accompanied the raspy voice of the man now called Frank Costello. Castiglia had adopted an Irish name, and he married a Jewish girl.

Listeners would learn about a vast criminal organization, mafia or Cosa Nostra, and the man on their television screen was one of its architects. He was first called The Ambassador; and now, The Prime Minister.

Costello, Jack noted, disliked violence. Costello, like some of his peers, disliked attention. He did not want his name in the newspapers. Kefauver changed all of that. The man lived a modest life. Jack observed something else. Like Joseph Kennedy, Costello shifted from bootlegging to owning a distillery. Unlike Kennedy, however, Costello was a successful kingmaker. He owned judges, lawyers, and politicians.

Jack had heard a copy of Hoover's wiretap. Reclusive as an eccentric millionaire, shy as a Hollywood starlet, Costello had moved a man into a nomination for the presidency of the United States. Now, the guest of the taxpayer at Milan since August of '52, he folded socks in the prison's laundry while he waited for his lawyers to overturn the conviction for tax evasion.

Milan was a low-security facility, although one inmate did walk to the gallows in '38. After he'd parked his car, Jack climbed into the backseat to shut off the AC. Jack came to talk with Frank about Hell's Kitchen, where the diplomat once convinced Jewish, Irish, and Italian gangsters to work together. Jack wanted some of that diplomacy for Walker.

A guard, a Company man, greeted him. There was no log to sign, no weapon to surrender, and no name tag. Jack was escorted into a courtyard where the same guard whispered into Frank's ear. Costello's breakfast companion, "Bumpy" Johnson, a Harlem gangster, excused himself. Someone else would be folding socks at Frank's station today.

Costello sat there, in prison-issued gray slacks, a gray shirt, and lace-less shoes. His indulgences were limited to a nice watch on the left wrist and the comb in his pocket, which he used to comb over the thinning hair on his head. Someone said Frank Costello could pass for Bela Lugosi but Jack thought of an actor from Hell's Kitchen, George Raft, if George would pack on twenty-five pounds.

Jack approached the wooden table. Costello had sized him up. "You're not a lawyer?"

"No, I'm not, Mr. Costello. I'm not with the Bureau or a Treasury man, either."

"Good to hear, because when a government man shows up, it means they want a rat, and I'm no rat, mister." Costello's eyes measured Jack again and he almost smiled this time. "You have me at a disadvantage, since you know my name and I don't know yours."

"Jack Marshall."

"Have a seat, Mr. Marshall. What can I do for you?"

"We both work for a company, and we can help each other."

"How do I know I can trust you?"

"You don't, but I'd like a moment of your time."

"I've got nothing but time, Mr. Marshall. I am curious, though, as to what it'll cost me."

"Peace of mind."

"I do all right in that department if I say so myself. Tell me about your company."

"We handle foreign affairs, but my problem is a domestic matter."

"Forgive me for being so blunt, Mr. Marshall, but why should I help you?"

"Because I can make sure you don't get deported. Foreign affairs is my department, like I said. Whether your conviction for unpaid taxes is tossed out or not, the government doesn't need a compelling argument to give you a one-way ride to the Old Country. All they have to do is say is that you're unsavory. Moral turpitude."

"Nice choice of words."

"Moral turpitude?"

"No, one-way ride. You have this kind of pull, to put the brakes on deportation?"

"My company helped your friend Charlie Luciano."

"But he was deported." Costello exposed both hands, palms up.

"Deported, as opposed to doing the rest of his ticket in prison. There's a difference."

"You've made your point. What is it that you need from me, Mr. Marshall?"

"You like theatre, right?"

Costello's hands lifted and then dropped. "Yeah, so what?"

"I'm fond of *The Mikado* myself, especially the character Ko-Ko."

Costello leaned back and smiled now. He understood the code. Jack had, without saying the name, identified Costello's colleague and the man he'd tapped as his successor while he was in Milan. Within the inner sanctum of organized crime, Albert Anastasia was called "Lord High Executioner," another name for Ko-Ko in the Gilbert & Sullivan musical.

"You don't want trouble with Ko-Ko, is that it?"

"An associate of mine is doing a play off-Broadway. Any problems he might have with deliveries or suppliers, I'd like for them to vanish, like that." Jack snapped his fingers.

"His play means that much to you?"

"Not really." Jack leaned forward, both hands on the table so Costello could see that he was honest. "The play is a means to an end."

"Then, you need something bigger from me, don't you?"

"I do," Jack answered. "Let's say an important piece of paper needed to be signed. It would be nice if the pen ran out of ink, and the person signing it was either hard to find or uncooperative."

A moment of silence. Costello possessed an agile mind. Jack was counting on it.

"You wouldn't happen to have a Jewish problem, about yay tall?" Costello's hand indicated an approximate height.

Jack nodded.

Costello smirked. "You know powerful men back him, don't you?"

"I'm talking to a powerful man now, though there's something else that interests me."

"Interests you, how?" Costello asked.

"I'm curious, as to how it is that you've never run afoul of one of the powerful men behind my problem."

"Can I tell you a brief story, Mr. Marshall?"

The Prime Minister explained how J. Edgar Hoover, who denied the existence of organized crime on television, liked the racetrack. How the top lawman, the image of moral decency, would visit the two-dollar window and bet on a pony. A modest wager and never a problem. A little harmless fun, except, while he is at the two-dollar window, one of his agents goes to another window to place the real bet. The tacit agreement was that Costello and friends had their thing, and Hoover never went looking for what simply didn't exist.

"Impressive," Jack said. "And Ko-Ko?"

"You'll have no troubles with him."

"Appreciated. What should I do next?"

"Have your friend, the one with the play, go out to dinner."

Costello named the restaurant, the night, and the time. Jack said he'd take care of it.

"Now that we're clear," Costello said, "Two observations, if I may."

Jack shrugged. "Sure. It costs nothing to listen."

"Observation one is that I have an old friend with an unhealthy obsession, and he may run interference. I'll do my best to help you with that problem."

"And your second observation?" Jack asked.

"Your problem isn't Jewish; it's Irish."

In one masterful declaration, Frank Costello aired the names of Vito Genovese, Roy Cohn, and Robert Kennedy for Jack without saying them. Vito Genovese, Jack knew, was bent on narcotics, a lucrative enterprise that Costello, as a member of the older generation, was against. He believed drugs were fraught with problems, from politicians in the pocket to logistical issues such as distribution. Like grease that spattered, the drug trade dirtied everything. Money, however, blinded common sense, and Costello believed that greed and unnecessary risks were the first step into a prison cell or the grave.

"Any advice you can offer me, Mr. Marshall?"

"Step down."

"As in *retire*?"

"Or be retired. You can't change the future, Mr. Costello. You've had a good run."

It seemed hotter, despite the shade from the tree behind Costello. Sweat beaded on their foreheads. Jack could see that his advice wasn't what Frank Costello wanted to hear.

"You're right. I've had a good run," Costello said. A finger moved, invited

Jack closer. Jack did and saw the man's face up close. Serious eyes, honest eyes, which he hadn't expected.

"Your Irish problem is no different than the man at the two-dollar window. Both are moralists and they'll both use whatever they have at their disposal and justify the means later. You said you don't handle domestic matters."

"I don't. Why?" Jack asked.

Frank Costello's hands moved gracefully, like a ballet.

"Because the way you destroy your Irish problem is you attack those around him. Family, and let me be clear, it's not my way of doing things. I believe in rules."

Silence passed between them instead of a breeze. Jack did have something to say to the man, something that had no bearing on Walker, Cohn, Kennedy, or even Vito Genovese and the possibility of war between The Prime Minister, Anastasia at his side, and Genovese and his allies in New York and New Jersey.

"I wish you luck on appealing the tax charges."

"When someone wants you bad enough, Mr. Marshall, they'll become creative. People look at me and call me a crook, but if you ask me, the federal government is the greatest criminal mastermind of all. It was Shakespeare who said the Devil can cite Scripture for his purpose. Instead of the Bible, the government uses law books." Costello's smile was pained. "Anyway, I should've listened to my lawyer and pled the fifth more."

Jack's eyebrows jumped. His impression was that once a defendant said, "I refuse to answer on the grounds it may tend to incriminate me," the machinery stopped. There were consequences, but everything grinded to a halt.

"Plead the fifth more?" Jack said.

"My lawyer George yammered on about the diminished fifth. Know what that is?"

"Pertaining to law, no, but I've heard of it in music," Jack said.

"The Devil's music." Frank's hands opened. "But it's also a legal strategy. Lillian Hellman used it before the Committee. She offered to talk about herself but said that, in good conscience, she wanted an assurance from the committee members that she wouldn't be asked to talk about others before she entered the courtroom. Smart lady." Costello wagged his finger. "She put it in writing and said it publicly, too."

Jack considered Costello's words. "There's no way the Committee would go for that."

"Exactly, but she appeared cooperative. She claimed the higher moral ground about not being a snitch and threw the ball back in their court. Pun intended."

"Not sure I understand how diminished fifth works."

"Let's pretend you are before the House Un-American Activities Committee."

"Me before HUAC?"

Costello was serious. He folded his hands and looked up, stared at Jack as if he were Cotton Mather himself. "Are you now a member of the Communist Party?"

"No."

"Were you last year?"

"No."

"Year before?"

"No."

"Year before that?" Costello pointed a finger at Jack. "Plead the fifth now, and there's your diminished fifth, Mr. Marshall. See, there's a statute of limitations. You've answered twice, denied twice, and you can invoke your amendment right now and legally force your inquisitor to pursue another line of questioning."

"Cooperative and within the letter of the law," Jack said. "It's cagey as hell."

"But not illegal."

"Any advice you might have for me, Mr. Costello?"

"I do. Listen for the devil's music. A composer isn't supposed to use the dissonant note, but he will when it suits his purpose. Saint-Saëns did in his *Danse macabre*. Mahler's Symphony Number 9, first movement, is another example, and then there's Bach's *Saint Matthew Passion* when Judas is mentioned. That's my advice to you, Mr. Marshall."

"Listen to music?"

"Music is all around us, Mr. Marshall, especially the Devil's. Listen for that one discordant note, the one that offers no resolution, and you'll know when to act."

Chapter Ten

Leslie rented a Remington Noiseless No. 7 in black matte finish. Walker test-drove the petal keys and carriage bell. He teased her and Sheldon about whether she ought to lock up the ribbon at night. It was a joke between them from their days in Vienna. Leslie had typed two copies and used carbons so there were four available scripts.

Walker was hunched over, pencil clenched between his teeth, revising dialogue, while Vera practiced lines with Adler onstage when the payphone in the back hallway rang. Sheldon was busy on a list of items for the set.

Adler excused himself to answer the phone. It had to be his sister-in-law. The woman called every hour on the hour, hysterical with some new crisis with his son. Walker turned his attention to the piece of paper under the roll.

In the scene, he placed a Fox double-barrel Model B shotgun on the wall; not quite Chekhov's rifle, but it was classic, durable, and destined to go off at some point. His character reloaded the shotgun, set the choke for maximum spread, and the double-trigger was ready for a fast one-two. Walker sensed Adler approaching. He looked up and heard Adler. "Phone was for you. Your reservation for tonight is set."

"I didn't make any reservation."

"The Copacabana, eight, party of three. You and Sheldon."

"You said three. Was that someone from the Copa on the phone?"

"No idea. All he said was that his name was Jack."

The maître d' advertised a smile, and his hand included a gaudy pinkie ring this time. A man came up behind Walker and Sheldon. With three flat words, he was Bogart to the man at the podium. Mister maître d' didn't check his guest list. "Evening, Steps. Right this way, gentlemen. Your table is ready."

Steps was hatless and tieless, in black slacks, ordinary white shirt, and a jacket in a checkered pattern that was dull as soap water. Two waiters tended to their table.

Not that Steps looked intimidating, but his reputation preceded him like strong cologne. One server poured water in the glasses, while the other asked whether they were interested in drinks from the bar. Sheldon went virgin. "Club Soda with a twist." Walker requested a vodka martini. Steps ordered a Carling Black Label. After the waiters departed, he said, "A new beer I've wanted to try out."

His eyes owned every square inch of the Copa. Steps could tell how many people entered and left the room, whether the table across from him seated a lawyer, a politician and his mistress, or Dick and Jane on a first date. He could tell you how many times the fly circled the table before it landed.

"I recommend the filet mignon." Walker nodded, inclined to follow his lead and order the same. Sheldon continued reading the menu, so Steps small-talked.

"Since you're off-Broadway, I'd recommend Al Schacht's Restaurant, 102 East and 52nd Street, for lunches. Jewish ballplayer for the Washington Senators owns the joint. Good man, great food. Tell him I sent you."

They'd decided on three filets, and they each told the waiters how they wanted their meat cooked, and their choice of sides: creamed broccoli or mashed potatoes. The servers disappeared. Since their table afforded them privacy, Steps talked.

"Whatever you boys need, you get. The Prime Minister's orders."

"In that case, start with this." Sheldon handed Steps a piece of paper.

Steps read it. "Not a problem. I'll have carpenters and electricians on it in the morning." He turned to Walker. "About casting, I know local actors from all the art schools."

"We're good, except for one role. I need a young girl. She has to look under eighteen and special."

"I can find you a girl. She'll be legal and pass for young. My question is, special how? Blonde, brunette, short—what's the type?"

"She doesn't have many lines, so we need someone with presence. She's my gun on the wall." Both Sheldon and Steps gave him a curious expression.

"She's the linchpin to the whole play."

Walker looked away. "Here come our steaks."

Three waiters carried sizzling plates, while a fourth man cautioned them that the plates were hot. The trio put down the plates in a synchronized presentation that would've made Esther Williams proud. The sides arrived and the entourage left.

"I might have someone for that role," Sheldon said.

Steps and Walker looked at each other. "Who?" Walker asked.

"Tania."

Walker explained to Steps, "His niece."

"If she's the right age and up for the job, then we're good."

They ate like family, in absolute silence, except a band played in the background instead of a radio. The only nuisance was the waiter who interrupted them to ask whether they were enjoying their meal. They were. The maître d' then came over and asked whether they were happy with the service. They were.

Near the end of their meal, Steps reiterated his earlier point, that anything they needed, they'd get, and added that it was on the arm. No cost to them. On his dime.

"The Prime Minister spoke with your friend. Tell him that we're holding up our end."

"Is that so? I haven't talked to him yet," Walker lied.

"It seems our bosses have no great love for committees and lawyers."

The guardian angel Jack sent him had knocked on his door earlier in the day. Walker found the nearest payphone. Jack painted the conversation in Milan and it included more of Robert Kennedy. He also heard Jack discuss music theory and legalities. The devil existed, and he was out and about in the world. Walker listened intently to Jack explain Costello's lawyer's take on ways around testimony, the idea of a diminished fifth. Jack called it "an absolutely Homeric way around an amendment right."

Walker indulged Steps with a comment about love for the legal profession.

"'The first thing we do, let's kill all the lawyers.'"

"*Henry VI, Part Two*," Sheldon said. "Why does The Prime Minister dislike lawyers?"

"Because his cousin met an unfortunate end, on account of one. This cousin of his shouldn't've been subpoenaed but was because a snot-nosed lawyer had a judge ink a bunch of subpoenas. This lawyer's father pulled on a string so his kid could impress a certain senator from Wisconsin."

"Thought this senator already had a lawyer of his own," Sheldon said.

"He does." Steps sipped cold beer, and then put the glass down. "The lawyer you're talking about couldn't get the subpoenas on his own. His colleague could because of his old man. Call in a marker and the next thing you know, a judge was squeezed like a lemon. The senator's Jew lawyer didn't take it well, that some tony Irishman did what he couldn't and in a hurry."

Sheldon looked to Walker. "Who are we talking about?"

"Robert Kennedy."

"The one and only," Steps said. "Subpoenas signed in '50, and Kennedy is assistant counsel to McCarthy in '52, thanks to daddy and he reports to Roy Cohn."

"What was he doing between '51 and '52?" Sheldon asked.

Steps cleaned his hands on his napkin. "Worked Internal Security Section in '51 and handled fraud cases in Brooklyn. He joined McCarthy after his brother John was elected to the Senate."

Walker filled in another detail for Sheldon. "The Internal Security Section investigated Soviet spies."

"And The Prime Minister's cousin?" Sheldon asked.

"Kennedy convinced a judge there was some kind of Fifth Column working the New York and Jersey waterfronts. Why? Because there wasn't one strike or act of sabotage during the war years. Imagine that? There's no trouble and he thought there were Commies on the piers. You'd think with the people around him in DC, the judge who signed the subpoena woulda known The

Prime Minister's good friend Lucky guaranteed the safety of the waterfront."

Sheldon wouldn't have known this tidbit, though Walker did. After Lucky Luciano's conviction for prostitution, the US Army approached him in Dannemora and asked for his help with the Allied invasion of Italy and, later, asked him to recruit his associates in the underworld to secure New York Harbor and the piers, on both sides of the Hudson River. The OSS, the Company's precursor, and not Hoover, underscored the importance for domestic security after the SS Normandie inexplicably caught fire at Pier 88 in '42. Thanks to Lucky & Company, Generals Eisenhower and Alexander took Salerno in '43.

"Luciano did all that from a prison cell," Steps said to Sheldon. "How about you. You work for Mr. Marshall?"

"Independent contractor. You didn't say what happened to the cousin who was subpoenaed?"

"He was called up before Kefauver, like The Prime Minister was. It shoulda never happened because the man was sick."

"Sick?" Sheldon said.

"Insane in the brain. Advanced syphilis." Steps tapped his temple. "He had to go, so he went."

Steps explained. Instead of taking the Fifth, like his cousin did, Willie Moretti made a spectacle of himself. The damage done, the Commission issued a contract. The man who'd convinced Tommy Dorsey to release Sinatra from his contract, the guy who was supposed to have lunch with Dean Martin and Jerry Lewis on the day he died, couldn't get a stay of execution. Cousin to Frank Costello or not, Moretti was executed at The Elbow, a restaurant in Jersey. "It was a mercy killing, more than anything."

"Explains The Prime Minister's love for Kennedy," Sheldon said, folding his napkin.

A waiter refilled Steps's water glass. Steps thanked him and continued the diatribe after the man left. "Cohn is a son of a bitch, but this Kennedy, he's unrealistic. He hasn't learned what The Prime Minister learned years ago, that you make compromises. Kennedy shoulda learned that from his father. Joe Kennedy made serious money because he worked with us; not against us.

He made millions importing gin and scotch, and then more in Hollywood with RKO. Little Lord Fauntleroy gets a law degree and thinks if you don't go to church on Sundays and pay your bills early, you're un-American and a criminal."

What Steps had excluded and what Walker had learned from Jack was that it was Vito Genovese who had initiated the request to have Moretti put down and, seeing the opportunity to amplify the narcotics trade, suggested they ask Frank to retire after his appearance before Kefauver. The Prime Minister refused.

The sound in the room turned boozy, with the slow syncopation of drums and wheezing horn section. The musicians looked like they'd pulled an all-nighter with a female rhythm section in Harlem. It all changed when a trumpet punched the air with squeals and the drummer banged the kit faster than a heartbeat.

Sheldon asked Steps, "Whatever happened to the judge who signed those subpoenas?"

"He liked to walk his dog." Steps reached inside his jacket for his cigarette case. He chose a cig, put it between his lips, and closed the case. He lit his cigarette with a Zippo lighter. "His Honor slipped on some ice and fell down a flight of stairs. He broke his hand, too."

"And the dog?"

"The Prime Minister loves dogs. The dog did fine. We should leave. I don't like our new friends across the room."

Walker looked to the mirrored wall. Behind him were two men, two tall men in long coats, too long and too heavy for a muggy June night.

Hoover's men.

Chapter Eleven

There was the clang of a dropped hammer, a profanity with a Jersey accent, and the call for nails and more wood. One of the carpenters mumbled an apology since Vera was onstage with the male actor cast as Joseph. Walker watched, Steps observed, and Sheldon sat off to the side in the audience.

This was the domestic scene, Rose and Joseph at war over money that wasn't there for their sick child. Vera as Rose set in on husband Joe, fresh through the door from work. He's distressed over reductions at the ad agency. Like any good husband, he doesn't want to burden the wife. Adler directed. "Do it again. Top of the page, Miss Williams."

Vera's voice competed against the noise the carpenters were making and the voice of her leading man. Rage and the words fit the scene on the pages, her volume and delivery matched her frustration with the cacophony of dings, bangs, and crashes.

"Stop," Vera yelled.

The startled cast looked at her, but the carpenters continued hammering. Vera screamed but the carpenters kept at it, until a loud, shrill whistle from Steps arrested the noise.

"Boys, take a break and let the lady have a word with the director."

"You don't want me to lose my voice, do you, Mr. Adler?" Vera said.

"Of course not, but we need to rehearse our lines."

"Then let's do it elsewhere, somewhere quiet."

While Adler and Vera argued, Walker asked two actors to stand in front of a backdrop, the shadow of a lone carpenter and scaffold behind them.

Walker, script in hand, requested a minute with the same men and showed them some pages. He pointed to the top of the stage set and shared some words with the lone worker on the scaffold. Vera and her male lead resumed the scene, their argument on a low flame, the steam in the kettle building. Walker nodded to the foreman.

The hammering restarted, a blow here and another there. Some men struck wood; others whacked metal. Little by little, the orchestra of hammers achieved a steady rhythm of percussions. Behind the two actors, everyone spied the silhouette of a man, his arm cocked, the hammer raised and delivered. Rose and Joseph lifted their voices until at the pitch of the battle, Vera rebelled. "I can't do this."

Walker shouted, "Don't stop."

He rushed the stage and confronted Vera. "I need you to fight him," pointing at Joseph, "and that hammering behind you is the world outside, against the both of you."

Walker shouted to the carpenter on the scaffold, "Raise your arm and hold it to the count of five and then strike. That ought to slow the music down. The rest of you, as you were."

The man with the hammer raised said, "Like this, Mr. Thompson?"

"That's right. Hold for a count of five and then hit the metal."

"Will do, Mr. Thompson."

"What's the meaning of this?" Adler asked.

Walker pointed to the man on the scaffold. "See for yourself."

"Not that," Adler said. "I meant you undermining my play. I'm the director. I'm the boss."

"You mean, the boss of Jack Warner's play. Relax, Mr. Adler." He pointed to Vera and companion, on stage. "Her husband is getting grilled at work like a cheese sandwich and his wife is worried about their daughter. She's frustrated and he's angry because no matter what they do, they're drowning in a teaspoon. Their fight has to be authentic."

"And that is your solution?" Adler pointed to the man with the hammer. "Nobody will ever accuse you of having the Lubitsch Touch, Mr. Thompson. All we're missing is a sickle and a poster of the *Daily Worker*. There has to be a subtler way."

"Subtle?"

Steps whistled again. "Sit this one out, pal. Get the steam out from under your collar." The gangster pointed Walker to an empty seat within the sea of seats. "Mr. Adler, a word, please."

Steps unshelled a peanut, ate the nut, and placed the shell inside his jacket pocket. He was wearing a different ensemble from the one he'd worn last night at the Copa. Tailored slacks, tan, a white shirt without a tie, and two-toned shoes, shined and buffed. Adler braced himself. He clenched his fists.

"Relax, Mr. Adler," Steps said. "You gotta ask yourself a question here."

"And what question is that?"

"You wanna run a racket, or do you wanna make art? I listened to the two of you from over there." Steps turned and faced the empty seats, and then to Adler. "A racket makes money, art not so much. You have a choice. You could sell tooth decay to the folks from Nebraska off the tour bus, who can't afford Broadway prices, or you can give them something they can't see back home in Omaha."

"Your kind is only interested in money."

"My kind? That cuts, brother." Steps put his hands up. "Come over here." Steps put one arm around Adler's shoulders and pulled him close. Adler flinched, expecting a punch to the gut, but there was none.

There was no mistaking Steps for a son of Park Avenue. He was a Bowery boy, a kid from Five Points and an East Ender. The diplomacy, his art of the walk and talk with Adler, he'd inherited from his boss, The Prime Minister.

"This isn't radio, Mr. Adler. There's nobody in our lobby handing out copies of *Red Channels*. There's no station manager worried about subscriptions and sponsors. My boss guarantees whatever you need for this show, including more money than you'll ever see from Jack Warner. Now, Walter over there isn't O'Neill, but he has a story worth telling. Trust the story, trust him to steer you right. You have a chance to create art. Knock yourself out." Steps lowered his hand, rested it on Adler's back as he guided him back to the stage. "You've got Miss Williams, a great cast, and your set design is coming together; and most important of all, you've got protection."

Steps said something into Adler's ear. Whatever it was he said to Adler was between him, Adler, the one, true god, and the future messiah.

Delivery boys arrived with lunch. Steps had Artie Cutler put together some sandwiches for the cast and crew. Turkey, corned beef, and several pastrami sandwiches were laid out. A pastrami and corned beef, with Swiss cheese, coleslaw, and Russian dressing was hand-delivered to Steps.

The theatre filled with the sounds of deli papers being unwrapped. Cast and construction crew talked about pickles and messy sandwiches. The last of the delivery boys ushered in an assortment of soda pop in ice buckets. Hires Root Beer, Nehi in a variety of flavors, some RC, and Sun Crest. Steps tipped the boys five dollars each, but the young man who handed Steps his special sandwich and a bottle of Carling received ten.

A carpenter brought out a record player and a pile of records. The break-hour passed with songs from Jo Stafford, Frankie Laine, and Sinatra from the portable. When Patti Paige started to skip on the player, Steps stopped eating and visited the carpenters. "Boys, let me show you a trick I learned in Newark." He reached into his pocket for change. "Place a nickel on top of the arm and voilà, the record don't skip no more."

After lunch, as everyone returned to their stations, the door at the top of the stairs opened and a wedge of sunlight widened and then narrowed and vanished when the door closed. Nobody but those sensitive to unexpected sounds looked. Steps slipped his hand inside his jacket. Walker lowered his hand, inched it towards Grable under his arm. Sheldon watched and waited.

A woman stood there. She was slim, tall in white linen, a scarf around her neck, a belt around her waist. A small purse hung from her shoulder. She held a travel case in faux crocodile in one hand and in her other hand, a hard-sided suitcase.

Her makeup wasn't derivative, taken from a how-to article in *McCall's*. Her look and fashion sense hadn't come off the screen or the pages of *Look* and *Photoplay* magazines. She looked eighteen but could pass for younger.

Her hair was platinum, her eyes dark blue, her lips, soft and the kind to make a man feel guilty the first time he saw them, and very ashamed later when he thought about them again.

The carpenters stopped and stared. So did Vera, her eyes unable to stop looking at her.

Tania had arrived.

Chapter Twelve

Steps's remark to Adler that he wasn't O'Neill stung. O'Neill was good for relatives around the table with the booze in the wrong glass and the Bible an arm's length away on the sideboard.

Walker reread sections of the play in his apartment in Hell's Kitchen. He reread all the dialogue. None of it sounded like rain on a tin roof. Le Corbusier might've said "God is in the details" about buildings, but American theater was more like a game of baseball. The trot around the bases required a hit. The last thing Walker wanted was for the audience to think he was pitching them a spitball.

The floorboards creaked.

Walker looked over to the door behind him. He saw no shadows under the door. No voices either. He returned to the script and read his markups in blue pencil, Adler's suggestions for stage directions in red.

Another sound.

He eased Grable out of her holster. He glided to the door, ear to the wood and to the sounds in the hallway. A black shadow passed in front of the door's eyepiece. His left hand reached for the doorknob. A breeze chilled him. It was the same chill he felt before combat. He looked down. The shadow stopped.

Walker raised his right arm when the wooden door came off its hinges.

Leslie had returned to the hotel from a day of shopping, lunch alone, and exploring Manhattan. Vera was at her vanity removing her earrings and primping; room-service, her dinner, was in the first room. The silver dome was flipped on its back like a beetle, the dinner plate scraped clean, and a bottle of bubbly headfirst into a bucket of ice.

"How was work today?" she asked Vera.

"You should have been there. We could've used you."

"For what…more typing? No, thank you."

"I told you I was sorry."

"I see that you've had some champagne." Leslie put down a shopping bag.

The clerk who waited on her said the bag was a limited edition. It was a paper sack, with strong handles, a rose on one side and a gloved hand with an umbrella on the other side with the store's name in distinctive script: Bloomingdale's.

"You should slip into something comfortable, and please don't nag." Vera said.

Leslie shimmied out of her dress. "I don't nag."

"Like an old biddy, you do."

"It's just that you should refrain from drinking during the work week."

Vera dismissed the comment with a laugh. "Work week? In this business work is seven days a week, so you might as well have fun sometime. You go out and there are photographers. Work. You go to the set and there's the camera. Work. Here, I have a stage and I have my lines. It's work, all the same."

Leslie disliked the combination of self-pity and bubbles from champagne. She took off her shoes and put on her robe. "What happened at work today, Vera?"

"Nothing. Why do you ask?"

"I ask because there's a dead bottle in the other room. You also have that purr in your voice. You want to make love; and when you do, it's because you have something to prove."

"What an awful thing to say, Maggie."

Vera pivoted her bottom and straddled the chair, her long fingers curled around the top of the backrest. Leslie called it the Dietrich Maneuver. All Vera needed were a top hat, tails, and a cigarette in her hand. She had none of those props but talked anyway. "If you must know, the girl slated to play my daughter showed up today."

"And?"

"Every man in the house cracked his neck to get a look at her. You should've seen them. Half of them held their breath, while the other half sucked in their gut when she came near them."

"Now that we have her looks out of the way, what was she like?"

"Quiet, acted all shy and demure, proper and polite, impeccable manners, a soft voice and a figure that was sinful."

"You're jealous."

"I am. You wouldn't understand."

"I'll ignore that last part. So, she's young, Vera. You're famous and glamorous. Did you ever think that you might intimidate her?"

"Honey, if that was intimidated, I'd hate to see confident, although…"

"Although what?"

"Something's not quite right about her."

"You're imagining things, Vera. Besides, I read the script and she doesn't have many lines. You have nothing to worry about. The spotlight is yours."

Leslie embraced Vera. "I dislike it when you get this way. You're beautiful."

"I'm sorry if I sound so fragile, Maggie. I feel old. She's young. She's my daughter in this play and that alone makes me feel ancient. In the last three years my career has had something of a resurgence. Can you blame me if I want to hold on to it?"

Vera was "a woman of a certain age." She didn't look it, but when she turned forty, leading roles dried up and the cash crop was in playing dour matrons, or some forgotten woman.

"I really shouldn't complain," Vera said. "The girl was respectful to me. It's just that…there's something queer about her."

"It's all in your head. You worry too much," Leslie said as she stroked Vera's hair. Leslie touched Vera's cheek with hers, thought to kiss her lips, but the question rose to the surface. "What's this girl's name?"

"Tania."

Leslie hugged Vera. As she looked at the vanity behind Vera, her eyes in the mirror almost broke the glass. Vera was right about Tania. Something was not quite right about the girl, but that required a history lesson she couldn't discuss with Vera.

Leslie understood Tania. Leslie understood Sheldon. All three of them shared an act of violence in common. Tania was beautiful. She was polite. She was respectful. She was also deadly.

Walker came to inside a warehouse, seated in a chair, his hands tied behind him. The place reeked of tar and raw sewage. The wide door in front of him opened to a view of the East River and the Hell Gate Bridge. A few feet away from him, a seagull, the fisherman's vulture, sat on a stump. The bird's head turned, one black button of an eye watching him, pink legs and webbed feet doing a small jig of forward and then back on the small platform.

The last time he'd enjoyed this spa treatment was in Vienna. The one positive out of the negative encounter then was that he quit smoking. A tall man appeared in front of him.

"How you doin'?"

His host took a slow puff from his cigarette. The man was square as a lineman, and the shape of his head suggested he'd forgotten to wear his helmet one time too many.

Another man, a short one, came into view. "I hear youse a writer."

The seagull stayed for the show. The taller man initiated the interview. He had hands that could chip ice. "Me and my associate here have questions, and we're counting on you havin' answers."

Walker looked up at his inquisitors. "You could've asked me at my place."

"We were worried youse run."

"Ask your question then."

"You play straight with us, and you might not take a swim."

"Ask away."

"What's Frank's angle?" the giant asked.

"Frank who?"

The shorter man delivered a punch to Walker's midsection.

"Frank, as in The Prime Minister," the little man screamed into Walker's ear.

"Never met the man."

"Why is Frank Costello so interested in this play?"

"Patron of the arts?"

Walker braced, but there was no blow. The tall man leaned over, eye to eye with Walker.

"Hows come you don't pay protection money? How does it add up that a no-name like you comes into town and you don't have no problem with any unions? You show up and Steps is all lovey-dovey."

"I'm just a writer."

"Not one problem with the carpenters, electricians, or the garment industry."

"Look, I am a writer from the West Coast."

The two gangsters stood there. The big one cracked his knuckles and grabbed a handful of Walker's hair. "You go back to your director, your producer, whomever, and you tell them there's an insurance premium. Fifty a week. Understand me?"

"I'm a nobody."

The big man's fist came down like a power shovel. Walker had no fillings, but he anticipated loosened teeth after that blow. The runt spoke into to Walker's ear. "Between us, Steps don't have to—"

"Don't have to what?" Walker heard.

The sounds of numerous footsteps suggested Steps had arrived with reinforcements.

"Nuttin,'" the small man said.

Steps pointed to Walker in the chair. "This how you treat a guest? You size up my friend here for a kimono and a long swim?"

"We were having a conversation," the short man said.

"A conversation about what?" Steps said. "Looks like he was listening with his face."

"Why The Prime Minister was so interested in his play. It don't figure."

"Since when does what The Prime Minister thinks concern you?" The big lug laughed the way a fat man heaves. Steps punched him in the solar plexus and talked to the man when he doubled over. "Tell your boss that if he orders a civilian pinched while he enjoys The Prime Minister's hospitality, he will hear about it. Now scram, and you…" Steps grabbed the short man by the lapel. "You, hold on."

"Whataya want from me?"

"Hand over whatever you crumbs took off my friend: wallet, watch, whatever."

"Nothing like that," the short man said. "Only thing we lifted was his forty-five."

Steps admired Grable before he returned it to Walker. "You're a peculiar man, Walter. You take a beating and you don't spill a word about The Prime Minister or your boss, Mr. Marshall. The average joe would've handed over his own mother. Then, there's this nineteen-eleven." He held up Grable. "Now, this here makes me wonder."

"Wonder what?"

"How you came by a piece like this?"

"Army, like most guys," Walker answered. "Those guys who left, who's their boss?"

"Vito Genovese."

Chapter Thirteen

She asked him to indulge her, and he agreed to it. She warned him that it'd be expensive. He agreed to it anyway. She said she would make the reservations. He agreed to that too. She gave him the time for a mid-day meal, a time that was late for lunch and too early for dinner, but he agreed to that also. When he had arrived, he told the maître d' the name she had given and followed a tuxedoed gentleman on the expedition to the private table in the back.

He had never seen so much red. Red leather banquettes, red lampshades, a red rug with an Oriental pattern, and red dessert plates—and all of it was just a drop of blood compared to the amount of gold. Gold-leaf ceiling, gold firebird, gold statues, and the soft golden glow of sconces against gold veins in mirrored walls.

He walked past an acrylic bear that weighed the same as a real bear, past a luminous tree with Fabergé eggs hanging from the branches. The bear and the tree reminded him of the Greek heroine, Atalanta, whose father abandoned her on the mountainside, to be reared by a protective mother bear. The huntress swore to a vow of virginity, refused marriage, and killed two centaurs who tried to rape her.

Tania had picked the Russian Tea Room.

Her gauntleted white hands rested on the pink tablecloth. She closed the book she was reading when she saw him. She stood up and they kissed each other on both cheeks.

They spoke the language they had always used with each other, Russian. They could've spoken in any of the other languages they both knew: French,

German, or Hungarian. Though English was a distant cousin to her, she spoke it well and without a discernible accent.

Sheldon pulled out his chair and sat down. He set his water goblet aside. He heard the table of Brighton Beach mobsters behind him, speaking bad Russian, which they ruined with street slang. He observed them in the mirrored wall. To him they were thugs who wouldn't survive a day in the Butyrka prison. He turned his attention to something more pleasant: her.

She was wearing a peach-and-blue lace dress, with a simple necklace. She was discreet as to how she displayed her cleavage. Tania made American women her age seem tawdry. Her name in Russian meant "fairy queen."

"Thank you for indulging me. I've always wanted to visit this restaurant."

He pointed to the empty glass. "They served you vodka?"

"They did because I didn't order it in English. We should have a drink together later, in honor of my father and the promise we made to each other."

"We'll have that toast, but food first, please."

The waiter handed him a menu, recited the specials, and said he'd return to hear their decisions. Sheldon stole brief, furtive glances at her over the menu while she read the description of the veal and lamb dumplings in broth. She knew what he was doing and rewarded him with a smile each time. They ordered appetizers.

Sheldon noticed the book on the table. "You're reading Dickinson. America's Sibyl."

"Enigmatic, yes, but I enjoy her for her violence with language. I find most American poetry either sentimental or bombastic. She's forthright. 'Tell all the Truth but tell it slant.'"

The first course, dumplings for him and a salad for her, arrived. Tania spoke with a student's passion for a favorite author. He appreciated her intensity, her enthusiasm. The scared, vulnerable child he remembered in Vienna was long gone. Everything about Tania had become refined and honed to precision, from her diction to drinking water from crystal without leaving a trace of lipstick. As they ate, he noticed how her eyes admired the splendid combinations of colors throughout the dining room, from the red scalloped curtains to the silver trays and bowls for the cream and sugar.

"I wish that you had had a childhood," he said.

"No need to dwell on what can't be changed. I'm fine."

"Are you?"

They paused to let the waiter take away the dishes. They both had decided on salmon in a pastry with a champagne sauce for their entrées.

"Would you prefer that I be 'a shy little wren, a sweet little thing,' as Miss Dickinson described herself in her letters? I can be if you want me to be that way."

She said it with determination. Tania had survived Nazis first, and then the Communists. Both groups hated each other. The Nazis, Sheldon knew from personal experience, didn't waste bullets on Russians; they ran them into electrified fences. Stalin was the titan Saturn who devoured his own people, and now his apparatchiks were following the same bloodied path. Tania's father's name was an entry, a ghost, in the ledger of human cruelty. He had disappeared into the gulag system.

"I simply wish you had known some silliness earlier in life."

She tried to smile. "I enjoyed silly moments with my father, although I don't understand why he pursued politics when it endangered his family."

"One day you can forgive him for that. Maybe, when you become a mother."

"And what about you?" she asked Sheldon.

"What about me?"

"Has time healed your wounds? Do you feel guilty?"

"Guilty that I survived?"

"Not that." She sipped some water. "I meant how we met."

"Him? No. You were a child then. That's different, Tania."

Tania was speaking about the man who had abused her in Vienna before she had met Sheldon. She also spoke of the day Sheldon had saved Jack and Walker, and how she had exacted her revenge on another man who had hurt her.

Waiters set down the second course, while a busboy refreshed their water. They started in on their meals with the slow scrapes of knives and forks.

"And now, you work with Jack and Walker."

"Jack is the reason we were able to escape from Vienna. Are you mad that I asked you to come to New York to help them?"

"No. I'm here because you asked me. You saved his life and he helped us in Vienna. I ought to pay my part for him helping me, and I'm grateful to you because you saved my life but when is the debt settled and paid in full?"

"The salmon is delicious. Isn't the pastry flaky and ingenious?"

She looked at Sheldon with a royal intensity, those blue eyes demanding an answer. "When do I repay my debt to you?"

He searched for a waiter. He wanted to toast her father and distract her.

"You repay me by living a good life, by getting an excellent education, having a family, if that is what you want, or by having a career."

"A career in this country?" Her lips twisted in amusement. "I'm not cut out to be a housewife, teacher, or a nurse. You know that." Her last words were said with all the seriousness of a physician to a patient with a grim prognosis. "There is an alternative path."

His eyes confronted hers. "Jack won't allow it. You're a child. Where is that waiter?"

She held up her gloved hand and a waiter appeared. Tania ordered two vodkas, in perfect Russian, and instructed the server to bring them to the table after dessert. He nodded and disappeared.

They ate in silence. The Brighton bunch had left. They waited for their final course, a crème brûlée with a berry salad for him and chocolate cake with a molten center and pistachio ice cream topped by raspberry syrup for her.

"This play should offer me some of that silliness you think I'd missed out on as a child," she said.

"The role you play is far from silly. I regret that I hadn't read the part until after I'd invited you. The part as Rosemary might prove cathartic for you."

He cracked the glazed sugar with the edge of his spoon. She let the fork slide slowly between her teeth, to take the chocolate off the tines. She wore the raspberry syrup in the corners of her lips. "Cathartic sounds fun," she said.

"Tell me about this promise with your father."

"He said that if we survived the war he'd take me to a fancy restaurant, and we'd toast each other."

When their vodkas arrived, she rotated the small-stemmed glass and asked him why they weren't staying at the same hotel.

"A young lady needs privacy," he said.

"Maybe I don't want to be alone." Again, she gleamed at him. Eyes, a show of teeth, those lips, and he became uncomfortable.

"It's not that simple, Tania."

"You can change your mind."

Sheldon raised his glass, "To your father."

She raised her vodka and said, "To you."

Chapter Fourteen

Steps handed Walker a bag of ice from the back of the car.

"First-aid in the trunk? I'm impressed."

"You should see the repair kit for the tires. C'mon, we'll take you to your place."

The car interior reeked of rubbed leather and Caswell-Massey's Jockey Club. The leather belonged to the customized Shoebox sedan; the aftershave, to the driver. Steps sat quiet as a date next to Walker during the healthier version of a one-way ride.

It was one of those long sultry nights, humid as a sauna. One take of the knuckles on the chauffeur's hands said he belonged to a very real and adult world, the kind that'd seen and survived bright lights, a phonebook, a rubber hose, and maybe, if the cop was creative, a hand-crank and copper wires. Walker hedged his questions with care. "So, that was Vito's subtle way of welcoming me to the neighborhood?"

"Vito is never subtle. How are you feeling?"

"Tenderized, like a club steak. Good thing you showed up. You have the gift of foresight, or something?" Walker touched his side. It felt like Ezzard Charles met Jersey Joe Walcott. Steps looked down at the bag of ice against the ribs. "Your associate Mister Marshall is interesting."

"Interesting how?"

"You say you're from the left coast, and your boss said he was from DC."

"Technically, he's from Virginia," Walker said. "You haven't answered me. Interesting how?"

"You think you're the only one capable of research? I've got friends, Walter, if that's your real name. Your friend Mr. Marshall visited The Prime Minister in the joint."

"And that's the sum of your research?"

"No, I'm only getting started. You show up, script in hand and with a pad in Hell's Kitchen, the month's rent paid in advance, and then there's the Loudmouth you're carrying." He looked down at Grable on the seat between them. Steps picked up the gun. "Care to tell me why a guy like you carries a piece like this?"

"I heard New York was a dangerous place. Look, I'm a writer and that's it."

"Yeah, and I go to mass every Sunday."

Walker shifted the ice to his temple. "I forgot. The door to my place."

"Don't worry about it," Steps said. "I had one of the carpenters fix it."

Walker climbed the stairs. His hand used the railing like a skier used a rope tow, until he reached his apartment. Steps was behind him, the restored door in front of him. The carpenter's work included the original lock because Walker's key turned it. The door swung inward without a squeak.

"Say the rest of what you've got to say, Steps. I need sleep."

"Say *writer* all you want, but this world around you is non-fiction, my friend. Life is about to become complicated with Vito Genovese. Whatever angle you and your friend Marshall are playing, it'd better not hurt The Prime Minister."

"Because you two are such good friends?"

"We are."

"And Vito?"

"Business."

The bag of ice on his desk, Walker held Grable up for Steps to see. He ejected the mag, racked the slide, ejection port up, and popped the round and caught it in mid-air with his support hand. "Eject and catch is not recommended."

"Just a writer, like you said."

Walker placed the forty-five next to the typewriter.

"You can trust me, Steps, and you can trust Jack Marshall."

"Get some rest. I'll tell Adler you're under the weather," Steps said as he opened the door and left.

Taking his shirt off was as pleasant as a full nelson, but Walker managed. He fell back on the mattress. His jaw hurt and his ribs were bruised. He lay there, pillow behind his head, counting his toes. Sleep swelled in his veins and his eyes became heavy then heavier.

He thought about his writing. First, there was the screenplay for Warner last year, and now this play. He wasn't a poet or a philosopher who conjured with metaphors, but he did dream about love and time, about Peggy of yesteryear and Leslie, too.

Sleep dripped like morphine, line by line, like Keats and his nightingale, but there would be no singing bird tonight. He had a seagull on his mind, and it wasn't Chekhov's.

The next morning, he wanted coffee, but had none; he wanted some eggs, but had none of those, either. He craved bacon. He looked at his watch and realized the time. He remembered Steps and the man's suggestion to take the day off when he heard a soft rap on his door.

He ignored the peephole, swung the door open. His ribs hurt when he did that, and his jaw could move but no words came out.

There was food and there was Tania.

Chapter Fifteen

His contact said twenty-four hours. Jack had one day and one night to review the contents of two folders before Hoover's file clerk noticed they were missing. His daughter let herself in.

"What is it, Elizabeth?"

"We need to talk."

"Please, take a seat."

His daughter, unlike his son, was assertive and deliberate in her choice of words. Elizabeth possessed a disarming smile, and she pinned her hair back, unlike girls her age. She sat down, shoulders back, head erect, and folded her hands on her lap. The nuns at St. Mary's Academy had taught her comportment and poise, but the confidence was all Elizabeth Virginia Marshall.

"I want to know the difference between a girl, a lady, and a woman."

Jack glanced at the two folders, the mountain of information in front of him. He could take the coward's way out and tell her that now was not a good time. He opted for the more diplomatic, "Don't you think you ought to discuss this with your mother?"

"No."

Jack had handled Nazis in Vienna, established the government's interest in British India, but his own daughter was harder and more complicated than the Durand Line.

"What prompted this question?"

"A girl at school called me an awful name," she said, not looking at him. This conversation was going to require either pliers or delicate tweezers.

"And you won't tell me what she called you?"

"No." He admired that she was not a snitch. Her hands remained folded.

"Will you tell me what happened then?"

"I'd rather not say."

"How can I help you then?"

"Afterwards, she said that I'd never be a lady or a woman."

"Since you can't tell me what she called you, or what happened, then my answer is another question. What's wrong with being a girl for now? You have your whole life ahead of you. What do you say to that?"

She blinked and her face betrayed no emotion.

"Jack Junior talks about becoming a policeman, a fireman, or a pilot. I wonder what there is out there in the world for me, because I don't want to be a nurse, or a teacher."

Jack understood. This had nothing to do with her classmate.

"When do I stop being a girl?"

This was a question for Dr. Kildare on the radio, he thought. She expected an answer from him, and she'd pursue it with all the ferocity contained within that small body and dress of hers.

"You've already stopped being a girl," he said, and watched her face register surprise, then pride, before the inevitable question.

"When?"

"Remember when I used to put you on the table?" he said. She nodded. "I used to tell you to stay still and be careful because you might fall off and get hurt. Remember that?" She nodded again. "Remember the time you reached for something, and you fell? You cried and cried, and you said you hated me."

"I can never hate you, Daddy," she said, a flash of panic in her face, and then she composed herself. "I don't remember saying 'I hate you,' but I seem to remember you stopped putting me on the table. Did I apologize?"

"No."

Her eyes had moistened. She was sensitive. "I'm sorry that I didn't."

"I know, and that was when you stopped being a girl. You made a mistake, paid the consequences, and moved on. I think that's more important than worrying about whether you're a girl or a woman."

"Why?"

"Because you decided, then and there, that you weren't a victim."

She looked straight ahead, did some internal calculation, and jumped down from the chair. "Thanks, Daddy."

Jack returned to the file on Adler and sister-in-law Judith née Kaplan Nussbaum.

"Come on in, Tania," Walker said, door opened.

"I brought you some breakfast. Here, hold this while I put my purse down." She handed him a brown bag, full to the brim with groceries. He could feel something warm inside the bag. "Those are biscuits." She had already surveyed the small room, the kitchen, desk, and bed. "I'll leave my purse on the bed."

"I wasn't expecting you."

"It's called a surprise."

"Does Sheldon know you're here?"

She had stopped to admire the holster near the bed. "It's been so long, hasn't it?" Her smile was bright, the sun behind her, brighter. Her hair, platinum, looked like snow on fire.

"I remember Grable from Vienna and from the last time we saw each other in California. You haven't changed."

"You have."

She reclaimed the groceries. "Let me have this, before the biscuits go cold."

"I'd like to know how you found me, Tania."

"Steps. He said you might not feel well and since I don't have many lines, I asked him where I'd find you. He insisted that one of his men drive me over. Interesting cologne, not-so-bright fellow. The scent didn't match the face. I'd describe the scent as patrician, and his line of work is hardly aristocratic." She removed items from the bag while she talked. "While I shopped, he waited in the car. Ford Tudor Sedan. I hate to think what you might find in the glove or boot. I sent him away after I arrived."

"You shouldn't be here, Tania. It doesn't look right."

"I don't see why not. I don't have lines to rehearse. Why should I hang around and be a dartboard for Vera Williams? We both know she won't miss me, and I doubt Leslie will."

"You know that's not true."

Walker realized that he must look terrible. He hadn't shaved and his hair was a mess. She pretended not to notice. She carried on, as the British say, a dervish of activity and with purpose, in a peach summer dress. He rubbed his chin. "I'll go shave."

"Make it quick," he heard her say behind him. He made his way out of the kitchen to his closet, where he snatched a fresh shirt and headed to the bathroom.

He heard the metallic groan of the stove door closing, heard something slide out and then back into the oven. He imagined jam or butter slathered on hot-from-the-oven biscuits. The crisp scent of coffee drifted from the kitchen to the bathroom. He heard noises. She jostled dishes and a pan from the cupboard. He could hear her cracking eggs.

The bathroom was cold, square as a matchbox, white with linoleum and porcelain. He squeezed out some toothpaste and brushed his teeth until his mouth felt minty. He wet his hair and combed it. He splashed his face with hot water, stropped his razor and lathered up. He used the mirror to see where he'd place the blade. He shaved in controlled strokes, stretching the skin, and kept the steel wet, until he was done. He shocked his face with cold water next, then patted it. No cuts, no blood. He put on his fresh shirt, hungry for breakfast.

He entered the kitchen to the sounds of bacon blistering. "Excellent timing," she said.

He confirmed that everything in the room was where he'd last seen it. Grable was on his desk. The holster hung from the bedpost. Her purse was on the bed.

He offered to help but she shooed him away and told him to take a seat. She poured coffee, warning him it was strong and hot; the bacon, she said, was drying on some paper towels. The flame was low, and the eggs were sputtering. With a spatula, she moved the eggs to the plates where the biscuits were waiting. He watched her from behind as she worked at the small counter space. The sunlight came in at a slant and her dress darkened from peach to orange. He saw the pale calves and the rest of her legs disappear under her skirt.

They sipped coffee. They ate like a couple; each started from the whites of their eggs and worked their way to the centers. They each cut their strips of bacon into smaller sections, and they grinned at the mess their buttered biscuits made.

"Enjoying your eggs?" she asked.

"They're great, thank you."

Coffee cup to her lips, her eyes considered the last untouched yolk on his plate. "Don't forget the best part."

He took his biscuit, tapped the last part of each egg, and let the yolk run. He ran his bread through the wet mess and mopped it up. "We should talk, Tania."

"I don't want to talk," she said, collecting the dishes. "Finish your coffee."

He did. She returned to the table and stood there in front of him. She had noticed the bruise on the side of his face. "Does it hurt?"

"It's nothing."

"May I?" she asked, her hand up near his face. He said nothing, but he felt the heat from her fingertips. The dishes, the warmth from all the cooking, he told himself. Her touch explored the recent violence. He tried not to look at her face and tried not to look at the rest of her in front of him, but she kept moving into him while her fingertips lingered on the bruise. Her hand drifted, her thumb came near the corner of his mouth. He closed his eyes. He felt her hand sliding down, her hair falling, and then her lips on his.

Chapter Sixteen

The first kiss was nice, slow and memorable. Somewhere between the second kiss and the lazy slip of her shoulder strap he found his conscience. He had to say no. He had to say *no* to that blonde hair, to those eyes, to that lower lip, *no* to the mild taste of lipstick, and especially *no* to a peach in a sundress.

No. No. No.

Her arms around his neck, her mouth slightly open after she pulled back, a smirk formed on her lips as if she were pleased with herself. His hands on her hips, she moved in to straddle him in the chair, her legs parted. Her smile said she thought all of this was some delicious game to her. His hands pushed against bone and slipped. She had strong, firm hips and thighs.

He stood up, pushed her off and that was when she must've felt ugly because the expression on her face changed. He felt ugly; the room and the entire world turned ugly and meaningless. He looked out the window, saw fog in the skyline, and wanted to walk into it and disappear forever.

She said something low and sweet, but he wasn't listening. He had said it. "No."

"Why not?"

"I can't."

"I'm eighteen."

Her eyes searched the room. They found the holster and then the revolver, but she picked up her purse. He went to say something. She told him to shut up.

"Let's talk," he said.

She said something impolite. Tania stood there, her eyes full of schoolyard hurt. She headed for the door. He didn't know why he felt the need or the urge, but he blocked her from leaving. He mumbled something stupid. She held the top of her purse with both hands, asked him something he didn't hear, and he said "No" again. She lowered the purse with her left hand, looked up at him. She asked again, why not.

"Because you're a kid."

She slapped him hard across the face with her right hand, pushed him aside and walked out. She slammed the door behind her.

He collapsed backwards, his shoulders against the wall. His eyes swept the room, as a photographer would, and composed the scene. He saw the table and chairs, the breakfast scene. He crossed the room and touched a dish on the counter. A simple, innocent dish that he grabbed and threw against the wall. He needed to give a sound to all that had been broken.

"Fuck!"

Walker returned to the theatre, but he didn't go inside. He felt hung over, exhausted, and empty. He was tired of the high road, of doing the right thing, and being left with the feeling he had done something wrong.

He scribbled a note and gave it to one of the boys Steps parked in front of the theatre to take inside to their boss. In the time it would take Steps to get to the soda fountain across the street, he'd place a call to Jack from one of the payphones there.

The soda jerk was polishing the real estate to a high shine when he asked, "What can I get you, brother? You look like you need something stronger than what I've got behind this counter."

Walker ordered a Bromo-Seltzer. When it arrived, he watched the bubbles, the sizzle and the effervescence. He took his sip when the front door opened and tickled a little bell overhead.

Hot summer air mixed with the refrigerated air-conditioning air, and the two weather fronts felt like thunder. It was Leslie.

He chose not to look. The sight of her burned more than the fizz inside of his mouth.

"A man came in with a note for Steps," she said. "I asked him where you were, and he said I'd find you here."

"So much for privacy. I thought it was a federal offense to read someone else's mail."

"Smart remarks aside, what's going on?"

"Everything and nothing. Look, if you don't mind, I'd asked to see Sheldon, not you."

He realized talking to her that way was his second mistake of the day with women.

"There's no need to be rude," Leslie answered.

"This world is rude."

She stepped forward, stopped. "What happened to your face?"

"I'd rather not talk about it."

Leslie wasn't wearing peach, but still looked as welcoming as fruit. He tried not to think north of the hemline. He had wanted her once. Her rejection had laid him out flat as a fish on a bed of ice, and it hurt to look at her sometimes, just like his ribs when he breathed.

"What's gotten into you?" she asked.

"Nothing you can fix, Maggie."

"I could at least try and be your friend."

"Try? It's always the same with you women. You try to realign a man's system to see if the blood'll flow the other way, and when it doesn't play out the way you wanted, suddenly everyone is a friend."

Leslie glanced over at the soda jerk, who'd made the face of a man who heard a riddle. "You're not making any sense. I came here to tell you Sheldon will be here in a moment, and to discuss something else with you. We have a problem."

"We?" Walker swallowed the last of the Bromo-Seltzer and made a sour face. "What's with this *we*, all of sudden? Let me guess. Vera is unhappy with a scene."

"No."

"Something with the set design?" Nothing. "The script? Did I end a sentence with a preposition?" He pushed the empty glass away from him. "Nobody cares that I might have a problem."

"Self-pity is never attractive," she said, the voice higher and frustrated. "I came here to talk to you about Adler, but let's hear this problem that has you all bothered and inconsiderate, you big jerk."

"My problem is a woman, and it ain't you this time, sweetheart. One problem and one name." He stepped away from his seat and faced her. "Tania."

She walloped him across the face. Hard, and she had used her left hand. His hand flew to his cheek. "What the hell was that for?"

The soda jerk whistled.

Leslie stormed out of the shop. And before the heat on his face reached his brain, he'd heard the silver of the bell. Customers. With the imprint of her hand fresh on his face, he resumed his place at the counter, like a boxer at the end of a brutal round. The soda jerk set another Bromo-Seltzer in front of him. "I'd offer you something stronger if I had it, pal."

The customers through the door this time weren't kids in a rush to ruin their stomachs before lunch. Walker turned to his left, saw his visitors, turned away, eyes clenched. It was Sheldon and Steps.

Walker threw a bill on the counter for the soda jerk. "Thanks for the cure." One look at them, the barman took the money and migrated south of Walker and his guests.

"Gentlemen," Walker said. "This day doesn't get better, does it? Heard there's a problem with Adler."

"There's that, and more," Steps said.

Walker tilted his Bromo back, drinking it all in one toss. He waited, scowled, and shook his shoulders. He pointed at Sheldon. "This is your fault. You never should've—"

"My fault? What the hell are you talking about? We're here to tell you that Adler flew the coop for Jersey. His sister-in-law rang, all hysterical."

"And how's this different from a million other phone calls?"

"She said men were outside her house in a parked car."

Walker shot a look over to Steps who had his answer out before Edwin R.

Murrow could light one of his Camel cigarettes. "I've already sent my boys over to Jersey."

Steps looked placid as the executioner who'd received the go-ahead from the governor. "Now, there's this other problem. We need to find the girl Tania."

"What?" Sheldon looked shocked. "She should be at her hotel."

"She's not. She was with him last," Steps nodded to Walker.

"Him?" Sheldon pointed.

"All I know is one of my guys drove her over to his place, after she heard our playwright here was under the weather. My guy sat on Shakespeare's address until she left, steamed, according to him. He tailed her, offered her a ride wherever but she refused. She ditched him. He came to me because he didn't know what to do. I knew the name of her hotel, naturally."

"Naturally, and?" Walker asked.

"My boy talked to our business associate there and gave him a description of her. The connection said she left with two men. My guess is they were Genovese's men."

"Your guess?" Sheldon said.

"This contact at her hotel knows everybody there is to know, and he's good at spotting cops and government types. These two joes were imports."

"Imports?" Walker said.

"Chicago Outfit."

"I thought you guessed they were Genovese's men. Did I miss something?" Walker asked.

"On loan, freelance, perhaps?" Steps said. "I'll look into it."

Walker took it all in and thought back to Jack's dossier on Frank Costello. He looked to the phone booth, but this wasn't the time. He said to Steps, "She's a civilian, and I thought the Commission doesn't believe harm should come to women or children, like it's a cardinal rule or something."

"You did your homework, friend." Steps stared hard into Walker. "Problem is you haven't dealt with Vito Genovese."

Chapter Seventeen

Steps occupied one of the phone booths. Sheldon eyeballed the soda fountain while Walker whistled a snatch of *Bonnie Blue Flag*. Steps dispensed with privacy and left the booth door open. He dropped his nickel in and gave the operator instructions and waited. When the connection was made, he said something fast and cold in Italian and then hung up the receiver. Neither Sheldon nor Walker asked for a translation, but Steps paraphrased anyway. "I invited a friend of mine to join us for moral support. Let's head back to the theatre."

"What about Adler?" Sheldon asked. Steps reminded him that he'd sent men over to Adler's home in Jersey. Sheldon offered a suggestion. "Why don't we send Maggie to Jersey?"

"The secretary? What good'll that do?"

Walker agreed. "It's not a bad idea, Steps."

"The secretary? Something you boys not telling me?"

"A distraught woman, an unwell child," Sheldon said. "Miss Gardner could lend a woman's touch."

"Look, my boys aren't family therapists, but they're better than a secretary."

"I wouldn't count on it," Walker said.

"So, there is something about her that you didn't tell me. Drop the dime and tell me."

"Think of her as moral support."

"Right, like Tania is his niece?" Steps didn't point at Sheldon. He walked towards the front of the drug store. The way he yanked the door open the silver bell overhead ought to have cracked like the Liberty Bell. Outside,

Steps whistled, held up two fingers, a signal to his man across the street to call for two cars. The first car was a maroon Buick Roadmaster, its body waxed and buffed, and all the metal in the car's molding and front grille had someone in accounting at GM counting millions in sales for General Motors. Steps said the Buick would ferry Maggie to Edgewater. The muscles on the driver said he was the kind of guy who could change a tire without using a lug wrench or a jack.

The driver behind the wheel of the second car, a Chrysler Imperial Limousine, was a big man sitting down. His hair matched the black paint job. He wore a dark double-breasted suit, and his tie provided some contrast to the car's gray interior. Pale skin, pale face, and his white Arrow shirt matched his nickname, Jimmy Alabaster. The one item that didn't square with all the elegance was the toothpick between his lips.

Steps instructed Sheldon to find Miss Gardner inside the theatre. Walker understood the ploy. Steps wanted a private word.

"The secretary rides in the Buick. We ride with Jimmy."

"And Sheldon?"

"With us, and a word of advice about this friend of mine from uptown." Steps checked his watch for the time. "He's not what I'd call sociable. The less you talk, the better."

Sheldon returned with Leslie. Her purse tucked under her arm, Leslie appeared annoyed. "Jersey, at this hour?" she said.

"There's never a good time for Jersey," Steps said, and pointed to the Roadmaster. "The maroon car takes you to Adler's. Now, let's make this next part quick. Are either of you carrying?"

"Why would we be?" Sheldon said.

"We live in uncertain times," Steps said, deadpan. "How 'bout it, Mr. Set Designer?"

Sheldon unbuttoned his jacket and opened it up. Steps approved. "Excellent."

"I don't see any reason for this," Leslie said.

"I'll give you two," Steps responded. "My drivers are law-abiding men."

Those boys outside Adler's house are either local or not-so-local law enforcement, and they're itching for the slightest excuse to collar Adler. Either of you armed gives them probable cause and that's trouble for everyone. How about that purse of yours, Miss Gardner?"

Leslie handed it to Steps. He held it from underneath like a newborn and he tweaked the brass bulbs and peeked inside. He removed a small-caliber pistol and pocketed it. "I'll be holding on to this. I'll see that you get it back. Enjoy your trip."

The Roadmaster drifted into traffic. Sheldon saw Leslie's profile in the window. A gas-blue Cadillac Eldorado pulled up. A man was sitting in the backseat, behind tinted glass. The car was a rare, limited edition, and the driver handled it as if he were the curator of the Smithsonian. Steps put one hand on Walker's shoulder, the other on Sheldon's when their Chrysler eased up behind the Cadillac. "Gentlemen, we ride with Jimmy Alabaster and follow the Caddy."

The conversation during the ride out of Manhattan was a silent film without subtitles. Walker read signs for New Jersey. Sheldon saw them, too, and said nothing. Steps ignored them. Sometime later, they journeyed down a country lane on which they saw fewer and fewer cars. It was a flat ribbon of monotonous asphalt, endless trees on both sides of the road, and fewer white lines every few feet.

"Sheldon?" Walker said.

"Yes."

"Tania and I had breakfast together. Nothing more."

Sheldon didn't answer. He admired the bucolic scenery. Sheldon's silence haunted him.

"We had an argument. She left angry. I should've followed her."

The head turned and the eyes, cold as the ocean, appraised him. "Following her would not have been wise. I do have one question, though. If she was with you for breakfast, then does that mean she was with you the night before? Tell me the truth."

"She showed up with groceries in the morning."

Sheldon's fingers strummed leather. The sunlight should have felt warm.

It didn't.

"Given her childhood, I'm not surprised. I should get her professional help."

"We should talk about this, Sheldon."

"That won't be necessary. I asked you a question and you answered it. I have no reason to believe that you were dishonest." Sheldon's eyes returned to the greenery outside his window. Cars sped by and the passengers in them gawked at the Chrysler and then the Cadillac.

"Where to in Jersey?" Walker asked Steps.

"Atlantic Highlands."

"What's in Atlantic Highlands?" Sheldon asked.

"Vito Genovese. I have an idea, thanks to Walter."

"What did I say?"

Steps twisted in the front seat so he could look at the two men behind him.

"What you said about rules, that the organization doesn't touch women or children. This thing of ours survives because we have rules. Let our visit to Don Vitone be a test, to see if he took the girl." Steps raised a finger. "If he did, then he'll answer to the Commission."

"And if he didn't?" Sheldon asked.

Steps turned and faced forward. "Then we have a bigger problem."

"Meaning?" Walker asked.

"Meaning those men we saw at the Copa and the men in a car outside Adler's place play on the same team. It's a hunch. Like I said, Cosa Nostra has rules. The government, not so much."

"I still don't understand," Sheldon said. "Why would he take Tania?"

Walker answered instead of Steps. "To create trouble. Tania is a guest of The Prime Minister and on his territory. Her disappearance makes The Prime Minister look weak in front of his peers. Of course, Vito Genovese assumes that nobody can trace Tania's abduction to him."

"Say you're right," Sheldon said. "Then what?"

Steps pointed at the Cadillac in front of them. "That's why I brought him."

Sheldon and Walker looked to the car in front of their Chrysler.

"The man in the backseat is Albert Anastasia."

The way Steps pronounced the last name in proper Italian assured everyone that Albert was not missing Russian royalty. Jimmy Alabaster turned his head and his smile included the toothpick dance.

Chapter Eighteen

The ferry ride to Bergen County was a slow churn over dark water. People in cars, people on deck, people like ants on a cork suffered in the humidity. Edgewater, on the other side of the river, was busy with factories for those anxious to own the clean and shiny things in life. There was the factory for aluminum, Alcoa; a factory for automobiles, Ford Motor; a factory for soap, Lever Brothers; and a factory for oil, Valvoline.

Adler's place was a modular cottage, straight from the Sears catalog for homeowners on a budget, for folks who hungered for a castle, a green lawn, and a picket fence instead of a moat. A short brick pathway led to an entry with columns, gables, and double doors. Two-stories high, the house glared from all the glass—bay windows out front, bow windows on the side, and box windows on the second floor for all the Jersey sunlight. The only thing missing was a railing with the snap of an American flag in the wind.

It was all cozy as the vicar's house in the village, except for a dark Ford sedan. Two men in dark suits, white shirts, and black ties fried in the front seat. Sunglasses covered their eyes, and their windows were lowered for ventilation. Everything but a cherry light on the roof said Hoover-issued.

The Buick pulled up. Leslie gave them enough time to see her. She exited the Roadmaster and began her voyage to the front door with her driver. Both suits left their car, and the two men started the slow approach.

"Who are you two?" one of the men asked.

"We're friends of Mr. Adler. Who are you?" she answered.

"Patriotic Americans."

They were fresh off the assembly line of government men. They both stood the same height, wore the same haircut, fashioned the same tie-knot, and both chewed the same gum. Dentyne. The smell of cinnamon preceded them.

"Are you gentlemen the neighborhood watch?" Leslie asked.

"We ask the questions, Miss. Is this man here your husband?"

"He's my boyfriend for today. I switch them out at night."

"You two have names?" the second man asked.

The driver gave his name, and she gave hers. The suits didn't ask for identification. They introduced themselves as Special Agents Doherty and McKenna and showed their badges.

"The reason for the visit?" Doherty asked Leslie.

"I'm working in a play and hoped to speak with the director, Mr. Adler. I was told this is his house. Is the man in or not, gentlemen?"

"Go inside and see for yourself," Doherty said.

"Doesn't your boyfriend here talk?" McKenna asked. "From the sound of all those vowels in his first and last name I'd wondered whether he spoke English or was limited to dago-speak. While I'm at it, you have yourself a nice Brit accent there, Miss."

"I wasn't aware I had an accent," Leslie answered. She looked to her driver. The man hadn't taken the bait. Smart customer, experienced shopper. He didn't give them any lip, otherwise he'd risk a dented fender, a busted taillight, or be told that his car didn't have enough screws holding the license plates. Leslie excused herself and asked the driver to accompany her. Doherty lifted his hat, while McKenna played to type, sullen and unable to scratch his itch for confrontation.

Her back turned, Leslie had no doubt that one of these men had taken out a little notebook, licked the lead on a pencil, and written down the four yellow numbers and one letter on the Buick's black license plate and underlined NY·THE EMPIRE STATE·53.

Adler was at the door, his sister-in-law, Judith, at the window. The kid, Leslie learned, was named David. He was on a davenport, staring off into space and mumbling gibberish to imaginary friends. The red bullseye around his lips was from drinking punch. Adler introduced Leslie as Margaret

Gardner to Judith.

"Some lemonade for you and your friend, Miss Gardner?" Judith asked. She had moved over to the cocktail cart for two clean glasses, not waiting for an answer. She was wiry, wore a yellow sundress, and her red hair appeared to be her natural color. Ice cubes rattled in the tall glasses of lemonade she handed to Leslie and the driver.

"I came when Judith called," Adler said to Leslie as an excuse for his absence.

"Was something wrong?"

"Those men outside have been there day and night," Judith answered, back to sentry duty at the window. Judith didn't pace. Her eyes did everything.

"The same men?" Leslie asked.

"No. Another car comes around six, but it's the same kind of car and the men always look the same."

Adler went over to David, who seemed to be working himself up into a fit, and picked him up.

Leslie asked Judith, "They ever come to the door?"

"Never. I go out for the mail. They take notes. I fetch the newspaper. They take notes."

"Pardon me, Miss," Leslie's driver spoke. "Do they follow you when you go grocery shopping?" Judith appeared as if she was about to cry, and David began making loud, incoherent noises.

"Yes, and those two beasts out there have gone around the neighborhood. I could see them talking to my neighbors. One of the men takes notes while the other one talks to their children. It's awful, just awful."

"Have you spoken to any of your neighbors on the telephone?" Leslie asked.

"No…no, I haven't. It's Margaret, right?"

"Maggie will do."

"I don't dare use the phone. I remember what that was all like."

"What all what was like?" the driver asked.

Judith looked over at Adler, who gave her permission with a slight bow of his head. These two understood each other. David's head rested on his father's shoulder. Leslie marked the kid to be about twelve and one who sucked his thumb for comfort. Judith explained.

"I used to work at the Signal Corps' headquarters at Fort Monmouth. I was a secretary. When Julius—that's Julius Rosenberg—was arrested, the authorities questioned everyone. There was a Kaplan in town at the time—Kaplan is my maiden name. Because this fellow was politically active and we shared the same name, my life became a living hell." She pointed to the window. "Men like them followed me everywhere. I was cleared, of course, but my phones were tapped, or at least I thought they were because I'd always hear these clicks on the line. Cleared, they said, but the damage had been done. My neighbors stopped talking to me. My husband left, Irwin's wife left—who knows, those two might've become a couple before then. Anyhow, I tried to rebuild my life. I watch David for Irwin while I try to piece together what's left of my life."

"What about you, Mr. Adler? Anything you'd like to add?" the driver asked.

"I left radio when the issue of Red Channels broke, and the PI reports mentioned Judith's name. I left CBS because I was worried that someone would take my son away from me."

Leslie turned to Judith. "Were you Kaplan when you worked at Monmouth?"

"Of course not, my married name is Nussbaum; not that it mattered. Employers do a background check, and the whole fiasco resurfaces. The few jobs I manage to get interviewed for, they treat me like I'm a box of broken eggs."

"Mr. Adler?" Leslie asked.

"Yes?"

"We do need you at the theatre."

"I can't leave Judith and David here like this, with those men outside."

"Mr. Adler?" It was the driver this time, and not Leslie. "How about I have groceries delivered to the house? If Judith wants to take David to the playground or to a movie house, my men will escort her. They'll keep an eye on her and David for you."

"What kind of men?" Adler asked.

"Private hire, authorized to carry firearms. The kind of men who are bonded and above reproach, enough so that a judge will sign for them."

Judith paced now. "It won't stop those men out there from asking questions and—"

"No, it won't, but it'll make them think twice, Mrs. Nussbaum," the driver said. "These men will protect you and David."

"And these men are legitimate?" Adler asked.

"They are."

"Who'll pay for their service?"

"A friend of the arts."

"A friend?"

"A friend."

"Okay, then. I'll be at work tomorrow morning."

"Thank you, Mr. Adler. Now, if you'll excuse me, I'll return Miss Gardner to the city. I do advise you, however, not to use the phone."

"And the neighbors?" Judith asked.

The man smiled for the first time that day. Leslie admired the quality of that smile and what he said even more. "Those neighbors ain't your friends. I'm your friend now."

Leslie and her chauffeur walked across the lawn. He tipped his hat to Doherty and McKenna. They seemed to stop chewing their gum in unison and forgot to note the time of departure. He opened and closed the door for her. He opened his, got in, put the key in the ignition, and turned over the engine. As he pulled away, he handed Leslie a card.

"The number is my direct line. If you need something, you call me. You need to talk, call me. If you don't want to talk, I'll listen to you breathe. Someone bothers you—"

"Call you."

The man stepped on the gas pedal and the car became a blur to catch the ferry for another swim across the river.

Chapter Nineteen

New Jersey wasn't the only state with the mafia, but it was the only one where one of its county seals depicted a murder. While Jimmy drove, Walker thought about another difference between the coasts, here and his home in Malibu. People on the East Coast were kind, but not nice; the folks on the West Coast nice, but not kind. Steps asked Jimmy to dial down the music so he could have a word with Sheldon.

"Let me do the talking with Genovese."

"Tania is my niece. Don't I deserve a say."

"Your presence is symbolic."

"Symbolic?"

"You're a civilian, Sheldon, and Vito needs to be reminded of that."

"And your friend in the Cadillac, is he symbolic, too?"

"More like insurance. Again, let me do the talking, please."

"I'll be quiet as a statue until I see or hear a pigeon."

Walker tried not to smirk. Steps had no idea what his friend from Vienna was capable of. "It'll be okay, Sheldon."

"Like marble, understand?"

If the outline of the Garden State resembled the profile of a lady on a map, Atlantic Highlands formed the back of her neck, and Vito Genovese's digs in Middletown was the boil her hairline couldn't hide. He'd once owned a forty-acre estate in the town, but it burned down a few weeks after he'd left the country for Naples.

Genovese had fled the country, wanted for murder. Like the artist

Caravaggio, Genovese had killed a man after a game of chance. Ferdinand Boccia and Genovese had sharped their victim during a high-stakes poker game, cleaned the man's pockets out. When Boccia asked for his share of the pot, Genovese had him shot and killed at a coffee shop. With Genovese in Italy, The Prime Minister became the boss of the Luciano crime family.

While Vito vacationed abroad, he entrusted a colleague named Steven Franse to look after his wife, who controlled the bar scene on the West Side and in the Village. Word got back to Vito that his wife was having an affair, that she wanted a divorce, and that the Feds were squeezing Franse for information. Everyone assumed Franse was doing Anna. He wasn't. Anna liked women. Everyone, including Vito, assumed Franse was singing a song to Hoover's men. He wasn't. Franse died of lead poisoning in a restaurant in the Bronx.

Vito returned to the States after one witness was found dead in a car in Norwood, New Jersey, shot to death. The second witness died in protective custody. If all of this seemed ancient history, it wasn't. Franse checked out the day before the Rosenbergs were executed, which was why Vito Genovese was the recluse of Atlantic Highlands.

He rented a mansion, with the option to buy.

Anastasia's Eldorado stopped first. With a steely gasp, the Chrysler braked next. A massive wrought-iron gate spanned the driveway. The Colonial revival rested on a hill. Steps said the property reminded Vito of the estate he'd lost in the fire. The design for the grounds was half English garden, half Italian villa. All the topiary worked grooves into the hillside. Though they were nice for show, they also doubled as trenches, like the kind used in the Great War. The house itself held more weapons and ammunition than the local armory.

Jimmy Alabaster tooted the horn. Security sauntered over. The guard's eyes took an inventory of the passengers in both cars before he returned to a phone inside his pillbox. One quick person-to-person call; the gate yawned open, and the cars entered.

As the cars traveled to the house, several men appeared on the sides of the road, the business ends of their shotguns pointed skyward. Steps seemed oblivious. His eyes stared straight ahead.

The cars stopped in front of a set of wide steps, which led up to two magnificent doors.

Valets emerged from a small shed. A tuxedoed Negro appeared at the top of the stairs, his face sad that his morning tea had gone cold. Once inside the foyer, he asked for their hats and jackets and for them to surrender any accessories on their person. He had to be the only black man in the entire country who could ask white men for their weapons and expect them to oblige. Steps said that nobody was carrying. The servant looked to Albert Anastasia. "Would the good gentleman care to be relieved of his coat? It is unseasonably warm."

"No, thank you. Your boss gives me the chills."

"Very well. Mr. Genovese has company. Follow me, please."

They walked down a corridor, past museum-size rooms, one with a dead fireplace and another with a gallery of portraits and nature scenery. Genovese, like most immigrants, compensated for the lack of a formal education with an art collection. Tasteful, expensive, and extensive, his choice of artwork suggested that Vito Genovese had not made it past the sixth grade. They arrived at a set of French doors.

"Who shall I say is calling?" the man asked Steps.

"I gave the guard our names, thank you."

The doors slid open and the four of them walked into darkness, a lamp ahead of them as a beacon. Walker recognized the opened box, off to the side, as a Victrola. A record spun and an aria filled the room. Sheldon squinted, as if he recognized the music.

Steps said hello to a squat, balding man. Walker and Sheldon heard the man's name as Carmine Galante, or Lilo, for short. Lilo nodded to Anastasia. A thick unlit cigar bobbed between his clamped lips. Galante removed the stogie from his mouth and pointed to Sheldon and Walker. "I don't know these two. You ought to know better than bringing civilians here, Steps."

"This is an emergency, and it affects Don Vitone."

"What makes them special?"

"They're guests of The Prime Minister. You know how hospitality works."

Galante walked over to Anastasia, looked the man up and down, like an officer reviewing a field grunt. Anastasia played the part, except no subordinate in the military would ever make eye contact with his superior. Albert did.

"Are you cold, Umberto?" Lilo said, calling Anastasia by his proper name.

"Not cold enough that I can't light your cigar."

A door slid open and closed. Genovese entered the room, dressed like a character in a Damon Runyon story: silk shirt and tie, hair slicked back, large ears, longish face, and dark circles under his eyes.

"I was in the middle of eatin' my sammich and listening to music. I heard the word *emergency*, but before we get to the matter, introduce your friends, Steps."

"Think we could turn the record off?"

"And miss the best part?" Genovese said, from behind his desk.

"I wouldn't know the best part, Don Vitone."

Sheldon spoke, "It's Purcell's Dido's Lament, the aria in *Dido and Aeneas*. It's a beautiful example of—"

"Thank you, Sheldon, but please let me do the talking here."

Genovese held up his hand. "Let the man speak. Beautiful example of what?"

"Ground bass and melodic line. Your countrymen would call the bass line a passacaglia."

Genovese put on his eyeglasses and studied Sheldon. He'd seen British tailoring before and detected European manners, but couldn't place the way with words, the slight accent. It wasn't English filtered through one distinctive European language. He took off his glasses and used them to point at Sheldon. "In the aria, Dido orders a funeral pyre before she commits suicide. Why? I think it's because she wants her despair and grief to become our own. What do you think?"

Sheldon considered the rug with his foot. "I can tell you what you want to hear, and agree with you, or I can tell you what I think?"

"What you think I want to hear?" Genovese's grin was as cocky as that of the smartest kid in the class. "I'm used to that, in my line of work. I could use a little honesty and sincerity."

"She wants Aeneas to see the smoke, so he knows that she killed herself. That's the reason for the fire, but don't forget her words, 'Remember me, but forget my fate.' You want to believe she did it for love, possibly because you yourself are a romantic, despite appearances."

"Despite appearance? You've got stones, my friend, but I asked for it. Now, your answer, your interpretation?"

"What she thinks or feels is immaterial. Aeneas is father to an empire, to a civilization, and he must abandon Dido, his Queen of Carthage, because the gods expect him to fulfill his fate. The gods come before personal wishes. Duty is what matters, Don Vitone."

"And love means nothing then?"

"I didn't say that, but don't forget that Rome survived, and Carthage was destroyed."

Genovese tossed his glasses onto the blotter on his desk. Genovese's finger lifted, up and down while he considered Sheldon. "Clothes. Culture. Refinement. You must be a teacher."

"I'm not."

"What do you do for fun, for entertainment?"

"You might find me in any one of the bars in the Village."

Genovese's face twitched. "Pansy bars?" Both of Genovese's hands touched his chest. "You know what I do and what I am. Who are you, and what do you do?" The vein in the man's forehead bulged.

Sheldon stared into the hard and coarse face of Vito Genovese. "If you must know, then tell your friend Lilo, and your colleagues, Steps and Anastasia to step outside for a minute."

"And your friend next to you?"

"He stays."

Genovese, silent at first, said, "Boys, if you don't mind. A moment alone."

Walker walked to the door and opened it. Steps seemed stunned and went to say something to Walker, but Walker tilted his head. Anastasia was the last to leave the room. When the door clicked shut, Genovese stood up.

"Who the hell are you?"

"Sheldon."

"That, I know. Who do you work for?"

"Rome."

Genovese absorbed Sheldon's answer. "The government? And people say that our thing frightens them. What is it that you do for the empire?"

"You can say I'm its Anastasia, but I'm more silent and much more prolific. Now, let's not keep our friends waiting outside."

Genovese nodded to Walker, who walked to the door and opened it. Genovese sat down at his desk. He picked up his spectacles. "What exactly can I do for you?"

"My niece has disappeared. Last seen in Hell's Kitchen."

Genovese motioned for Lilo Galante to approach the desk. "Before they leave this room, I want the girl's name, what she looks like, and where she's staying. Have our boys ask around."

The man with the cigar bowed his head and stepped back.

"Anything else?" Vito Genovese asked Sheldon.

"My friend here," Sheldon said, meaning Walker. "Your men will discover that he was the last person to see her."

"And you're sure he had nothing to do with her disappearance?"

"Certain of it."

"Because you're friends or colleagues, is that it? I mean no disrespect when I say this, Sheldon, but friends may not be what they seem. My wife ain't Dido and I'm sure as hell no Aeneas, but I've been deceived, nonetheless. I'll admit it. Why do you think I listen to music?"

"You're a romantic, remember?" Sheldon smiled. "You might be correct about deception, but I know he wasn't involved in her disappearance. Know how I know?"

"How?"

"Look at him, Don Vitone. If you were him and you tried to harm her, you would not be here today."

"Why not?

Sheldon leaned down and whispered into Genovese's ear. "Because she would have killed you."

Chapter Twenty

It was late afternoon, claustrophobic, and hot. The humidity was relentless and inescapable as the cloying stench of orchids in a greenhouse. A hotel doorman opened the door for her, and she walked into polar air, the kind of cold where you'd expect slabs of meat on hooks and men in aprons sharpening knives. What she did find instead was a lobby, alive with activity. Bellhops racked luggage, a concierge scribbled something frantic in his notebook with his pencil, the phone tight to his ear.

A hat box from Henri Bendel passed her. Deliverymen from local retailers, such as Bloomingdale's, Macy's, and Saks Fifth Avenue headed for the freight elevator for private deliveries. Near the newsstand, a group of men, all of them tailors, chatted as they waited for appointments with clients. Leslie had read somewhere that the American man of means desired bespoke fashion, and tailored suits from the Brioni line and custom shirts from Ascot Chang helped him become his best version of Cary Grant.

She took the elevator up to her floor. The corridor appeared longer, the door to her room distant, because of the gold-framed mirror at the end of the hall. She was tired and her head throbbed like a bass drum. She wanted ice, something cold, since the rooms, unlike the lobby, were not air-conditioned.

She closed the door behind her, turned around, and rested her forehead against the dark wood. This was one of those days when even a hotel room could feel like home. She composed herself upon hearing Vera.

"Ah, there you are, dear. Did you find Adler?"

"In Jersey as expected. I need to change, Vera. This heat is dreadful."

"Is Adler all right? What about his son?"

"Adler is fine. David is fine. Judith the sister-in-law is high-strung, but who can blame her. Two FBI agents were camped outside her home for 'round-the-clock surveillance."

As Leslie undressed in the bedroom, she noticed two dresses on the bed.

"Those are for tonight," Vera said. "I've made reservations, and there's no need to fret. I thought about what you said, and I was careful."

"How are reservations careful, Vera? Anything with your name on it becomes public record."

"The reservation is for an early dinner. Who eats dinner at four pm?"

Vera stood in the doorframe. Her shoulder leaned into the wood, a glass of clear something in her hand, the ice long gone. Her voice was sweet, as if she'd eaten jasmine petals all morning. "Let me make it up to you," she said.

"Make up for what?"

"For being inconsiderate…the whole secretarial nonsense."

"You've already apologized. How did rehearsal go?"

"We managed, but we are coming to Tania's part. What do you think happened to her?"

"Wish I knew." Leslie splashed some water on herself in the bathroom, toweled off, and returned to the bedroom. Vera had moved the dresses aside, so the bed was now unclaimed territory, and she was the island in the middle of the map. She patted a landing spot with her hand. "You're incorrigible," Leslie said, amused.

"Do you find Tania attractive? I think she is."

"Why do you torture yourself like this? I told you what I thought. Aren't you the one who told me she was off?"

"I haven't seen platinum hair like hers in a long time," Vera said, softly. "Swathe her in silver lamé and you'd have Carole Lombard."

"Lombard was funny. Tania is deadly serious, or seriously deadly. Take your pick."

"How would you know? Never mind." Vera stretched and her fingernails etched claw-marks on the top bedsheet. A small part of her robe slid up and Leslie saw the white of her thigh when the phone rang. Leslie answered it.

It was her driver. She didn't like what she heard. She turned her back to Vera and mumbled something and hung up.

"Who was that?" Vera asked.

"Did the concierge make the reservation?"

"Yes. Isn't that what they do?"

"In addition to dinner reservations, we have a ride to the restaurant."

"Remind me to tip him well."

"The concierge or the driver?" Leslie asked.

"Does it matter? Why not both? Please come to bed."

It mattered to Leslie that her driver to New Jersey had known about the restaurant before she did, and it mattered to her that someone else knew where she and Vera would be tonight.

Leslie walked over to the bed. Vera's hands ran up the back of Leslie's legs, and pressed her lips against her stomach. Leslie glanced down, knowing what Vera would do next. Vera kissed her again, this time lower, much lower, and for Leslie it was the croupier's rake, pulling her towards trouble.

Le Café Chambord on Third Avenue was French haute cuisine. The menu required a degree from the Sorbonne. The restaurant captain wore no diamond pinkie ring. The waiter translated the menu items, and not with the standard Parisian accent. The sommelier waited his turn to recite his list of fine wines, ports, sherries, and spirits. Another waiter sped by with pommes soufflés, the house specialty. From the way their waiter spoke about the Dover sole, you'd think the Queen of England's personal pilot delivered it.

They decided on a double order of fresh oysters for a starter. Their server promised that they were the best in the city. Vera wavered between the Maine lobster or Lobster Newburg for her entrée. The more the waiter explained the two dishes to her, the more she became indecisive. Leslie was hungry and anxious for a good night's sleep. At last, she took charge and decided that they'd split an entrée and accept the sommelier's recommended pairing with champagne. Vera listened as Leslie used the words, homard du Maine flambé au cognac and blanc de blancs champagne. She used French to instruct the waiter to tell her when the kitchen would start their dessert, an order of île flottante, a floating island of meringue on top of vanilla custard, topped with caramel. He suggested a sauterne, but she said she'd prefer an Eiswein. The man collected their menus, bowed his head, and disappeared.

"You never told me you spoke French?"

"I don't," Leslie said. She refrained from telling Vera that their waiter had complimented her on her French and she confirmed her suspicion about him; he was from Marseille. She couldn't tell Vera how she'd acquired a taste for German iced wine in Vienna, or that, while with the OSS, she had worked with the French Resistance and was awarded the Croix de Guerre for her service.

Vera discussed the play, the scenes she'd rehearsed, and how the stage set was coming together. Cocktails and appetizers came and went. Except for them, there was nobody in the restaurant, until the captain approached their table. He'd heard Leslie speak French and conversed with her in the language. Vera watched the tennis match, at a loss as to what they were discussing. Vera asked, "What did he say?"

"He said we have guests."

"Guests?"

"Sheldon and Walter. Here they come."

"How did they know we were here?"

"I'd like to know the same thing. The concierge, perhaps?"

Walker apologized for the intrusion. A waiter arrived with a silver cloche and lifted the dome to reveal the orange crustacean. He poured them champagne and left them to their feast. Sheldon requested a menu. "May we join you and order something?"

"Might as well. You're already here," Vera said, at work on her lobster.

Leslie ate. Sheldon and Walker shared a menu, made their decision. Sheldon ordered in French. Vera stopped eating and shook her head. "Another one who speaks French. I went to all the wrong schools. What about you, Walter? Do you speak French?"

"No, I don't."

"Any word on Tania?" Leslie asked. She looked to Sheldon to include him in the question. "I assume that's where you two disappeared to."

"We've got something in the works," Walker answered.

Sheldon kept quiet. The waiter placed a glass of sparkling water on a cocktail napkin in front of him, and Walker's champagne cocktail onto another. They'd ordered drinks before they had ambushed Vera and Leslie.

Leslie noticed her driver had walked in and braced himself against the wall in the corner of the room. "Dare I ask what 'something in the works' means?"

"We visited an associate of Steps in New Jersey."

Sheldon watched solemn faced as Vera devoured her portion of lobster tail.

"Does this associate offer any leads?"

"Ask Sheldon since he did most of the talking."

The hors d'oeuvres for Sheldon and Walker arrived. Leslie tried some of the lobster Vera had placed on her plate. The waiter asked whether the kitchen should start their dessert. Leslie apologized, canceled the île flottante, but asked that he'd still bring her the glass of Eiswein.

Two men entered the room. One of them was Steps, the other man walked in confident, with purpose, and he emanated strength in a tailored shirt, silk tie, and fresh fedora.

"We have more company," Leslie said.

Vera asked, "Who is the scary-looking gentleman with Steps?"

Walker looked. "Albert Anastasia, a friend of The Prime Minister."

The restaurant's captain set his course to intercept the two men but one hard look from Anastasia stopped him.

"Evening, and my apologies for interrupting," Steps said.

Vera prepared to say something sarcastic, but Anastasia stepped forward, hand out. "It's an honor to meet you, Miss Williams. I'm a big fan of yours. My name is Albert Anastasia."

Vera's hand disappeared into Anastasia's.

"Any word on Tania?" Leslie asked Steps.

"Not quite."

"What then?" she asked. Sheldon and Walker finished their hors d'oeuvres.

Steps leaned down to Walker's ear. "I thought you said she's a secretary."

"Like Albert is your personal assistant?" Walker answered.

Anastasia responded. "Remember the gentlemen from the waterfront?"

"How could I forget? They work for Genovese," Walker said.

"Who is Genovese?" Vera asked.

"An unpleasant man," Leslie said.

"Unpleasant is right," Steps said. "I was right, Walter."

"Right about what?"

"They're from Chicago, involved in extracurricular activities."

"In other words, Vito didn't know?" Walker said.

"I wouldn't go that far," Steps said. "Like they say, ignorance is no excuse. Our Labor Relations Board has rules, and Mr. Anastasia is in charge of the Disciplinary Committee."

"Would you care for something to eat, Mr. Anastasia?" Vera asked.

"No thank you, Miss Williams. I don't eat before I work. Excuse me, I should be going."

As Anastasia exited the dining room, he tipped his hat to Leslie's driver.

"He seems like Gary Cooper, the strong silent type," Vera said.

Amused, Steps said, "I don't know about silent, but something like that."

The dishes were taken away. Waiters swept their table clean. There was a loud commotion moments later. All eyes locked on the door to the main room. The captain tried to prevent several men from storming the dining area. A few rough types emerged from the kitchen to assist their boss with the intruders.

"Good thing I canceled dessert," Leslie said.

"They must be fans," Vera said with a prepared smile for cameras. Leslie and Walker exchanged anxious looks. Both Sheldon and Steps focused their eyes on the mirrored wall to understand the reflection. Vera pulled a pen out from her purse, ready for autographs.

"They're not fans, Vera," Leslie said.

"They're not?"

"Government men," Sheldon said.

The captain and his crew formed a line in front of the table. One of the suited men shouldered his way through, with a piece of paper in his hand.

"Miss Vera Williams?"

"Yes."

"Consider yourself served."

Chapter Twenty-One

Outside the theater the next morning the sky had darkened, and rain pelted people and sidewalks. It was a day to stay inside. When the sun did show up later, it would bring with it the inevitable steam bath.

Adler's kid David was sitting with Judith in—to lift a recent phrase from a newspaperman in Philly describing the Army-Navy game in November—the nosebleed seats. Everyone was busy. Adler was coaching thespians. Vera, preoccupied with her subpoena, listened. Leslie imitated Lady Macbeth, in that she paced and paced, while Walker sat between Sheldon and Steps in another section of the theater.

"I thought The Prime Minister knew all the judges?" Walker asked Steps.

"He did and he does, but a federal judge in DC signed Vera's subpoena."

"Does he also walk a dog?" Sheldon asked. He remembered what Steps had said the night they'd met at the Copa about Kennedy, a judge, and the sequence of events that led to the death of The Prime Minister's cousin, Willie Moretti, a boss in the Genovese organization.

"I'll see what else I can find out," Steps said. He rose from his seat, headed up the stairs for his raincoat and umbrella. Sheldon waited until he was out of earshot before he spoke to Walker.

"History has taught us never to fight more than one enemy at a time."

Sheldon was correct, and Walker didn't disagree. No one had ever emerged victorious from a two-front war: not the British in the Seven Years' War; not Napoleon against all of Europe and Russia; and certainly not Germany in two world wars. Sheldon may not have served in any army, but he'd worn the striped uniform of an inmate at Auschwitz and understood strategy. He'd survived to exact his revenge on Nazis in Vienna. He enumerated the targets. "Front one is Adler, with Hoover on their doorstep. Literally."

"Second is Cohn." Walker watched the actors.

"And again, Hoover will endorse whatever Cohn puts into play."

"And then we have Tania's disappearance."

"Which lifts the lid on a feud between The Prime Minister and Genovese. I need to ask you one last question about Tania."

Walker saw Sheldon's cuff on the armrest next to him, and then the sleeve and the rest of his Birdseye suit. The unbuttoned blue jacket revealed a patch from the Savile Row tailors H. Huntsman & Sons. Perched on the other armrest was a Tremont instead of a Panama hat for the rain.

"We've been over this, Sheldon. I'm not sure there's more I can add."

"Was she suggestive?"

"Yes, and I rejected her. Is that your question?"

"I'm afraid not." Sheldon scratched his temple. "The thing is I talked to a reputable analyst. He said to expect inappropriate behavior as a consequence of her trauma. We both know what Tania experienced in Vienna. He also mentioned that there might be another manifestation."

"Your question, please."

"Was she violent with you? He said the other manifestation is rage."

"Yes, she was violent."

Walker faced the stage. The slap he'd received was nothing because he knew she was capable of so much more. He remembered himself and Jack, both half-dead, on that green lawn in Vienna with Tania ahead of them. It still haunted him, gave him nightmares. He remembered looking up, bloodied and battered, seeing the sunlight filter through her hair. In that fatal ecstasy and frenzy, she was enraged, on fire. Her hair. Her clothes. All that light, all that blood. He'd seen something similar with men in combat. They'd become so intoxicated and infuriated that they continued bayoneting or shooting the dead. The snow turned red with blood.

Sheldon's voice snapped him back from the gruesome reverie. "Is there any chance that we're being played?"

"Played? By whom?"

"Take your pick. Let's start with Hoover. Is it possible that he's targeting members of the Syndicate? In my opinion, he'd rather deal with The Prime Minister than Vito Genovese."

"Are you suggesting that Hoover is setting up Genovese?"

"You heard from Steps himself about the boys from the Chicago Outfit, mercenaries."

Walker had read Jack's file on members of La Cosa Nostra on the plane and discussed Hoover and the Bureau numerous times with Jack. Hoover had disavowed the existence of organized crime. His exact words to the American Municipal Association in '49 were, "There is no mob."

"Let's hear your theory, Sheldon."

"Let's examine the fact. Hoover backs Cohn and Senator McCarthy. Kennedy is a new addition to the team to hunt Commies, and we know Hoover is cautious around the Kennedy name, but it's not beneath him to use the man."

"Like having Kennedy get a subpoena signed," Walker said.

"Exactly. It never hurts us to evaluate the person we'd least suspect and consider their endgame." Sheldon's finger tapped the armrest. Walker watched the polished nail shine under the lights overhead. "What does Steps stand to gain in all of this?"

That question jolted Walker. It reminded him of his childhood in Middle America, of what it was like to open a barn door. First there was the scent of hay, and then the smell of manure. He listened to Sheldon.

"Steps is The Prime Minister's man, but both men are fighting for their lives against Don Vitone. If Genovese convinces the other families to side with him, then The Prime Minister and Steps are dead men. Treachery is a way of life in the mob."

"What are you saying, Sheldon?"

"Steps might want his boss's job."

"You think he'd form an alliance with Vito Genovese?"

"Mercenaries or not, how did he know that Genovese's men kidnapped you that night?"

"I'm not sure, but the man saved my life."

"Even if Steps were loyal to The Prime Minister and not looking to replace him, one thing is clear and that's—"

Walker completed Sheldon's sentence. "Vito Genovese has to go, for them to survive."

"But in order for that to happen, the Commission has to okay the contract."

"They'd need a reason, since they haven't clipped him for his interest in narcotics."

"No, they have not," Sheldon said. "The drug trade is compelling money."

"I don't know, Sheldon. Genovese did seem surprised when you told him about her disappearance."

"All I'm saying is that with The Prime Minister in prison, Steps is vulnerable and he'd need a powerful ally to take out Genovese."

Walker observed the stage and actors. "Albert Anastasia is one powerful ally."

The theory intrigued him. Opportunist or mere survivor, Steps might well be a better hoofer than Fred Astaire or Gene Kelly, dancing between raindrops. The man was keeping the beat.

Walker heard nothing but the actors onstage now. The rain had stopped. He turned his head towards the door, saw an arc of sunlight trying to break in but even that didn't seem so warm, so welcoming, so inviting. The sunlight suggested a clearing, a break in all the bad weather, a brightness and clarity, proof that the worst was over.

He doubted it.

Chapter Twenty-Two

Walker stopped at the deli to order a hobo sandwich and a bottled beer to go. Thoughts of what Sheldon had said played in his head while he waited for his scrambled eggs and sliced potatoes on grilled bread. He paid and left, his dinner in a paper bag that reminded him of Tania and breakfast.

Same stairs, same hallway, the same key and lock, and once inside his apartment, the same view of the river. The door was new, and on his bed sat someone unexpected.

Leslie.

He placed the paper bag on the table. He stared at her as he took his jacket off. "Remind me to get you a spare key sometime."

"We need to talk."

"The four most dreaded words in the English language from a woman. Allow me to make myself comfortable first. You have. Shall I fix you a drink or have you helped yourself?"

"Thanks, but no thanks to the drink. I see you're still fond of Grable."

She sat there, one leg crossed over the other, on his bed, in a black dress pencil skirt from Christian Dior. The skirt stopped at just above the knee. The material hugged her figure, and the white satin top flattered it. The lipstick, red and bright as fresh blood, was a bold choice. Most women these days wore cat eyes for sunglasses, but Leslie preferred ovals, her lens tinted green with tortoise shell frames.

Leslie was one of those women, modest about the looks, about her long legs and the entire ensemble, unless she had a purpose. She'd used her looks to lure Nazis, seduce them for a secret, or kill them, if necessary. He was too tired to guess what her mission might be tonight. He noticed that she had cleared his table and washed the dish he had left in the sink.

"Thanks for the housekeeping. Would you like to see my sock drawer, too?"

"No need to be fresh, Walker."

"Fresh? I'm not the one who invited myself in. How did you get in? Jimmy the lock?"

She didn't answer him. He fetched a plate and slid the sandwich out of the bag. Like his milk on Fridays in Malibu, he decided to forgo the glass for his beer since it was his place. He sat down and watched her. He figured she'd cased the apartment and could tell him which floorboard creaked. The sip of beer tasted good, the chair felt better, and there on his bed, she looked the best he'd seen her in a long time. He glanced at the door. "I assume you finagled an extra key from Steps, or from the carpenter at the theatre who fixed my door."

Still no answer. He walked over to the window. He parted the curtain near the desk to make it look as if he were interested in the river. He wasn't. He wanted to see whether there was a car parked outside. Nothing too obvious or unusual on the street below, except for the Buick down the block, lights off, and the shadow of a man behind the wheel. He let the drape swing closed. "Cute chauffeur," he said.

She stared at his sandwich. Another sip of beer and he put the bottle down, not one to worry about leaving a water ring on the wood. He visited a drawer and took out a knife. He cut the sandwich in half. He placed her half on a plate and handed it to her. "Here," he said. "You look hungry."

"I shouldn't," she said, but accepted the dish anyway.

"It's a far cry from lobster whatever-it-was-called from the other night. Nothing fancy about the hobo sandwich there. It reminds me of back home when we were poor. If you're hungry, you should eat."

She looked to his bottle of beer. Walker read the cue and got her a glass. When he returned with it, she'd taken a healthy bite out of her sandwich and was sipping his beer. "Help yourself," he said.

"Why don't you sit and eat with me?"

He grabbed his half of the sandwich and was thinking egg, potato, mother and home, and the farm. He swallowed his first bite, about to take another when she said, "Did you offer her something to eat and drink?"

"Is that what this visit is about?"

He took that bite, reached over, and washed it down with beer from the bottle that he had taken out of her hand. When he returned the bottle to her, he told her, "No. She cooked for me."

"I cooked for you in Vienna."

"That was Vienna, this is Hell's Kitchen."

"She's a kid."

"In age, yes. In other things? Far from it, and you know it."

It wasn't exactly Jack Benny repartee, or choice dialog for Jack Warner, but he dished it out to her, just the same. She absorbed what he said and didn't say a word. Leslie had trained herself not to show emotion, another strategy she used when there was a purpose.

"I don't get you, Leslie. You have your girlfriend, a nice house on Mulholland, and you're here with me in my flat, as you would call it in England. What does your boyfriend out in the car have to say about all this?"

"Boyfriend?"

"Buick parked down the block."

"Is she a good cook?"

Walker ate another bite. The potatoes tasted starchy, and the pressed bread, like cardboard. "To answer your question," he said, "she's excellent."

He swallowed the last bite of his dinner and wanted more beer, but she was holding the bottle, and he was afraid of taking it away from her. The hard and cold stare from her was a deterrent. "What happened between you and Tania?"

"A gentleman never tells. You should appreciate that, Leslie. And what is it to you? Like I said, you have Vera and you've got your ride outside. I can't see his face from here, but I'm confident he's handsome. One of Steps's men, right? You like glamour in your women and dim and dangerous in men."

"She's a child, Walker. A mere child."

"Save it. She's not and you know it. What's with you and Steps, by the way?"

That question made Leslie's forehead crinkle. "What do you mean? There's nothing between us."

"What's with the driver outside my window? He's not out there stargazing. He drove you here when you could've taken a taxi. Maybe a little smile from you was all he needed to become your knight. You ought to know better. Him outside has Steps knowing where you are, or maybe that's what you want. Speaking of being seen in places, does Vera know you're here?"

Leslie stood up and Walker stood up. There were no corners, no bell, and no referee this time. This was a rematch after their last dinner in Vienna.

"I left Vera after she fell asleep."

"And you'll be there to wake her up like nothing ever happened, right?"

"You're rude."

"Good. Why don't you slap me again? This time make sure you use your right hand. I'll ask you again. Say why you're really here."

She put the beer bottle down on the desk and sat back down on the bed. He sat down, too. Diplomatic relations between them had improved, or so he thought.

"I think Steps is playing an angle."

Walker wanted to say that it was the second time in the same day that he'd heard that theory. He didn't, though he wondered whether he was too blind, too simple in the head, and in last place in the strategy game. "Why do you say that?" he asked.

She smoothed out her dress with her hand. "He has an opportunity to take over The Prime Minister's territory. All he has to do is neutralize his opposition and form the right alliances."

"Or he could remain loyal and look out for his boss."

Walker examined how much beer was left in the fridge. Not enough. He offered her the last bottle. She shook her head. "When you say neutralize, you mean kill Vito Genovese."

She kicked off her shoes. Walker watched them fall, hit the floor, and her long legs fold up under her skirt. He tried again. "Think Steps will try and knock off Genovese? The way I understand politics, that would require approval from the Commission."

She had scrunched a pillow and rested against it. "The Commission won't issue a contract on Genovese. The man has a far-reaching and lucrative business plan. Money talks and virtue walks."

"You mean his interest in narcotics. And The Prime Minister?"

"He should retire. If The Prime Minister doesn't retire, then there's a possibility of a mob war, and that would be bad for everyone. The Commission faces a conundrum—"

"A dilemma, you mean," Walker said.

"You're right. Dilemma is the better word because there are two choices. Does The Prime Minister retire or not? He should because he isn't the future of the mob. Narcotics is."

"And the other choice?"

"The Commission needs all the judges, politicians, and police The Prime Minister owns. It's why the man remains alive. No matter how much money Genovese makes for everyone, no politician or judge wants to be associated with the drug trade."

Walker weighed what she had said, worked off the last of the beer and watched the suds blister inside the bottle. She possessed a fine tactical mind. He leaned back in his chair. He played the squeak in the floor to effect. She stood up and stretched out her legs.

"That leaves Anastasia," he said. "The man is loyal to The Prime Minister, according to Steps, and Albert isn't fond of Vito. The question is whether there's enough money in narcotics to sway Anastasia against The Prime Minister."

Leslie returned to the bed. She punched up the pillow and did her imitation of Cleopatra on the barge. The Hudson was not the Nile, but Walker was not about to argue for historical accuracy. He appreciated her light-brown hair, those red lips, and the leaf-green eye shadow too much.

"That leaves one of two possibilities," she said.

"Either Steps or Genovese has to kill Anastasia."

"Walker?"

CHAPTER TWENTY-TWO

"Yes."

"What happened between you and Tania?"

"Nothing."

"Be honest."

"I am being honest. She tried. I said no. She became upset and left. I should have followed her, but I didn't. You know, Sheldon said something about Cohn and Hoover and—"

"Walker?"

"Yes."

"Come over here."

She was lying in his bed, in his apartment, and on his pillow. She pulled him down by his tie to join her there. He wasn't complaining and hoped that there would be no broken pieces to sweep up in the morning.

He stopped thinking.

Chapter Twenty-Three

Walker waited outside for Steps. True to his name, Steps had stepped up security. The theatre's latest sentry was as obvious as a New York pigeon, a factory-issued mobster in a dark tailored suit, loud tie, and fedora. He was blowing the smoke from his cigarette into the street, and the sparkle from the diamonds in his pinky ring added to the glare of a hot summer day.

A red light seemed to irritate the driver behind the wheel of a Hudson Hornet in the street in front of him. The man rolled his car into the middle of the crosswalk, ready to blaze through the intersection. He waited instead, despite the nasty stares from pedestrians, including one elderly lady who stopped in front of his car. Walker wasn't sure whether she'd spit on the car or rip the hood ornament off.

He spotted Steps. In gabardine slacks, no jacket, and a blue dress shirt, Steps walked fast. The mobster behind Steps held an opened umbrella to shade Steps from the punishing sunlight. Kelvinator made refrigerators as tall and wide as he was. Walker said hello and Steps was short and curt. "There's a diner up the street. We need to talk."

"Privacy include Rocky Marciano behind you?"

"Don't mind Aldo. He'll wait outside. He's quiet."

"Yeah, quiet as a solar eclipse."

The diner was all Art Deco, a cube of chrome and stainless-steel. The glass was so clean it could squeak in the sunlight. Aldo opened the door and a cold front punched Walker in the face and chest.

A waitress in a pink uniform led them to a booth and handed them laminated menus. She recited the specials. Steps kept it simple and ordered two bottomless coffees. She doled out two napkins and a smile and said she'd be back. The scent of perfume left with her.

It was the two of them, two men sitting on frigid leather, and a Formica countertop between them. With or without the coffee, Steps itched to talk and did.

"The heat is on, and I'm not talking about the weather."

"Care to elaborate?"

Their waitress returned. She placed cups and saucers on the table with one hand and poured their coffees with the other. She borrowed a sugar holder and creamer from another table and set it down between them. Then *L'Air du Temps* drifted away.

Steps tipped sugar from the dispenser and then some cream into his coffee. Walker pulled his saucer and cup towards him. He liked his coffee black. He took a small sip of it. "You were saying."

"I need to clear the air, so to speak. Allow me to remind you of the ground rules, my friend. You are a stranger in a foreign land and a guest of The Prime Minister. Let me do my job and keep you alive for the time you're here. You want to die, then do that on your own time, but try not to take others down with you."

"Where's this coming from? I think I do all right."

"Like the night at the pier?"

Walker held up both of his hands and conceded. "I deserved that, but level with me and tell me what's got you so steamed?"

"Miss Gardner's little visit to your place is what." Steps changed gears. "I'm curious. You mentioned Marciano earlier. I wouldn't finger you for a fan of the gloves. Did you ever see the man live?"

"I watched The Rock feed Jersey Joe leather in Philly."

Municipal Stadium. September 23, 1952. Walcott was ahead of Marciano in points, giving the New Englander a grammar lesson. Round 13 proved unlucky for Walcott. Marciano leveled the most devastating KO in the history of the sport. With Walcott against the ropes, Marciano delivered a right hook from General Electric and turned off his opponent's lights, leaving his victim caught up in the ropes until gravity brought the body to the canvas, crumpled and unconscious.

"You were at the fight?"

"Do I have to repeat myself?"

"Were you in Philly before or after LA?"

"After, and what's that got to do with anything?"

"I suppose, like the Brockton Blockbuster, you have your own Suzie-Q, that devastating right punch."

"Again, what's with the interrogation?"

Steps slurped some joe and set his cup down hard, emphasizing the clink of porcelain against Formica. "I'll tell you. A friend of mine in LA dropped it into my ear that you had a run-in with Johnny Stompanato and laid him out. Few people, and none of them writers, survive an encounter like that with Stomps. If you're a writer, then I'm Father Sheen and this is The Catholic Hour. I like to know who I'm dealing with, and nothing about you has added up right since day one. I also heard about your tea party with Roy Cohn at the movie studio."

Impressive. Steps had moved dirt, like an archaeologist.

"You said earlier the heat was on, and I assume by that you meant Genovese."

"Don't turn the page on me," Steps said. "I'll get to Vito in a second, but I want to get one more thing off my chest. You and women."

"You already mentioned Maggie. I get it, you think I put her in danger."

Steps held up a finger. "First, Tania brings you breakfast and then vanishes." He presented a second finger. "Second, Miss Gardner blows in and out of your place in the middle of the night." His hand dropped and slapped the table.

Steps, for all his fancy threads and streetwise bravado, had acquitted himself. He'd done both reconnaissance and surveillance. Walker wouldn't take the bait or cut the line. He pressed on, like a good infantryman.

"Talk to me about Genovese. You mentioned boys from the Chicago Outfit at the French restaurant. Mercenaries. I assume they kidnapped Tania."

"Hold that thought. Let's discuss the subpoena and Miss Williams first. I told you and Sheldon that a federal judge signed it. What I didn't tell you is that The Prime Minister is feeling a sense of déjà vu all over again. Wonder why?"

"Because it reminds him of his cousin, Willie Moretti."

"Correct," Steps said. "Guess whose name popped up behind the judge who signed it?"

Walker sipped coffee. "Robert Francis Kennedy."

"Correct again."

"What do you want me to say about Kennedy? The man is looking to make a name for himself. He's ambitious."

The waitress swept in to do refills. Walker thought about a breakfast pastry. He'd seen a man at the counter eating a jelly doughnut. Powdered sugar stuck to his upper lip. Soon as she left, Walker continued. "Kennedy's old man wants a son in the White House. Nothing you can do about it."

"Wanna bet?" Steps reached into his shirt pocket. He tapped his pack of cigarettes. He offered Walker one. Walker declined, but pulled an ashtray in front of Steps, who lit the cigarette with a lighter. Chesterfields and Zippo. Walker paraphrased an earlier conversation with Jack. "Let me guess, Big Business won't allow it."

"We are Big Business," Steps answered. He turned his head and blew smoke. He held his cigarette over the ashtray. "I would've thought it'd be his brother, the senator, and not the runt of the family. You might disagree with me but, in my book, Kennedy is as dangerous as Anastasia. Their methods may differ, but both share the same mentality."

Walker sat back in the booth, surprised but not stunned.

"Anything else, gentlemen?" the waitress asked.

"Two doughnuts for my friend outside. You choose them and bring them to me in a bag, please." She nodded to Steps and walked to the display counter.

"Remember what I said at the Copa?" Steps said. "The first time Kennedy made his presence known in New York was when he said the waterfront was unsafe. This time, he says he's hunting Commies, but I think it's a smokescreen. You said it yourself. He's ambitious. You're the writer. How do you see the scene playing out?"

The perfume and waitress returned with the two doughnuts in a bag. Steps thanked her, asked her for the check. She reached into her apron and tore the slip from the pad and placed it face down on the table and thanked them.

"Write the scene for me, Mr. Thompson."

"He'll come after what people in the street can understand, things like unions and trucks, and it'll be big theatre on television, which will make people in your world uncomfortable and vindictive. I wouldn't be surprised if he leaves Cohn and McCarthy to do it. What do you think?"

"I think you and Mr. Marshall and whoever you work for better count the ways Kennedy will be a headache for you."

"Thanks for the advice, but you said we'd talk about Genovese. I want to find Tania. Do you know where she is?"

"I do," Steps said. "When people think of us, they look to New York and Jersey, but they forget the other mobbed up city, the City of Brotherly Love."

"Philadelphia?"

"She's in Philly."

"That's why you asked me about Marciano in Philly."

Steps winked. "Ding-ding. It's time to get into the ring."

Chapter Twenty-Four

Walker blue-lined the script, Adler added red ink, and Leslie retyped it in black at some unknown hour and redistributed it to all the players.

Adler coached. Adler coaxed. He heaped praise and issued directions. The cast read their lines. They rehearsed their roles. They recited their lines for the umpteenth time with this tone or that pitch, this style or that interpretation; enunciated from this spot here, that spot there, under this light, away from that light, until every actor had hit his or her mark with an athlete's trained memory. Everything was as it should be minus one actress and her scene.

Adler also fretted as any parent would about their child. The government men outside the house in Jersey had followed him into the city. He couldn't walk a city block without their car following him, like slime behind a snail. They tracked him to the theatre, and he was surprised they hadn't invited themselves in to audit the play. They chose to remain outside, parked in their dark Ford Crestliner. They'd gone so far as to tail Judith and his son to Central Park, where David tossed bread to the birds. At Walker's request, Leslie accompanied them and reported back to him that there'd been additional detail added to the initial surveillance team, which she believed was for Vera and they ought to expect men in the lobby of the Sheraton Hotel soon.

Adler ordered a recess, and the actors fled for coffee and cigarettes outside. Vera lingered. She approached Adler and Walker and stated the obvious before she walked away. "Gentlemen, we need Tania."

"I don't understand how someone like Steps can't find her," Adler said to Walker.

"Steps did find her."

"He did?"

"She's somewhere in Philly."

"When were you planning on telling me?"

"It's complicated, Mr. Adler."

"We're days away from our first show. Does Sheldon know?"

"Not yet. Where is he, by the way?"

"He said he'd be late." Adler checked his wristwatch. "I'm going to get some coffee."

Adler walked off while Walker thought about what Steps had provided for details about Philadelphia on their way back to the theatre. While there was a mafia presence in other parts of the country, New York was home to five mafia families. Walker understood as much from Jack's dossier, but he listened to Steps anyway. Steps sketched in nuances that Jack's research lacked, a layer of complexity in the power struggle between Vito Genovese and Frank Costello.

Prohibition would derail Arnold Rothstein and Meyer Lansky's dream of a corporate criminal empire. When the country was wet again, Luciano, Lansky, and Costello worked at the slow crawl away from gambling, loansharking, and prostitution towards legitimate enterprises. Meyer Lansky managed casinos in Florida, New Orleans, and, later, Cuba. The Prime Minister owned poultry and meatpacking plants.

Genovese's interest in narcotics kept the mob on the streets. There were two problems, as Steps saw it. First, narcotics was an international business, and it required a network for smuggling. This conclusion was in line with what Frank Costello disliked about narcotics, but Steps saw something that either The Prime Minister didn't think of or kept to himself, and that was no matter how much they wanted to distance themselves from violence, the revenue for organized crime would always depend on unsavory fundamentals. What nobody in the five families in New York had anticipated was Vito Genovese forming a partnership with South Philly's crime boss

Joe Ida. This alliance extended Genovese's reach into Pennsylvania and southern New Jersey.

Walker had held back from Steps a nuanced observation of his own. Vera had been served with a subpoena and not a summons. The two legal terms were used interchangeably. A summons implied a lawsuit. With a summons a defendant had a prescribed amount of time to answer the complaint. A subpoena, however, lacked urgency, though it was technically a call for a deposition.

A deposition did not become part of the public record unless the lawyer filed it with the court. If Cohn and Kennedy filed, then her testimony became a matter of public record. Walker expected the lawyers to pocket her testimony at the deposition and use it as evidence in a future criminal trial. The more Vera talked about her time in New York, the more likely she'd mention or hint at "criminal elements" that interested Kennedy. Walker was certain that was the young lawyer's endgame.

Walker also realized that Cohn understood the spotlight as much as Vera did. Warner had been right to send her back east. Vera had too much history, too much of the wrong color around her. Her Friday night parties hosted every type of subversive over the years. Blacklisted writers. Lavender types. Reds. Warner had bought time for his studio. To Cohn, Vera was the easy apple on a low branch. No stepladder required.

Walker recalled how Cohn had ambushed him at Warner's. Leonard Moore, Jack Warner's clearance man for studio talent before HUAC, had prepped him for the meet and greet with Roy Cohn. Lenny asked his questions while Cohn sat wise as a Solomon at the table, in his expensive suit, slicked back hair, and smug smirk. Moore had no idea that Cohn would attack Walker's military record, which backfired on him in front of Moore and Warner himself.

Adler returned earlier than expected. Walker called him over.

"What can I do for you, Walter?"

"Now that we know where Tania is, I'm obligated to warn you about what might happen. You and Judith might get squeezed. They'll take advantage of the opportunity."

"Who is they?"

"The government men outside your house."

Adler wasn't drinking the coffee in his hand. He wanted an explanation.

"Come now, Mr. Adler. Don't be a hayseed. You know what they want. They're interested in what you have to say about Communists in radio and theatre. They're interested in Judith, for what she might have to say about the Rosenbergs during her stint at Fort Monmouth."

"The Rosenbergs are dead."

"But fresh on everyone's mind and they want to capitalize on the fact."

"But Vera is the one with the subpoena," Adler said.

"And you don't think they can print one up for you and Judith?"

Walker assumed Cohn was like any lawyer who didn't ask questions to which he didn't already know the answers. With Vera, there was ancient history and dust from parties on Mulholland Drive, and he'd parlay all of it into the volume entitled *The History of the Decline and Fall of the Hollywood Empire*, with J. Edgar Hoover providing the voice-over. Adler, however, was Cohn's railroad ticket to East Coast communists. Cohn had to resent it that he couldn't dent the Red wall on the eastern seaboard. While Cohn foraged, Walker suspected Kennedy would reveal his objective, and there might be an opportunity somehow for the Company to work one lawyer against the other.

"You're right, Mr. Adler. The subpoena belongs to Vera, but I'll wager if the person behind it is happy with whatever you and Judith tell him, he'll quash her subpoena like it'd never happened and Vera might, and I emphasize, *might*, not have to testify."

"And if you're wrong?"

"Then we'll know who or what they're after. I thought you deserved advance notice, so don't be surprised if they come for you and Judith. Until then, focus on the play."

"There's nothing for me to tell them, Walter. I swear. There aren't any new names."

He wanted to tell Adler it was the same song in Hollywood, that half the names that HUAC called up were informants for Hoover.

"And Judith was interrogated years ago about the Rosenbergs," Adler said. "There's a record of it somewhere."

"You can count on that, but Roy Cohn wasn't the one asking the questions then. Sorry to say this, but you'll have to play the naming game again. Old names are good because you look like you're cooperating and you're consistent. Look, Mr. Adler. I'm sorry to have to put the scare in you, but Mr. Cohn is the kind of man who'll take away your son and make him a ward of the state if you or Judith don't play along."

"He can't do that. I won't allow it."

Poor naïve Adler, Walker thought. Laws are made and the same people who make them break them when it is convenient to them. They might not believe him if he parroted the same names they'd read in the *Red Channels* or they might, but he had no choice. He was being handed a dead rose and asked to say it smelled good.

"The man is a reptile. Someone ought to turn him into a suitcase or put him in one."

"The day someone does I'll tip the porter, Mr. Adler."

The door opened and the conversation stopped. Sheldon appeared first, followed by another man. Sheldon and the visitor walked down the steps to Adler and Walker. This other man was tall and lean, in an olive-green suit, tawny Sleuth hat in his hand. He was wearing a crisp blue shirt, simple tie, and brogues on his feet. No pocket square. He introduced himself to Adler.

"Pleased to meet you. I'm Jack Marshall."

Chapter Twenty-Five

The Horn & Hardart was an all coin and chrome eatery on Broadway, instantly recognizable for its limestone exterior, scratchy granite and bronze entrance, its blue-green-and-tan terra cotta capitals, and the gaudy floral frills and zigzags on the third floor. The mezzanine was a mess of arches, fluted moldings, spandrels, and mullions, back when somebody knew what a spandrel or a mullion was. There was enough architectural excess in the building that a doctoral degree ought to have been awarded with the building permit.

The Automat inside was a DeMille production piece but reproduced to scale to bilk the Upper West Side of its income, one nickel at a time. The most expensive meal was one dollar, macaroni and cheese was the most popular dish, the New Orleans drip coffee put out more than most revelers did on Fat Tuesday, and people could see the food without a menu. It was Visual Arts and dining without the adjectives, the waiter's baritone swoon, or the waitresses' bare skin.

The Automat had a rectangular mess hall inside, numerous lacquered tables and red vinyl seats wiped down with a nurse's love for neatness. It also had thousands of daily customers. It was democracy in action. And behind the registers were the "nickel throwers" working inside booths. These ladies were not fit for fancy Macy's on 34th Street, its cosmetic counters; they would never be candidates for a fancy pension, but they were fancy in their own way, wearing white lace aprons and rubber tips on their fingers for all those nickels. The future for them was likely to involve carrying walking sticks, with knitting needles in tow. They counted out change for customers who fed the coins into slots for the food behind small glass windows in the wall as drones behind the wall kept the honeycombs stocked. For a few nickels a play a man could feel like a movie star as he ate his pumpkin pie on any day not Thanksgiving.

Jack chose a table for him, Sheldon, and Walker. Steps arrived with Leslie. They navigated the crowd with ease. Steps pulled up a chair for Leslie and she sat down. After the firm handshake with Jack, he joined them at the table. They had not exchanged names, which suited Steps fine because he initiated the conversation.

"I assume Walter has told you about Philadelphia and the G-men outside Adler's door."

"He has."

"I was informed you've spoken with The Prime Minister."

"I have."

"Tell me, how does The Prime Minister look these days?"

"Healthy and behaving like a Boy Scout. He says folding socks soothes him. He's offered to conduct a seminar on how laundry could be more efficient for the warden and other prisoners."

"A sense of humor. He relayed the message to do whatever I can to help you."

For a man in prison, The Prime Minister had more conduits for communication than Murrow and Paley. CBS should give the man a by-line. Western Union could learn a thing or two from the mob circuit.

"The Prime Minister says I can trust you." Steps pushed his hat forward on the table to make room for his elbows. "I've been loyal to the man since I got into the business."

"An admirable quality, but where does that leave you when business is changing?"

"The Prime Minister and I don't care for where the business is headed, or for the man behind that change in direction. I'll retire when The Prime Minister retires, even if it means a box instead of a gold watch."

"Friends to the end," Jack said.

"Mind me asking a question?"

"Not at all."

"You're not the law, are you?"

"Not in the conventional sense."

"And your associates here aren't actors, or interested in producing a play."

"I don't know about that," Jack said. "Each person around this table possesses a talent. Walter is an excellent writer. Sheldon is a tailor from my days in Europe after the war." Jack was dealing cards, the truth without his thumbs getting in the way.

"And Miss Gardner there? You seem to have forgotten her."

"I haven't forgotten her."

"I haven't worked with women before."

"You should," Jack said. "She's excellent at analysis."

"Really? What kind of things does she analyze?"

Jack asked Leslie, "What do you think Steps is carrying?"

Leslie put her elbow on the table, rested her chin on her hand, batted her eyelashes at Steps, and gave him a delicious smile. "I don't know. He doesn't seem the type of man who has the need to overcompensate. He's a cash-and-carry man with cold bills in his billfold in his left breast pocket and a .38 in a holster under his left arm. It's not a glamorous gun, but it's excellent for the draw. From the looks of him, I'd say Steps makes certain that the job is done. He'll put a tight group in someone else's chest before he delivers one to the head."

Steps gave her a queer look. "How would you know all that, sister?"

Leslie put her purse in front of Steps and undid the snaps for him. "Look inside."

"What are you carrying this time?" Steps stuck his hand inside and touched a Smith & Wesson Chief's Special in a blued finish. He smiled. "Similar to the one on me."

"Except she's a better shooter than you," Jack said. "I can guarantee it."

Steps closed the purse and slid it over to her. "I've seen his gun." He pointed to Walker and asked her, "What's your analysis there?"

"He's sentimental. Can we talk about Philadelphia?"

Sheldon raised a finger. "I'd like to ask a question. Do you know where in

Philadelphia?"

Everyone turned their attention to Steps.

"I have two leads on an address, but I've got to level with you. I'm not sure which one has the girl, though I can tell you one of them has men in cheap suits who have a not-so-nice boss in Washington, and a lawyer I can't stand."

"What about the second address?" Jack asked.

"A known safe house for Genovese's men. I've confirmed that they're the same fellows who poached Walter for a midnight swim. These men have a reputation for doing odd jobs on the side."

Jack contemplated the answer from Steps, long and hard enough to make a diamond out of coal. Jack's jaw tensed, his finger tapped the table, up and down, the way a metronome keeps time. "I see three possibilities," he said. "One is that Genovese ordered the kidnapping and these soldiers are expendable, so there'll be no trace of Tania to him. Possibility number two is a slight variation of number one, and that is Cohn was behind the kidnapping, and Genovese didn't know about it."

Steps asked, "And Kennedy?"

Walker answered. "Steps said Kennedy and Anastasia are alike, so if that's true then it's not Kennedy's style."

Steps nodded. "I agree. You said three possibilities. Option three?"

"Hoover hired the mercenaries, without either Cohn or Genovese knowing it, so he'll have Genovese pinned to the wall for whatever he wants and needs. Hoover does that, and he's in like Flynn, regardless of leadership within the mob."

Steps weighed Jack's answer. "As much as I don't like Genovese, option two or three makes the most sense. Genovese is thick as a bull, but even he knows the Commission is against harming civilians and he can't jeopardize his play with narcotics over an actress."

"Then join us in Philly and help us put an end to this," Jack said.

"I need to put this on the table. The Commission holds bosses accountable for anything their subordinates do, which means if this trip goes wrong, there's a contract on me and The Prime Minister. You do this and it flies south, the Commission won't consider you civilians. Everyone around this table is dead."

"You have to decide for yourself where you stand," Jack said. "I'm certain The Prime Minister will respect your decision."

"He promised you that he'd help you, right?"

"He did."

"I'm the only way he could keep his word," Steps said, eyes bright and intent. "There's more at stake here than politicians in DC and a subpoena for an actress. There's the possibility of an all-out war between The Prime Minister and Genovese. Don't forget that."

"I won't, but come with us to Philly," Jack said. "If you can't or won't, then all I ask is that you delay Mr. Anastasia from disciplining those independent contractors."

"I'll join you and I'll keep Albert on the leash. With The Prime Minister in the pen and everybody salivating over Vito's business proposition, I don't have a lot of friends, or room for mistakes, Mr. Marshall."

"I know, but you have friends now."

Chapter Twenty-Six

Jimmy Alabaster was driving the first car, the Chrysler Imperial, with Steps on the passenger side, and Jack, Walker, and Sheldon in the backseat. The second car, the Buick Roadmaster, had Leslie in the front seat with her favorite driver and Vera, Adler, and Judith with David in the back. The third car was the blue Cadillac Eldorado.

They were not itinerant Bennies, the Bayonne to Elizabeth to Newark to New York travelers; not Shoobies from Pennsylvania, their packed lunches in shoe boxes for the trip, but the lowest of the low, the Foots, the fill-the-expletive-here out of towners.

Steps was calm and ready for business. Jack debated whether to make Steps his point man, the soldier with an Auto-5 shotgun, or the last man with the Browning machine gun. The former drew first blood, while the latter offered the sound an infantryman welcomed like Handel's *Messiah*. Jack expected trouble with whoever held Tania captive.

"Swap out the plates like I asked?" Jack asked Steps.

"I did. Albert got a kick out of it. My guy in the car with Adler ditched the watchdogs in Jersey, but do you think it's a good idea bringing the kid along?"

"Do you think it was a bright idea to bring Anastasia with us?"

"You wanted him on a leash. The best way to do that is to include him. Besides, he's loyal to The Prime Minister," Steps answered.

"But he might tell the Commission everything."

"That wouldn't be a bad thing," Steps said. "He's our insurance. Albert with us gives him eyes on what's what, so if orders come down from the

Commission against me or The Prime Minister, he'll have his say and the board members will listen to Albert. Insurance, like I said."

"What if the Commission hires irregulars?" Walker asked.

"Outside contractors?" Steps looked up into the mirror to answer Walker. "It don't work that way. If Albert Anastasia wants no part with the order, his crew will stand by his decision. Whoever receives the contract will have to contend with Anastasia. It doesn't stop a war with Genovese, though."

"Let's hope it doesn't come to that," Jack said. "The minute anybody starts talking about a contract on The Prime Minister, Genovese will attack, and his first target will be Anastasia. He does it fast enough, he won't need the Commission's permission, so maybe it's good that Albert is with us."

"Think he can scare Kennedy back to Boston?"

"I doubt it, and don't underestimate his family when it comes to retaliation."

"What is it you propose we do with him then?" Steps asked.

"I'll leave that to our playwright in the backseat."

Walker didn't bother to look at Steps, choosing instead the view of the new Turnpike, the flashes of trees speeding by outside his window, the sun against his face. Jack had paid him the high compliment as the scene-maker. Jimmy Alabaster stepped on the gas for Quaker City. They were not Magi under a star in search of a manger in Philadelphia. There was no guiding star in the sky today. The sun didn't count.

The Buick Roadmaster carried on its own conversation as it barreled down the blacktop, second in line behind the Chrysler. Vera didn't like sitting in the middle of the front seat, but she had insisted on sitting with Leslie. She did not want the driver alone with her girl. The man had taken it in stride. He and Leslie gave each other the occasional fugitive smile over Vera's anxiety about meeting Roy Cohn. Though they had never met, his reputation preceded him as oil incarnate.

David slept on the backseat. They rode the asphalt past a series of industrial towns, and some bodies of water now and then. A truck rumbled past them. Its freight banged and buckled and swayed on the flat bed behind it. The trucker had a schedule to keep, bad food to catch at the next roadside stop, and a rendezvous with his gum-smacking mistress before he laid his weary head down in his cab for the night. He'd repeat the whole routine the next morning.

A sign at the side of the road displayed the miles left to Philadelphia. The driver noticed Vera's hand searching for Leslie's. Leslie gave Vera's hand a slight squeeze. Leslie searched for the Cadillac in her side-view mirror. The two men in that car looked as comfortable as insurance salesmen about to sell ten-thousand-dollar policies to a stick of paratroopers.

"Why do I feel like this will be the performance of my life?" Vera said to Leslie.

"You'll do fine. Follow Mr. Marshall's advice."

"Keep my answers simple and maintain a neutral tone."

Jack prescribed the same advice to Adler and Judith. Adler sat there, quiet since they had left Manhattan, a resigned weariness etched into his features. Judith's stoicism was admirable but was undermined by a slight tremor in her hand. Her eyes were moist and terrified.

Vera's voice was soft, almost inaudible. "There's no script here. I'm nervous, Maggie."

"Breathe and don't forget what he said about the Fifth," Leslie said.

"Easy for a man to say," Vera said. "Name a day a woman doesn't incriminate herself. What do rights matter when there are no witnesses present?"

If he could, Cohn would steal Vera away as his Academy Award, Adler as his Pulitzer, and Judith would be his ticket to a political career if he wanted it. Leslie touched Vera's hand. "You have people around you. You're not alone in this."

"I understand, dear, but consider the entourage. Steps in one car," she said, pointing to the Chrysler in front of them, "and then there's Murder Incorporated behind us. Some company. And what's Jack Marshall's story? The same goes for Sheldon and this fellow on my left here. I don't even know his name."

His hands on the wheel, eyes on the road, he leaned over and said, "The name is Johnny Mercuro. Friends call me Johnny Mercury."

Vera gave him a weak smile and whispered to Leslie, "See my point. Stage names everywhere. Two mystery men in front of us, and the Mad Hatter behind us. Our driver has a name out of a comic book. If I am the company I keep, then some credibility I'll have."

"Jimmy Alabaster."

"Excuse me?"

"The mystery man driving the car in front of us is Jimmy Alabaster. His real name is Giacomo Alabastrianni. Jimmy Alabaster is easier to spell and pronounce. He shortened his name just as I did mine."

"Charming."

"You need to lighten up, Miss Williams. You've got friends, like your girlfriend said. That's better than most people. Go and answer this Cohn character's questions. Same goes for you two in the back," Johnny Mercury said, looking into his rearview mirror.

"Let me guess," Vera said. "You think that because you answer some questions with your hand over your heart, the flag will wave bright and right, and life will be all normal again."

"Sure I do."

"Oh, brother. This one is a dreamer," Vera said.

Mercury gripped the wheel and punched the gas.

Leslie pulled on Vera's hand. "You don't have to be rude."

"I find little comfort in the company of gangsters on my way to meet Satan's best. I might as well have asked for a glass of wine from Lucrezia Borgia."

"You know what your problem is, Miss Williams," Johnny said.

"The man behind the wheel of the luxury Titanic has words of wisdom."

"Please stop, Vera."

Mercury gave Vera a sidelong glance that could have shaved inches off a cigar.

"I'm listening, Mr. Mercury."

"You're not a very bright dame, are you?"

"Did you just call me stupid?"

"Whad'ya know, the dye has worked its way down to the roots?"

Leslie put her hand to her mouth to stifle a laugh. Johnny Mercury laid into Vera.

"Ever cross your platinum brainpan that this shyster Cohn could haul you into a New York courtroom? Subpoena or not, he'll think twice before he does that because of this company of gangsters, as you so put it, and because we have judges and politicians on retainer, thanks to The Prime Minister. No, it couldn't have because you think only about yourself, sister. We're nothing but the express train for the great Miss Vera Williams."

"I beg your pardon," Vera said. "Do you have any idea who I am?"

"Yeah, I do. You're an actress nobody remembered until a few years ago when someone either gave you a break, or you gave someone a good time." He spoke the truth about the casting couch with the moguls in Hollywood. Mercury spared Vera no quarter. "The folks who are in a real jam, Miss Williams, are the ones sitting in the back seat. They've got to worry about their kid there. Like the idea crossed your mind."

Vera sat there mortified, put in her place. Ice could've cracked and thawed for the next long, silent mile of evergreens and bright summer sky.

Vera swallowed hard before she spoke. "Can't The Prime Minister help them?"

By them, Vera had meant Adler, Judith, and David.

"Sure, he can, but in the real world the very important people are taken care of first."

"That's unfair and unkind."

"Such is life," Johnny said.

"I'm sorry you think so little of me," Vera said.

"The biggest thing our friends in the backseat got going for them is they have a friend."

"The Prime Minister?" Vera said.

Mercury turned his head and ignored the road for a second. It wasn't a double take, but it was worthy of the camera. "Not him. I'm talking about Albert Anastasia."

"Anastasia?" Leslie said, shocked to hear the name.

"Didn't expect that, didja? The man is tough in public but a softie in private." Mercury focused his eyes on the road and picked up more speed. "Albert has kids. He takes them to the theatre every weekend and brings along the neighborhood kids on occasion. It's because of him there are rules."

"Rules?" Vera asked.

"Yeah, rules. Like you don't off a guy in front of his family, and you don't harm women and children. And if a guy goes down for the count rather than rat, Albert makes sure the wife and kids are looked after, taken care of—food and clothes, doctor's bills, rent and education."

"I didn't know that," Vera said.

"Ethics. That's why Albert and The Prime Minister get along."

"And Vito Genovese?" Leslie asked.

"Whad'ya think? The man offed a friend because he thought the guy was having an affair with his wife. Turned out to be the bunk. Even after he'd learned the truth, Vito wanted to have her killed but Albert drew the line and said 'No women.' Albert told Vito to either stay married or get a divorce, like everyone else."

"So, he's like David's guardian angel?" Vera said.

"You could say that."

Judith put her hand on the leather in front of her and pulled herself forward in the seat. In a soft voice, she said, "You mean that if something were to happen to me and Irwin, David wouldn't end up in an orphanage or institutionalized?"

Mercury spoke, looking into his rearview mirror. "Steps said that as long as your nephew lives in New York no judge in the state would sign the order if His Honor wanted to stay healthy or in office."

Chapter Twenty-Seven

Philadelphia is like a pair of shoulders. Wealth and poverty can see each other across the divide without much thought in between for city planning.

Georgian façades recall England, on streets named after trees, such as Chestnut, Locust, Pine, Spruce, and Walnut. Here, Old Philadelphians gather in rooms of white woodwork, behind the red bricks of the Philadelphia Club, under tall ceilings and large portraits of their ancestors. They play ruthless rounds of sniff, while Negro servants deliver food and drink. Their sons row for Harvard, play cricket at the city's club, or command the pitch at the Brandywine Polo Club. Their daughters attend Bryn Mawr and then embark on the Grand Tour, in search of a title and a husband. Wealth lives behind the iron gates of Chestnut Hill and the Main Line. Perennial Philadelphians winter in Florida and summer in Newport.

The less fortunate in Philly contend with narrow streets, live in row houses, and have no gardens to call their own. They have Germantown, Port Richmond, and the Mance. The quiet rich and the loud poor coexist in a city between two rivers, the Delaware and the Schuylkill. Lethe and Styx, forgetfulness and death. The landscape was dark and divided outside their window. For a city that was the first capital of the Union, the second largest English-speaking city after London during the American Revolution, there was no brotherly love among those who worked the steel mills or the coal mines for Carnegie or the Anthracite Aristocracy who owned them.

They approached a hilly town with the steeples of sleepy churches, dying factories and mills. Judging by the signs in the windows on Main Street, the decrepit lettering on rusted mailboxes, the poor part of town was made up of immigrants. German, Irish, and Polish.

Steps stopped once, to use a payphone. The call didn't take long, and he returned to the car with good news. Whatever spy network the mob used, Steps announced that he had confirmed Cohn's location in Philly. Genovese's involvement remained uncertain but intelligence from the field said that Tania was not with the lawyer.

The place was in northwestern Philly, an abandoned cotton mill not far from the banks of the Schuylkill River, which David kept calling School-n-Kill. Their three parked cars formed a cavalry line of American steel. Three suited men emerged from the old mill's front door. One of the men was dusting off his hands and chewing something.

"More mobsters?" Vera asked.

Johnny Mercury tried to reassure her. "Nah, we dress better. The only men who dress that way either live at home with mother, or they work for the Bureau. Let's not keep these ladies waiting."

Johnny Mercury exited the car. Anastasia remained inside his vehicle, engine and AC running. The three men from the mill stopped about four feet away from the Eldorado. One of the men, the tallest, stuck out his hand, but not for the handshake. He flipped his badge and asked for identification.

"You're kidding, right?" Johnny Mercury said.

"We're not. Identification, please."

The two men behind him spread their jackets, to show they carried weapons.

"Look, it's amateur cowboy hour," Johnny said to Jimmy Alabaster.

Jack Marshall stepped forward. "Excuse me. There are women here and we have a child with us, and it's hot. If you want to spend the next half hour taking names, then that is fine with us. We'll do the same and record your badge numbers, as it is our legal right, but I think it's a ridiculous waste of time when you and your men can go back inside and sit under that nice fan you've been sitting under all morning and enjoy the last of your breakfast."

The front man put his hands on his hips. Classic pose for asserting dominance.

"How do you know we were sitting under a fan and having breakfast?"

"You just told me." Jack squinted, the sun in his eyes. "None of you combed your hair. It's all windswept, and a fan will do that. As for breakfast—the fellow behind you was brushing his hands off and was chewing something as he came out. If you like I can point out the small coffee stain on the other fellow's shirt."

"You some kind of detective or something?"

"No. I'm not. Tell you what we should do. My friend over there," Jack said, meaning Johnny Mercury. "His name is sewn inside his jacket."

"What about the two inside that car?"

Jack didn't look at Anastasia's car. "One of them has a condition."

"Medical condition? Heat bother him?"

"No. He gets angry easily. Trust me, the Bureau didn't give you the training to deal with somebody like him."

"I've got a job to do, mister. Identification is part of inventory protocol."

"Take down the license plates and call them in. Meanwhile, I believe Mr. Cohn wishes to speak with two of our passengers. He's here, right?"

The agent blinked.

"Don't think too long," Jack said. "My friend and I would like to accompany our guest inside. Since we have a child with us, can you suggest a place for the others here to take him for ice cream or something? You can call the place you designate when Mr. Cohn is done, and we'll even bring you and your men some lunch. How does that sound?"

"That could be construed as a bribe."

"Son, sometimes lunch is just lunch."

"We'll take down the plate numbers. There's a Linton's about five minutes from here. Kids love when they put the food on these conveyor belts. The kid'll get a kick out of that. I'll call the restaurant there when Mr. Cohn and Mr. Kennedy are done speaking with Miss Williams. They'll also want to talk to Mrs. Nussbaum."

Jack accepted a slip of paper with the directions to the restaurant. "You boys take down the plates, while I join Miss Williams and my colleague, Mr. Thompson. Did you say that Mr. Kennedy was here?"

"Not yet. He's running late, but he'll be here soon."

The agent divvied up the task of writing down the license plate numbers while Jack handed the directions to Steps and instructed him to take the rest of the group to Linton's.

Judith approached Jack. "They don't want to talk to Irwin?"

"Looks like it."

The front door creaked when pulled open. Inside stood a standup fan a few feet away from a table. This was the agent's nest. Jack noticed the cards. Not much in the way of hands for poker and they were playing for pocket change. A radio sang in the background. The place was musty from the river, which had flooded the premises during the high season.

A stairwell led up to another office, in which the profile of another table and a small man in a chair awaited them. Jack peeked and spied black leather wingtips, buffed to a merciless shine, pleated dark slacks with cuffs to catch dropped change. The figure moved and flashed blue shirt and paisley tie, hair scraped back and wet. Roy Cohn.

Jack nudged Vera. She knocked on the doorframe.

"I'm Vera Williams."

"Have a seat," he said. His hand pointed at the chair across from him.

Cohn saw both Jack and Walker behind her. "I know you. You're that nobody, the two-bit writer in Hollywood. Is this other man a lawyer?"

"No," she answered.

"*Was* a Hollywood writer," Walker said.

"I'm Jack Marshall."

Neither Jack nor Walker offered a handshake. Vera took her seat. Jack and Walker stood at ease, like they did in the army. Cohn kept a legal pad and a ballpoint pen in front of him.

"I'll cut to the chase, Miss Williams. I'm fully aware of your association with listed writers in Los Angeles, aware of your generosity towards them in their time of financial distress. I have plenty of documentation of your numerous parties and all those who've attended them. You're quite the socialite."

"Thank you."

"It wasn't intended as a compliment, Miss Williams. You've consorted with Reds. I want to know why you are in New York."

"Mr. Cohn, when you say consorted with, you make it sound biblical. I can assure you that I'm a lady. True, I've had friends, many of whom were colleagues of various political dispositions, who have controversial opinions, but this is America, and our country was founded on certain principles that—"

"Miss Williams, when a lady has to say that she is a lady it usually means she isn't."

Cohn looked to Jack and Walker, expecting a reaction but found none. He continued. "We are now living in the Atomic Age and we're at war, a war to the death. It's Communism versus Democracy. Those principles you've alluded to are being subverted by sympathizers and traitors."

"I'm no traitor, Mr. Cohn. I may enjoy a martini like anyone else, and I happen to enjoy mixed company for intellectual stimulation, but none of my friends has plotted to overthrow the government. Their opinions may seem unorthodox to you, but they are hard-working and patriotic, and the only thing they're capable of subverting is my liquor cabinet. Actors and writers are curious types and—"

Cohn stared at Vera. His hooded eyelids falsified drowsiness.

"In my experience, actors are not intelligent. Writers on the other hand…" Cohn glanced over at Walker, surprised at the lack of response. Vera exhaled one of her signature sighs from her catalogue of characters. "I don't know what you want from me, Mr. Cohn. I'm in New York to do a play."

"What do you have to say about Mr. Irwin Adler?"

"A charming man, a consummate professional, and an absolute pleasure to work with."

"You do know that he worked for CBS?"

"Good for him," she said. Vera noticed with a downward flick of her eyes that he hadn't written a single thing on the naked paper.

"He was listed in *Red Channels* as a suspected Communist."

"That must be before my time, Mr. Cohn. Anything else?"

"Mrs. Judith Nussbaum née Kaplan?"

"His sister-in-law? A charming woman."

Cohn pulled out a sheet of paper that was hidden under the blank pages of his pad. He pushed it across the table. Vera did not look down. Cohn said, pointing at it, "That is a summary of her statement when she worked at Fort Monmouth. She knew Julius and Ethel Rosenberg. I believe that she still maintains contact with cronies of the Rosenbergs, and that she continues to do their work with Mr. Adler."

"Judith and Irwin and espionage? You do have a vivid imagination, Mr. Cohn. If you believe that to be the case, I suggest you talk to them about it."

"I will in due time. Like I said, she knew Julius and Ethel Rosenberg. The company one keeps says a lot about one's character, don't you think, Miss Williams? Judith has dined with traitors and spent hours with them in their home. I have affidavits. It might not have been the spirited benders you hosted in your home, but they are just as damning. The Rosenbergs were spies, tried and convicted as traitors, and executed. When I hear the name Nussbaum and Adler associated with a play and I see your background, it makes me think."

"Don't strain too hard, Mr. Cohn."

Vera's tone of voice was that of calculated but feminine indignation, one of the few weapons women had in the repertoire against men in power. She measured her words, each syllable a pail of calm and cold water from the Schuylkill. She poured her words.

"If we split a turkey sandwich for lunch, Mr. Cohn, I doubt it could be said that we shared Thanksgiving together. All I know about Mr. Adler is that he is a director. All I know about Judith is that she takes care of her nephew."

"You like to socialize. The Copacabana, the Café Chambord."

"I enjoy a nice meal and I like entertainment."

"Entertain Mr. Adler?"

"No."

"How about Judith?"

"What are you implying, Mr. Cohn?"

"The company of a woman. Intellectual stimulation."

"Have a good day, Mr. Cohn." Vera pushed Cohn's piece of paper back across the table. "If you have something to ask me then ask."

"I think that'll do." Cohn looked to Jack and Walker, at the door. "Please have Mrs. Nussbaum come upstairs. Thank you, Miss Williams. You may go."

"About my subpoena? Do I have to appear?"

"We'll see," he said, eyes shiny as he retrieved his paper.

"You're a bastard, you know that?" she said, standing up, the chair almost toppling over.

"I know."

"Vera?" Jack said.

"What?"

"Please have the Agent downstairs send Judith up. Mr. Cohn can wait."

Vera's heels stomped down the short hall and then stopped abruptly. The men in the room had expected more noise, of Vera taking the stairwell downstairs. The men heard nothing at first, then two soft voices, the polite and dry voice of a man and light laughter from her. Walker looked to the opened door. Jack did not.

There was the sound of feet. Not a woman's. A hand rapped on wood. A man, about five-nine and lean from years of swimming, stepped into the room, a bright toothy smile on his face. "Gentlemen, I'm Robert Kennedy. Pleased to meet you."

Chapter Twenty-Eight

Kennedy was a lean man in a dark suit, white shirt, and a black-and-gold striped tie. He crossed the room with grace and pulled out the empty chair at the table. Cohn did not get up and they did not shake hands. Cohn informed him Judith was on her way. Kennedy heard him but didn't respond.

Two lawyers, Robert Francis Kennedy and Roy Marcus Cohn, two men not yet thirty years old sat at the table before Jack and Walker. Cohn came from the Bronx, from a Jewish family, and spoke with a New York accent. His family money came from an uncle, the founder of Lionel toy trains. An alum of Columbia Law School, a loner, a bachelor, a man who still lived with his mother and who could recall the page number of testimony from months before, Cohn would enter the courtroom like a gladiator intent on killing, which is what he did to Julius and Ethel Rosenberg.

Though a lawyer, Kennedy carried no briefcase, relied on no pad of paper or pen. He was the seventh of nine children in the Kennedy clan, who had come from poor stock in County Wexford in Ireland and raised themselves from poverty to upper middle class. His family's wealth appeared to come from investments in the stock market and real estate, though there was no end to rumors of rum running and whiskey. His Mid-Atlantic accent dropped the *R* before vowels. A graduate of UVA Law, married with two children, he preferred the poets Shakespeare and Tennyson, and his lips moved when he read them.

They heard steps this time. Slow, soft, and sure. The sounds intrigued them. Kennedy was about to investigate when Judith appeared in the doorway with David at her side, his hand in hers. She stepped into the room, telling her nephew that it was okay.

Kennedy stood up, took his chair with him, and placed it near the door. He patted the seat to encourage David. The boy looked to his aunt for permission. He released his tight grip on her hand and climbed onto the chair, his eyes fixed on Judith. Kennedy introduced himself to Judith and asked that she take the seat in front of the table.

"What about you, Mr. Kennedy?"

"I can stand. It will do my legs some good. I've had a long drive."

"Thank you," she said, sitting down. Cohn didn't blink or acknowledge her.

"Counselor Cohn and I have some questions for you."

"If it's about Fort Monmouth, I've spoken to several FBI agents."

Cohn, with a tight smile, said, "That was a few years ago, Miss Kaplan."

"It's Nussbaum. I'm married."

"Where's your husband then?"

"He ran off."

"With Irwin Adler's wife?"

"If my husband and Mrs. Adler interest you, Mr. Cohn, I suggest you use your vast resources to find the two of them. If Senator McCarthy can spare the two of you to ask me questions, then I don't see any reason why he can't send the FBI after them. If Mr. Hoover can celebrate his success over John Dillinger and bank robbers, then my husband and my sister-in-law should be a day's work."

Jack touched his lips to cover his smile. Kennedy's grin betrayed an appreciation for Judith. Cohn's face was as indifferent as the mortician who'd made a sale on a casket. He pounced. "I'd like to ask you a different set of questions about the Rosenbergs."

"What good does it do, Mr. Cohn? They're dead."

"You knew them, correct?"

"Yes."

"Been to their house, attended some parties, and were present at some meetings?"

"Yes, and I've said it before that they were 'discussions' and not 'meetings.' I never heard a word about Communism. I made that explicitly clear to the Bureau's agents."

Kennedy this time. "Yet, in all your statements, you never mentioned what was discussed at those meetings or who attended them?"

"I just told you…I mean I told them—the agents back then, that these discussions were intellectual and over my head. I'm not a well-educated woman, but I never heard the words atomic, Communism, red, or Russia."

"Was there any discussion about work at Fort Monmouth?" Cohn asked.

"Sure, the usual shop talk, such as deadlines, bad coffee, the late hours—that sort of thing."

"You were a clerk at Fort Monmouth, were you not?" Cohn asked.

"Yes."

"And your job as a clerk involved typing, did it not?" Kennedy asked.

The lawyers had boxed her into a corner. Jack could sense it, and he waited for the knockout punch, and wondered who it could come from, Cohn or Kennedy?

Kennedy said, "Did you consider the Rosenbergs your friends, Mrs. Nussbaum?"

"I guess. I helped Ethel with the dishes, with the children. She was always in the kitchen and not around Julius as much when they had company. I told the FBI that, too. Not that it mattered to them."

Surprised. The decisive question, the punch, would come from Kennedy. Jack expected some soft footwork and light jabs that would test the air before the blow landed.

"Why do you say that…that it didn't matter to them?" Kennedy asked.

Judith stared at Kennedy. "A woman is supposed to take care of her home and Ethel did that. When the government went after Julius, they pressured her to turn on him. Problem is she wouldn't back down and that made her a B-I-T-C-H to the judge, the jury, and to Mr. Cohn here."

Kennedy seemed to admire her spelling out the word to save David's ears. Cohn snapped back with, "So she talked to you about being pressured?"

"Sure, at first, and then I didn't see her anymore."

"There was evidence against them, you must know that," Cohn said. "The United States government doesn't go around executing people because they're obstinate."

"Evidence? Julius was a machinist. He wouldn't know an atom from the marbles my nephew David plays with, but that didn't matter, did it? You're responsible for what happened to them."

"No, Miss Kaplan," Cohn said. "They brought it upon themselves."

"It's Mrs. Nussbaum."

"Excuse me," Kennedy said. "Did you tell the agents he wouldn't know an atom from marbles?"

"I did, and it should be in the paperwork somewhere. They didn't want to hear it, though. I wouldn't be a bit surprised if this one here," she said, pointing at Cohn, "erased it."

"Careful of what you accuse me of," Cohn said. "As for evidence, the Rosenbergs met a man named Harry Gold. Did you ever meet him?"

"Meet him? No, I never met Mr. Gold. I told the FBI that too. He helped your case. I'm aware of that fact from following the trial in the papers. Your evidence was based on a man who'd sent his own sister to the electric chair, to save himself and his wife."

"That's how it's done, Mrs. Nussbaum," Kennedy said. "Deals are made if the circumstances warrant it. It's how the government made its case against Julius and Ethel Rosenberg."

"Case? You had no case."

Cohn looked away, huffed, and snapped back with a raised voice. "Now you're a lawyer all of a sudden."

"If you have questions then ask them."

Kennedy sat on the table's edge near her. "But you were at these meetings?"

"Discussions. Read my statement."

"I asked you earlier if your position at Fort Monmouth involved typing."

"It did."

"How many words per minute?"

"Uh, I don't know," she said. "Seventy-five to a hundred."

There it was. Kennedy had set up the punch and combo, and he'd move in to finish her off. Walker turned his head. He had sensed it, too.

"Ethel Rosenberg," Kennedy said, "the wife and the hostess, who managed these social events, she cooked and cleaned and served drinks and food?"

"Yes…and?"

"Her work record indicates that she was a poor typist. Less than sixty words per minute." Kennedy bent over to convey intimacy. "I'm not asking about the drawings or what you thought of the trial, or the verdict. My question is the one the Bureau's men never asked you."

Harry Gold, Ethel's brother, testified that Ethel had typed up the minutes from the meetings for husband Julius. It was the damning act of the dutiful wife that would earn her an indictment for espionage and send her to the execution chamber in Sing Sing.

"Mrs. Nussbaum," Kennedy said, his voice gentle now. "I believe that Ethel typed those notes some of the time, but I think you were the person who typed them up most of the time. You were the better typist, the more accurate one, between the two of you." He stood straight, as if to impose his height. It was a standard tactic, but effective. "All I want is the names of those who were at those meetings. You slipped through the proverbial crack in the sidewalk the first time. You won't this time."

Judith turned her head towards David. Jack could see her eyes had filmed over, that the tears were about to fall, but he'd hoped that she wouldn't give either lawyer the satisfaction.

"Mrs. Nussbaum?"

"I refuse to answer that question on the grounds that it may incriminate me."

"You're invoking the Fifth?" Kennedy turned to see Cohn's reaction. Cohn smiled. Kennedy spoke, this time with an edge to his voice. "You do understand that your refusal to cooperate complicates your situation and that it could be perceived as obstructing justice."

"Justice? Then take me into a court of law, where there's a jury."

Kennedy's lips parted and he said in a softer voice. "Mrs. Nussbaum, I ask you to please reconsider. Think of your nephew, your brother-in-law, and—"

"Don't threaten me. There's nothing to reconsider, Mr. Kennedy. This charade is a veiled attempt at intimidation. I can't stop you from taking David away or destroying Irwin."

Cohn worked his pen, end over end between his fingers. "Defiant like Ethel."

Judith stood up, fixed her skirt. She took a step forward and took Cohn's pen out of his hand. She wrote a profanity on his notebook, underlined it, and tossed his pen onto the pad. "You want me then you take me into a court of law, you bastard."

This time, she didn't care that David heard her curse. His eyes darkened and he bared his teeth. She moved past Kennedy and held her hand out to her nephew and told him that they were leaving.

Her footsteps clattered down the hallway and thumped down the stairs. Kennedy pivoted to Jack and Walter. "Can you two talk some sense into her?"

"Doubt it," Jack said.

"What about you?" he asked Walker. "Can you persuade her to reconsider?"

"Me? I'm a two-bit writer, a nobody, like Mr. Cohn said. If I were you, I'd talk to him about the men downstairs. I'd also ask him where the young lady who is in my play is."

"What young lady?" Kennedy asked.

Jack answered. "The one who went missing, who was last seen with suits, similar to the ones downstairs. Find her and Walter here will invite you to the play."

"I don't have time for a play."

"You'll be interested in this one, I promise."

"And why is that, Mr. Thompson?"

"Tania plays Rosemary."

Kennedy's mouth dropped, but before he could say a word, a fast shuffle could be heard up the stairs and down the hallway. The tall agent barged into the room. The man stood there, a limp piece of paper in his hand next to his thigh. His face was pink from the heat and from the sprint. Crumbs stuck to his shirt, and a splotch of mustard stained his tie.

"Come over here, you idiot," Cohn yelled, his hand in the air for the piece of paper.

Everyone watched the man walk to the table, like a shamed child. He surrendered the piece of paper to the seated lawyer. "We called and double-checked," the agent said. Cohn read and let the sheet fall on the desk in front of him.

"What is it?" Kennedy asked.

Cohn gazed at the windowless wall. He pinched his lip with his right hand.

"What is it?" Kennedy repeated.

"Their license plates came back. All of them belong to the FBI."

Kennedy snatched the paper off the table. His finger traveled down the numbers and his eyes read the results. His chin lifted. His eyes met the mask of Jack Marshall, the army officer in Germany. Kennedy held up the piece of paper. "Explain this."

"I don't owe you or that salamander in a suit a damn thing," Jack said. "But I'll tell you this: if you talk to anybody again, it'll be in New York. My hospitality this time."

Jack made for the door but stopped. He turned to Cohn and Kennedy. He waited a few hard seconds. "Your men downstairs have the number to the restaurant where the rest of my entourage is waiting for me. I want the girl." Jack looked down at his wristwatch and tapped the crystal. "I expect a call. Don't disappoint me."

Jack and Walker walked down the hallway and before they reached the stairwell, they heard Kennedy behind them. "You son of a bitch! You have ten seconds to tell me what the hell he was talking about."

Jack and Walker smiled.

Chapter Twenty-Nine

Before they'd left the diner, Jack had them switch plates again. Bureau plates went into the trunk, and Empire State originals back on the cars. Jack dispatched everyone for New York City, except Walker, Sheldon, and Johnny Mercury. He figured if Cohn wanted to put the screws to them, it would be on their way to Manhattan. The cavalry, state or local police might have the make and model of their cars, but the wrong plates. It was a gamble as to how much of their physical details the agents at the mill scribbled down, so Jack swapped occupants in the vehicles.

The Buick drilled down the naked highway. There were fewer and fewer trees to be seen on the sides as they journeyed into the remote outskirts of Philadelphia. Jack sat in the front, Johnny drove, and Walker was in the backseat with Sheldon.

When one of Cohn's agents called Linton's, he had given them an address. The address matched the second lead Steps had for Tania's location, the one where they expected mercenaries who appeared to be working for the Genovese crime family.

Johnny told Sheldon to check the armrest in the middle of the backseat and take customer's choice. Jack had consulted a map. He pointed to a sign. "There's our exit up ahead."

The exit off the highway curved and threw their stomachs against one side of the car. The steering wheel banked hard until the blacktop straightened out and led them to another sign, this one with arrows that pointed left and right, and the lettering or numbers had disappeared around the time of King

George. A riser pole stood behind the sign, a constable of ravens watching them from where they sat perched on the wires.

Jack said he expected to see the house about a mile or two down the road they were on. Johnny Mercury asked Jack, "Does this Kennedy guy have any idea what a snake Cohn is?"

"If he didn't, he does now."

Johnny Mercury heard Walker with Grable behind him. Sheldon had slipped his preference into his jacket pocket. Jack had removed his weapon from his holster and did a last check. Johnny admired it. "Can't say I've seen one of those."

"Mauser Model 1934."

"Nazi?"

"Wooden grips have a pair of Uncle Adolph's eagles on them."

"Nice souvenir," Johnny said. He returned his attention to the windshield. "What's the plan before we get there?"

"I'll have a better idea once I see the place."

The area was so desolate that nobody but the birds would know if shots were fired.

Johnny Mercury brought the car to a noiseless stop. The house was a brown clapboard colonial on a meager hill. Tawny weeds everywhere. The fence was weathered. The gate, half-dead on the hinges, groaned in the breeze. The walkway had enough cracks to worry a seismologist. The front porch between two columns slanted to the right because the termites had decided the wood there tasted better. There were four shuttered windows, two on each side of the front entrance, and a chatty screen door. The front door was ajar.

Johnny tapped Jack's lapel. He pointed to the car moored in the driveway. It was a Packard Super Eight, green, with enough steel to patch the Titanic after the iceberg and enough cargo room for Patton's Third Army. "That car," Johnny said, coming up behind them. "It's part of Genovese's fleet."

"Walter and I will take the front," Jack said. "Sheldon, you go around back."

"What do I do?" Johnny asked.

"Shoot whatever comes out of that front door or those windows, unless it's Tania, or us."

"And what do I do, out back?" Sheldon asked.

"Shoot whoever tries to leave. If anybody goes running out that way, it won't be us."

Johnny Mercury seemed amused, as if Red Skelton had impersonated a seagull, crossed his eyes, and flapped his arms as wings.

"What's so funny?" Jack asked.

"I thought we were honoring the Geneva Convention and shooting them in the legs, but I guessed wrong."

Sheldon scurried down the side of the house, ducking beneath windows. Jack and Walker approached the front door. As they walked to the house, Jack indicated to Walker with sign language from their infantry days as to who would go low and who high. They made it to the door without having drawn fire from any of the windows. Jack crouched down on the left side of the door and Walker braced his back against the wall behind him. Jack held up three fingers. It was the count that said, "On one, we breach the front door."

Three.

Walker had Grable poised, and Jack, his Mauser out and ready.

The wind kicked the screen door open. It was yawning its way back towards Jack.

Two.

Walker swallowed hard. He waited for the decisive finger.

A hummingbird's heart could've exploded.

Jack kicked the screen door away from him. It slapped hard against the far side.

A shot ripped through the center of the door. Wood shattered and splintered everywhere. Shotgun blast.

One.

The high and low maneuver next. Jack pushed open the front door from his crouched position while Walker swung over on top. Jack fired first and

Walker second.

Two shots. One kill. Shotgun was out of the equation.

The shooter down, they had to sweep the premise for other bad guys. The disadvantage was that their shots had announced their presence, and whoever was inside the house knew the layout better than they did.

In two-by-two formation they rushed in to secure the room. There was nothing but motes of dust in the air, and awful furniture. The wood creaked, and the threat that their feet would sink into rotted-out timber was real. They passed through a small parlor. A doorframe confronted them. It led to another room, possibly a kitchen, bathroom, or a bedroom. Shadow and sunlight indicated that there was a rear door.

Another step and another creak and they paused. More dust lifted but they didn't dare cough. The smell of mold wafted up into the thick air. Walker had just taken another step when the profile of a man bolted across the room to the back door.

He opened it to escape, only to meet a gun. One shot.

The man fell screaming and holding his leg. Sheldon had chosen not to kill the man. Sheldon walked up the back steps and kicked the man's weapon away. The man howled and sobbed and spewed curses. Sheldon reached down and grabbed a handful of hair. "Where is she?"

"Let's get him into a chair," Jack said.

Sheldon shot Jack a stunned look. "Why?"

"Do as I say."

Walker helped Sheldon prop the man up into a chair. The room was a kitchen, after all. The man blubbered incoherent Italian.

"Shut up," Jack said.

Sheldon pulled the man back into the chair with a hard yank on his shirt collar.

"Get your hands off of me, you nance kike," the man yelled, and then spat on the ground.

Sheldon swiped the man's jaw with his pistol, knocking him out of the chair. He crashed to the floorboards and screamed. Walker picked him up and shoved him into the chair.

Jack stared into the man's face until their eyes met. "This is a non-denominational gathering, you dago guinea wop, so show some respect, or I'll shoot you in the other leg myself." He pointed to Sheldon. "This man here could have killed you. Understand?"

The man said nothing, so Sheldon punched him in the wounded leg. The man screamed.

"Keep him alive while we check out the rest of this dump," Jack said.

One dead body in the living room. Identification in the man's pocket revealed a name. Walker said he recognized the man as the tall inquisitor from his night at the pier.

Jack had noticed a phone and checked it. It was live, and he said to Walker that there was a good chance Cohn had called and warned them. Jack guessed that Genovese's men in the house were confident they could stand their ground.

The rest of the house was dead as Atlantic City in the winter. In the bedroom upstairs, there was a flop mattress. The toiletries suggested a woman's presence but there was no Tania there. They opened and closed closets. There was nothing except sad hangers that jangled in the air when the door opened.

No clothes either, in the room. Nothing but a cheap Shaker-imitation bureau.

No sign of an attic. Jack and Walker searched through the dust and the fading sunlight.

The man in the kitchen was screaming again.

Sheldon had taken to pistol-whipping the man. Jack rushed down the stairs and into the room. He caught Sheldon's arm before it delivered another downstroke.

"He's no use to us unconscious."

Sheldon ignored Jack and seized the man's throat with one hand and started choking him.

"Where the hell is she?" Sheldon screamed into the man's bloodied face.

Walker pulled Sheldon off. Jack tucked his pistol into the back of his belt, out of the man's reach. He eased the man back into the chair and anchored his knee into the man's groin. Jack, his hand under the man's chin, pushed his head backwards. "Where is she?"

"Floorboards," the man said, through spittle and blood. His eyes indicated where.

Sheldon and Walker crouched and worked the wood with their hands.

"Wait," Walker said. He lifted his pant leg and pulled his paratrooper's knife out of the ankle holster. He worked the knifepoint into an edge of the wood. One slat came up, then another, to access the cache. Tania was down there, in the dank soil, with her hands tied behind her back and a gag in her mouth, tight as a horse's bit. Walker and Sheldon grabbed a hold of her and pulled her up. Sheldon undid the gag.

She gasped, grateful for a full breath of air.

Walker handed Sheldon his knife so he could cut away the twine around her wrists. Walker's hand circled her waist and lifted her up. Her cheek touched the side of his face. Her hair smelled of earth and decay.

Tania stood up. Walker helped her find her balance. Sheldon hugged her and said something to her in Russian. All of them contemplated the man in the chair.

"What do we do with this one?" Jack asked.

Walker asked the seated man, "Vito Genovese?"

The man mumbled in Italian that he didn't understand English.

"The hell you don't," Jack said.

Sheldon punched the man in the face. "Tell me you don't know Cohn. Roy Cohn. You know—the other kike."

The man laughed in Sheldon's face and uttered a curse in perfect English.

Tania grabbed Jack at the elbow and pulled him back. She pulled Sheldon's gun, a .38 Special, five rounds left in the revolver, pushed Walker aside, and stood in front of the mobster. "He's losing blood. Take his belt off and tie it around the wound," she said to Walker.

While Walker undid the belt buckle, the man seemed confused and tried to resist as Walker worked the belt off his waist. "Stay still, you idiot."

"What's the matter?" Tania asked the tough guy. "You shy now? You weren't before."

She emptied all the bullets but one out of the opened chamber into her hand. Walker tightened the belt around the man's leg. The hoodlum grunted.

She hinged forward and said into his ear. "You're bleeding to death. You'll get weaker and sleepier. If you cooperate, we might get you to a hospital in time for them to amputate the leg. You'd be surprised how fast they can take a leg off these days."

She flipped the chamber over, snapping it into place. She pushed in the pin.

"Did you know in the Civil War a competent surgeon could take a limb off in seconds?"

The man sat there in total silence. Tania spun the chamber once more. She stepped back and checked the sight. "There is one bullet in the chamber. Don't understand English, do you? Bet you know math, don't you?" She showed him the .38. "One bullet means a one in six chance."

Her lips visited his ear. The Italian sweated as she whispered, "What was it that you told me these last few nights here? I know. Open your mouth and learn to love it." She flicked the muzzle under his chin. "Open up, sweetheart."

The man looked at Jack, at Walker, and then at Sheldon.

Tania repeated, "Open up that little hole of yours. I did. Your turn now."

The man's lips were quivering. He opened his mouth. Tania put the nose of the gun into it. "This is a .38 Special. Six-inch barrel. Most men aren't even that. You certainly weren't. Now, the gentleman here asked you a question. Do you know Roy Cohn?"

No answer.

Tania cocked back the hammer part of the way. "What was that you said to me? 'I'll try not to...'" The hammer clicked all the way back now and the chamber moved one groove over.

"Do you know Cohn? Answer me."

The man was shaking. He warbled "No" around the front sight in his mouth.

"I don't like being lied to."

She pulled the trigger and the hammer snapped forward.

No round.

"Oops. We'll have to play this game again until I'm satisfied. If you were a gentleman, you'd know it takes women longer. Less than a one in six chance. Odds are not in your favor, little man."

The man's eyes closed. She looked down into his lap.

"Looks like you wet yourself. At least I know which side you've placed it. You've proved me wrong. Most men usually put it on their left."

His mouth was trembling. His lips were white in the corners. She cocked the hammer again. "Do you know Cohn?" she asked.

The man's eyes teared up. He nodded. She pulled the gun away. "Speak," she said.

"He called here."

"Tell me more," she said.

The man started to cry and heave again. Tania raised the gun.

"I'll tell you. I'll tell you but get this crazy bitch away from me." Walker lowered Tania's arm. "What did Cohn say?"

"He said, 'Kill them when they show up for the girl.'"

"And what about me?" Tania asked.

The man was silent.

"What about me?"

Jack smacked the man's head. "The lady asked you a question. Answer her."

The man's face changed. He looked sad, as if all his life's regrets had coalesced, and he'd fallen short of repentance. "Cohn said, 'Do whatever you want with her and then make sure she's not a problem.'"

Tania lunged forward and stuck the gun back into the man's mouth.

"Stop it," Walker said, his hand on her arm.

"He's lying," she screamed. "What did Cohn say exactly?"

She pushed the gun further into the man's mouth. When he started to choke, she pulled back. "Like how that felt? Now tell me, what did he say. Word for word."

"Cohn said, 'Kill the little bitch.'"

CHAPTER TWENTY-NINE

Jack asked, "What about Genovese?"

"He's my boss."

"Him and Cohn have a deal?"

"I can't tell you that."

Tania raised her arm.

"Wait! For Chrissakes, wait! Yeah, the lawyer and Vito made some kind of deal, but taking the girl was not Vito's idea. I don't know what the agreement was word for word, but Cohn promised Don Vitone that he'd get no grief from the Feds, and that he'd take care of The Prime Minister for him."

"What does 'take care' mean exactly? Spell it out for us," Walker asked.

"How the hell do I know?" the man yelled back. "Kill him in prison, I suppose."

"What about Kennedy?" Jack asked.

"I know nothing about him. I swear."

Tania rolled the chamber with her fingers. "You know what happens now, big boy, don't you?" she asked. "We take you to a hospital. You heal up and your boss kills you because he'll think you snitched."

"You've got to help me," the man pleaded with Jack and Walker. "I'll never say a word. You can get me a doctor without him knowing. That can be done, right?"

"Him?" Jack slapped their prisoner. "Are you talking about Vito Genovese, or Roy Cohn? Or maybe his boss, J. Edgar Hoover? If it were up to me, I say we leave you here, and take your chances with whoever shows up."

"You can't. You can't leave me here," the man screamed, and then started sobbing. "You can't," he said. He lifted his head and said to Tania, "Please. You can't."

"Yes, I can."

A gunshot proved that she could.

Chapter Thirty

Walker considered the scene and how he'd edit it. He and Jack each sat in a chair in the spacious hotel room. Above them hung an unlit chandelier which glittered when the sunlight filtered into the room through gauzy curtains on a café rod. Sashes separated those curtains by day and reunited them at night. A small garden of pink roses floated in the center of the carpeting, dark and blue as the Pacific Ocean.

Walker cleaned Grable while Jack field-stripped his Mauser.

Before they'd left the house outside of Philly, two dead gangsters inside it, and before they'd rushed Tania into the backseat of the Buick, Jack changed his mind about the plates on the Roadmaster. He had stared at the monstrous green Packard for a long hard minute. He talked to Johnny Mercury behind the wheel. The car was running. Jack instructed Johnny to switch out plates again, theirs in the trunk for the Packard's. Johnny didn't ask questions. He did what he was told and siphoned off some gas from the big green car's tank. Dead men don't drive.

Jack revised accommodations once inside in the city. Everyone now resided at the Park-Sheraton. Walker didn't need the apartment in Hell's Kitchen, so he collected his things and left. Adler, David, and Judith were relocated to a room above them, and Hoover's surveillance team would have to adapt.

Everyone was close to the theatre and in The Prime Minister's protective care. Tania and Sheldon were in a room down the hall. Vera and Leslie retained their luxury-suite, not far from the one Eleanor Roosevelt used when she visited Manhattan.

Jack said Johnny Mercury would visit soon. Something was off about Johnny, and Walker didn't know what it was. Anastasia and Genovese looked the part of the sinister hoodlum, each in their dark suits and darker faces. Each man could level a stare that would stop a clock. Johnny Mercury was different.

Walker thought back to his studio days, to the time when Terry had handed him a pamphlet. *Screen Guide for Americans.* He thumbed through the thirteen commandments for Hollywood writers:

Don't smear the free enterprise system.

Don't smear the profit motive.

Don't smear an independent man.

He could recite the others because Jack Warner made his writers memorize them, but those three fit Johnny Mercury like pinstripes on a New York Yankee. Walker remembered the Southern California sun and how he'd searched through the worn bulletin for the name of the author. Terry, with his cigarette ablaze and the column of white smoke rising heavenward, told him, "Every studio head is reading her."

The her, Walker would learn, was a Russian named Alisa Zinovyevna Rosenbaum. Like everyone in Hollywood, she'd changed her name and become Ayn Rand, the priestess of a new alchemy called Objectivism. The three edicts he remembered reminded him of Johnny Mercury for another reason. Johnny and Jimmy Alabaster were the mob's version of her Howard Roark. They were shaved, glossy, and ready to steal or murder the future. Walker watched Jack with the Mauser. "Any word on Tania?"

"Steps took her to a doctor."

"OB-GYN?"

"Yes, and he's a Syndicate doctor, too."

"Gunshots to gynecology, in one generation. Who would've guessed? I hope Leslie went with her. She can, at least, relate and empathize. She'd understand."

"Because of Vienna?" Jack said, as he reached for his holster clip. "Relax, she's in good hands with Sheldon and Steps."

There was a knock on the door. Jack put his jacket on over the pistol on his hip. He opened the door and in came Johnny Mercury, tired but with enough jazz in his step for spare change and a smile. He breezed right into the room, his jacket draped over an arm. Jack closed the door. "Any news?"

"Steps says the girl is all right. I gotta say that broad is one tough customer. She eat nails for breakfast, or what?"

Walker stood up. "That broad has a name, so use it. What did the doctor say?"

"Little Miss Marker there cleared a man's attic out and this one has a crick in his neck about her name." Mercury grinned. He put his hand to his forehead. "She put one through the man's bean."

"You forget I was there, and you were outside?"

Mercury looked to Jack. "Someone iron his shirt the wrong way this morning?"

"Show a little compassion." Jack looked down to Mercury's hand. "Housewarming gift?"

"Whiskey. Heard you enjoy it. I figured we'd warm the glasses in this joint."

"Heard from whom?" Walker asked Johnny.

"Easy there and cut down on the coffee."

"There's no ice in the room," Walker said.

"No worries." Mercury eased past Walker. "I prefer my whiskey neat."

"I'll fetch glasses," Jack said. "Have a seat."

Mercury found himself a chair and parked it in front of Walker. Jack located another one for himself and sat down. "I think you ought to clear the air for Walker."

Walker for Walter tipped the scale. Jack handed out short glasses, one to Walker and the other to Johnny Mercury. Walker accepted his glass. "I'm in the dark here, and it's bad for work, and worse for friendships."

Jack poured splashes all around. When he'd capped the bottle of Powers Whiskey, he returned to sit with Mercury and Walker. He raised his glass and said he preferred a toast before they talked shop. They lifted their glasses, Waterford Lismore, crystal, and perfect for an Old Fashioned or their Irish firewater. Jack started with Walker.

"Ever think I'd put you in the lion's den without support? Tell him, Johnny."

"Wonder how Steps knew about you and the men on the pier?"

"No, but it'd better impress me," Walker said.

"How about, I'm Jack's inside man. Think of me as the insurance man, in the event Steps were to step out of line or get ambitious." Johnny Mercury raised his Waterford. "I watched over Leslie with one eye and checked in on you with the other."

"You were inside the rackets this whole time?"

"Long before you showed up, which is why I was able to utilize the chain-of-command without provoking any suspicion when I told Steps that we had to visit the pier pronto."

"How did this arrangement come about?" Walker asked, uncertain who'd answer, Jack or Johnny Mercury.

"Whittaker," Jack said.

Hearing the name slapped Walker. Even in death Whittaker played pool and put a shot across the felt without scratching it. If what Jack had said was true, Johnny Mercury had been embedded in The Prime Minister's organization before the man was cited for contempt and sent to Milan, and before Whittaker disappeared in Vienna in '48.

"Jack contacted me in Sing Sing, long before they fried the Rosenbergs."

Walker held out his glass for a refill. He needed one. Jack revisited the bottle, returned with it and refreshing Walker with a splash. "You were in prison?"

"I was doing a small stretch for illegal gambling. Is there any other kind outside of Vegas? Anyhow, I'd palled around with Whittaker before he went into the army. I'm a navy man myself, but that didn't stop Mr. Marshall here from recruiting me for the Company. I did my ticket, but before I punched out, the district attorney offered to shave a few months off if I ratted some names. I didn't and everybody in Brooklyn knew it, including The Prime Minister. The Commission looked kindly on my loyalty to The Prime Minster, especially after the Kid Twist Affair."

"Who is Kid Twist?"

Jack answered. "Abe Reles was a Brooklyn gangster who turned informant.

His testimony sent several men to the electric chair, and then he fell out of a window."

"Out of a window?"

"Five cops in the room," Jack said. "The canary flew out a hotel window on the day he was supposed to testify against Anastasia." Jack saved the best slice for last. "That was in '41 and it took ten years for a court to conclude: oops, an accident. Let Johnny finish his story. You'll find it interesting."

Walker heard the rest of it from Johnny. A DA had offered him a deal. He said no, and one of The Prime Minister's judge friends said yes and Johnny was sprung early for good behavior. "I've been in his good graces ever since," he said.

"With the mafia, you mean?"

Jack threw in, "Tell Walker who the DA was that offered you the deal in Sing Sing."

"None other than Kennedy."

And there it was: Johnny Mercury was a sleeper for Jack and the Company.

"What's next then?" Walker asked.

Mercury answered, not Jack. "We wait for Cohn to show up in New York. Jack's trick to put the Bureau plates on the Packard will get back to Hoover. Genovese has two dead men, and he won't be thrilled when he hears about those plates. Genovese is terrified of Hoover, and any love from J. Edgar won't endear Don Vitone to the Commission. With any luck, Vito will grab Cohn by the throat and choke him."

"And The Prime Minister?" Walker asked.

"He'll wait and watch to see whether Vito turns paranoid and violent."

"Assuming Vito Genovese doesn't take out Roy Cohn first?"

"He does that, and he signs his death certificate. The Prime Minister's friends in the judiciary and board members on the Commission won't tolerate that action. Dutch Schultz learned that the hard way. Vito does something similar, and he'll get clipped."

Johnny explained the history to Walker. The Dutchman had wanted to kill Prosecutor Thomas Dewey, ordered the hit, but the Commission learned about it and quashed it. Schultz ate his last meal at the Chop House in

Newark.

"What if Hoover protects Cohn and Cohn spits in Vito's eye?" Walker asked.

"Hoover doesn't shield Cohn from everything. He tolerates Cohn," Jack answered. "Hoover, like Genovese, will want an explanation from Cohn as to why Bureau plates were present at a murder scene, so don't think our lawyer is free and clear."

Jack relocated to the davenport and talked strategy.

"Isolate your opponent and alienate his allies. We wait to see what Roy Cohn does next. He has to answer to Hoover and we see whether Hoover reacts. If Cohn wants to act out his drama in the city, he'll have to find judges that are not with The Prime Minister."

"What if Robert Kennedy finds a judge?" Walker asked.

"He won't because it would help Cohn. Remember, it was his father who had helped him find judges. Twice, first with Moretti and then with Vera's subpoena. I think at this point, Mr. Kennedy won't accept help from his old man. He learned Tania was missing and the trip to Philadelphia proved to him that Cohn is a snake in a suit."

Neither Jack nor Johnny Mercury said anything. It was Kennedy and Cohn, together in a car now, on a one-way ride, and time would tell who would throw whom to the curb, while Genovese, Hoover, and all The Prime Minister's men watched.

Chapter Thirty-One

The stage lights were bright and hot enough to cook the dust in the air. Walker checked his watch again as Adler, script in hand, did his version of Moses coming down the mountain of stairs. His wristwatch said noon. The caterers had set up the sideboards and sprinted away.

With David and Judith absent from the rehearsals, Adler entered an obsessive phase, like Ahab after his whale. He wanted the play done right, perfect, and he wore everyone down with retakes, few breaks, and a barrage of unrelenting criticisms. He conceded the lunch hour.

Adler eased himself into a seat and Walker joined him. The velvet seat cushion seemed to have gone threadbare around the time Lincoln last saw *Our American Cousin.* The seat numbers were brass tags in need of a shine. Walker initiated the conversation with Adler. "Tania has her lines down cold."

"I'm glad someone does."

"Think you might find it in yourself to throw out a compliment every now and then?"

Adler leveled a stare that didn't require literacy. "Forgive me for my lack of praise, but I was the unfortunate recipient of a phone call at dawn from Jack Warner."

Daybreak in New York meant JL had called Adler during the wee hours of the night from his palatial estate on Angelo Drive. At that hour in Warner's Beverly Hills, sycamores wept and the mogul's Cupids either rode seahorses or made an obscene sound into any one of the numerous fountains.

The worry lines in Adler's face suggested JL had drawn a chalked outline on the ground and left Adler to draw his own conclusions. Warner's voice was known to stab people and leave them bloodied.

Adler tilted his wrist for Walker to see the watch. "Technical Week is about to start."

Technical Week was a time-worn tradition in theatre, about as pleasant as a nightmare. It called for non-stop practice until perfection was achieved with perfect lines, perfect lights, cues, prompts, and costumes. The thespian rite of passage included sleep deprivation, lots of sit and wait. The entire marathon of insanity included other superstitions of the theatre.

Nobody could say "Good luck."

Nobody could mention Macbeth.

Green and yellow costumes were not allowed.

Blue was allowed in spirit, but forbidden as a color, in any shade.

"Is there anything I could help you with, Mr. Adler?"

"Talk to Sheldon about his damn fireplace."

"Fireplace?"

"The man wants a real, honest-to-god fireplace, and not a prop. He says flames should symbolize persecution. He insisted that they must be red, and not any other color. What that means is I need a fireplace that hasn't been built, and an order of strontium salts."

"Strontium?"

Adler responded as if Walker were a slow child. "Strontium chloride; it makes the flames red as in the fires of hell, red as in Communism, red as in the blood of the Rosenbergs. Talk to the man."

Adler left, the crank despot of off-Broadway. Maybe Warner had threatened him, or maybe the studio head had promised him an acre of diamonds, a chair with his name on the back of it, a zebra clapboard, some lackeys to bring him drinks and vitamins by day, and a string of starlets in nothing but imitation pearls and easy morals at night. Adler had not revealed what Warner had said over the phone.

Walker heard a sound behind him. Tania had slipped into a seat above him.

Like the boatswain call, the only sound that could be heard above the waves, someone wolf-whistled. Whistling inside a theatre was another superstition. Adler heard the offense, and off he went in search of the culprit. He yelled out the time remaining to their lunch hour.

Walker assumed Warner called when his wallet had sensed a change in venue for accommodations. Warner was paying the hotel bill for Vera and Leslie. Word somehow may have floated back to him on the wings of seraphs that Adler and family and writer had relocated to the spacious Park-Sheraton. Warner worried about his money, from the humble penny to dollar bills, whether the seals on them were Federal Reserve Green, or Treasury Red.

Of course, Walker never ruled out Warner not having connections to the Syndicate. The man had spies everywhere in his studio. Everybody who was somebody in Los Angeles dealt with Mickey Cohen, even though Mickey was in the can for tax evasion. The game of telephone and switchboard operator was not a hard sentence to diagram. Warner did business with Mickey, and Mickey ran rackets with the Outfit in Chicago, and the Outfit had a seat on the Commission, and news must have arrived that one mercenary from the Outfit was on ice in Philadelphia.

Which meant everyone who was someone in New York knew Jack Warner had booked a string of rooms at the Park-Sheraton Hotel. Warner protected his investment.

One of Steps's security men unlocked the front door to the theatre to let Walker out. Foremost on his mind was a freedom meal, an unhealthy lunch at a spoon diner on 42nd Street and Lexington Avenue. His palate felt vulgar and adventurous.

Walker crossed the street and disappeared into the rambunctious New York crowd of fast feet and rude shoulders, men and women on a mission in the vast metropolis. Shoeshines and newsies cried invitations. Hawkers yelled "Get yer hot dogs" and "Pretzels and mustard! Pretzels and mustard!" The Chrysler Building loomed large above the streets. Steam wafted up through manholes and bathed his face in a fine mist before he opened the door to the diner.

He sat at the counter and ordered. People smoked and people talked. Waitresses worked the line and hustled food from the pit to the table. Walker's dish arrived, to the sound of pre-war swing from the jukebox. He dug into his plate of chicken and waffles and slathered on Cajun mayonnaise, while Benny Goodman's "Sing, Sing, Sing" with Gene Krupa on the drums sang, sang, sang.

On his way back to the theatre, the tenders filled his belly, and the Cajun spice burned a runway down his throat. He asked himself why the nice car was slowing down, the wheels so close to the curb. It was a shame to see whitewalls get smudged. He answered his own question.

Two separate hands belonging to two different men crooked his elbows from behind. He was escorted to the opening door of the luxury sedan that had come to a complete stop for him.

He heard "Shut up" in his left ear, and "Don't you make a sound" in his right.

Two faceless voices, both with the confident and masculine touch of all grip and no fingertips. Walker's right arm was losing circulation below the elbow from the longshoreman's pinch. He was bent headfirst into the waiting car. Pedestrians who saw the take stared straight ahead. On any other day, they'd debate the difference between a rock dove and a feral pigeon, and which borough had the better baseball team: the Dodgers, Giants, or Yankees. Today they saw nothing and thought nothing.

The door snapped closed. It was a spacious car with two facing seats in the back, big enough for a boardroom meeting. A hood went over Walker's head as the car parted from the curb. Someone bound his hands. In the darkness it was his warm Cajun breath against the black and calm. Hands frisked him.

"Look…" a voice said. "Membership to the Writer's Guild includes a .45 automatic."

"Semi-automatic," Walker said through the material.

"Shaddup. Who asked you?" A slap to the face accompanied this latest voice. The hand knew where Walker's jaw was under the hood. That took experience.

Walker counted voices and he knew there were at least two more in the car, someone who chose silence, the man behind the snatch and grab, and the driver.

The stop-and-go of the sedan meant the car was still within the city. A continuous, uninterrupted drive would indicate the highway or the tunnel to New Jersey. Smell would act as his compass.

"Heard you took a trip to Philly," the first and familiar voice said.

The formal request of "Fifty-cents, please" came and went, which suggested the car was taking the Holland Tunnel to Jersey.

One of his captors spoke. "Nice shooting and neat trick with those license plates. I oughta thank you for the headache with the Feds." An elbow then separated Walker's lunch in his stomach. The rough stuff was the way the Garden State greeted visitors.

"I kinda liked Tony, even if he owed me ten bucks," another voice said, and added his footprint to Walker's chest.

"Tony was the guy in the kitchen with the back of his head missing. Sammy in the living room took a .45 in the chest. I doubt it ain't no coincidence you're carrying a .45. I'd like to know who shot Tony in the leg before someone ventilated his melon, because the bullet belonged to a different gun."

Not answering earned Walker another elbow. The hood felt darker and the thrumming noise outside suggested they were still inside the tunnel, one hundred feet below the Hudson River. Walker wanted the hood off even if it meant seeing New Jersey. His two hosts talked Philadelphia, and the deaths of their compadres in arms. Walker listened to their conversation.

"I'm thinking two shooters."

"My money is on three, since it looked like Tony tried to leg it out the back way."

"I think you might be right. You were in the army, right?"

"Yeah, Canadian First Infantry, on accounta I couldn't get into the States."

"Right, and didn't you tell me you had to go house-to-house against the Jerrys?"

"That's right, Kraut hunting in Ortona. We mouse-holed our way through buildings. We'd pierce the side of a building, enter the hole, and clear the place of Nazi bastards with grenades and machinegun fire. When we'd run low on grenades, we'd do the high-and-low, like this skunk over here did to Sammy."

Another blow to the face, this time to the nose. Walker tasted blood.

"That's okay, friend. You got your girl back and we lost our buddies. Did you seriously think you'd get away with clipping our guys? You think The Prime Minister can protect you now?"

The car slowed and turned down an off road. Walker heard gravel. The first time he almost died in New York it was near water. The second time might be a bullet in the head, a shallow grave, or possibly buried alive.

All those years of combat jumps at night taught Walker's legs that they could find something solid in the dark. He flat-footed the man in front of him and elbowed the man on his left and pulled the hood off his head. He reached for a handful of hair and rearranged the geography of the face closest to him.

The car lurched to the side of the road and the driver jammed on the brake. Everybody in the backseat surged forward. Walker flailed feet and fists until he heard the sound of a hammer being cocked. No shooter ever did that. It was something you saw and heard in movies. Whoever was the author of the noise intended it as a cease-and-desist order.

Walker could see the damage to the men in the car.

The guy in front of him will talk to his date on Saturday night with a gash for an extra eyebrow. Walker had busted the lip of the man to his right, enough that he'd need soft foods and a straw. He read the scene outside the window.

Another nice and wide warehouse, like the one he knew by the pier. Walker was helped out of the sedan, a man on each arm. In front of him were two other men, one big and one small.

Vito Genovese and Roy Cohn.

Chapter Thirty-Two

The voice and question belonged to Lilo, the man Walker and Sheldon had met at Genovese's house. An unlit stogie, wet from hours between his lips, bobbed when he said, "Comfortable?"

Comfortable was a matter of perspective. Walker could feel his feet, despite that each leg was roped to a chair leg. His hands were tied behind him. His shoulders hadn't been this pinned back since Basic Training. His lungs hurt when he breathed. His face was intact unless they got tired of looking at it or the answers coming out of it.

"What's your name?" Cohn asked.

"It hasn't changed since we last met."

"We seem to run into each other, Mr. Thompson. First, in LA, with Leonard Moore and Jack Warner. Remember?"

"You questioned my patriotism is what I remember most."

"Yes, there is that," Cohn said. "You had quite the temper then, didn't you? And we met again in Philadelphia. I thought perhaps you changed your name like you changed zip codes."

Genovese stood there a bit confused about their history together. Neither Lilo Galante nor the other men were eager to interrupt the diminutive lawyer. Cohn was the boss here and Genovese was paying rent. Walker eyed the warehouse's interior. The walls were high, made of corrugated steel, and the flooring was basic concrete. No signs, no company name, or any tools of any trade or a single thing to betray the location or type of business here. Nothing here but four walls, and bad Jersey air. There was enough height to hang a side of beef and plenty of square feet to bounce or drag a man's broken body without the neighbors knowing it. "Found in New Jersey" was not how Walker imagined the headline to his obit.

"Where am I?" Walker asked, not expecting the truth.

"Lakewood," Genovese said.

Cohn spun faster on his heels than a DI on a recruit. "What are you, a moron?"

"He asked, and it's not like he's going anywhere."

Walker licked his lips for moisture. "Lakewood sounds about right for you."

"What makes you say that?" Cohn asked.

"There's a yeshiva and a synagogue in town, in case you discover religion."

Walker recalled the cruel picture of the Rosenberg children, taken in Toms River, New Jersey, and clipped from the *New York Daily*, reading about their parents. He'd consulted a map and saw that Lakewood was located nearby.

"Make sure Vito wears a yarmulke to temple," Walker added.

"Vito, in a beanie?" Lilo's cigar did the up-and-down of a polygraph needle.

Vito's mood darkened. "Shut it, Lilo."

Walker joined Lilo, laughing the crazy man's laughter until his ribs hurt and he coughed. Cohn started anew. "I asked you before. What is your name? Your real name."

"Answer hasn't changed, Marcus." Cohn's eyebrows twitched. Walker knew using Roy Cohn's middle name would surprise him.

"Sticking with Walter Thompson, is that it?"

"Worked for me in Los Angeles and it'll work in Lakewood. Two cities beginning with the letter L makes me feel lucky. Can't hurt, right?"

"We'll decide what'll hurt," Lilo said.

"Shut up, Galante," Cohn said.

"Thank you," Walker said. "Now, I have all the names to the party here. Lilo is Galante. Don Vitone is Vito Genovese. All the mobsters and their associates I've met seem to have nicknames. What's yours, Marcus? My guess is Short Stop, or Shrimp. No, wait. Shrimp isn't kosher, but I bet you don't observe traditions. Orthodox, right? Answer me this, Marcus, does Kennedy know about your friends here?"

"You've got a big mouth."

"I bet he must be wondering about those two dead mobbed-up stiffs in a house in Pennsy, and how they came to have Bureau plates on their Packard. I bet Don Vitone is thinking the same thing? I bet J. Edgar Hoover had a coronary, but I get it. You don't know a thing about that, do you?"

"Perhaps you can explain to us how you know so much."

Genovese turned on Cohn. "Those were my men, you dirty Hebe. If I find out that Anastasia did this, I'll—"

"You'll what?" Cohn yelled back. "Run off to your dago Commission and slip a note into their complaint box? Stand there and keep your damn hat on."

Cohn was brave talking to a mafia don that way. Vito Genovese must've really believed Roy Cohn would buy him time with Hoover and his men. Cohn's red face contrasted with his white collar. The vein in his forehead had popped and the ones in his neck looked as if they were trying to crawl up out of his shirt.

"And all you are is a writer, Mr. Thompson, is that right?" Cohn said.

"You oughta try it after you're disbarred. Jack Benny needs silent writers if you can afford the cut in pay. You can infiltrate the union for your buddies here. I gotta warn you, though, the writer's union is a tough crowd. They set a premium on the number of times you use adjectives or adverbs. It's called the Hemingway Clause."

Cohn waved over the two men from the car ride. The conversation was about to turn physical. One of the men cracked his knuckles and went behind Walker to keep the chair upright while his partner took something out of his pocket. He noticed Walker's curiosity.

"It's a roll of dimes. I left home without my pair of brass knuckles."

Walker absorbed the first blow. There went the face. It was a solid thud that lifted his tongue out of the groove. The teeth stayed the course. Blood gushed salty. The nose was still intact. Mr. Dimes delivered a decent right hook. If this continued, Walker would need an installment plan to put his head back together.

A round done, the man behind Walker released the chairback. Cohn pulled

Walker's head back by the hair. He whispered into his right ear: "You got the girl back, Mr. Writer. I want to know what that little bitch told you and I want to know all about Jack Marshall, too. And before we proceed, I wish to underscore the fact that I am a very, very patient and creative man when it comes to pain."

Mr. Dimes hit Walker again and again, enough times to pay for several roundtrips on the Tri-State bridge. All four terms of FDR in office put a lot behind a punch. A left hook arrived and departed from his jawbone. Another right reminded him that he should breathe through his eyes. Two body blows recommended an appointment with Epsom salts and a masseur. Then there was another break.

"What happened at that house, Mr. Thompson?"

"I plead the Fifth."

Cohn nodded. This time, two men inflicted multiple counts of assault and battery.

"Talk to me about Jack Marshall." Cohn returned like poison to Hamlet's father's ear. "Who do you work for, Mr. Thompson?"

"I'm a writer and you've met Jack Warner."

Another nod. Another three-minute round. Walter thought back to happier times and memories with each punch. He needed the distraction. Strawberry jam on Mother's French toast came to mind, then a sunset and Peggy in the hayloft. It'd been years since he'd thought about her and the barn together.

Blows tenderized flesh. There were pinpoints seen behind the eyelids.

Cohn's voice buzzed his ear. "What did that bitch Kaplan tell you?"

"Nussbaum. The woman told you her name is Nussbaum."

Genovese stepped forward and pulled on Cohn's arm. "This is getting us nowhere. I say we drive into the city and visit the Park-Sheraton. You said you served a subpoena. Act on it."

The knuckle men paused for a cigarette break. One of them offered Walker a smoke.

"Don Vitone is right," Lilo said to Cohn. "This guy isn't gonna spill a thing."

Cohn responded to the two mafiosi. "And I suppose you think we can prance into the lobby of the Park-Sheraton and one of The Prime Minister's men will hold the elevator door for us? Is that what you're telling me?" The soles of Cohn's shoes scratched the concrete. Not quite the sound of slippers, more like flint against stone. "And if either of you think you have the stones, I'll remind you that Anastasia takes his morning shave there in the barbershop every morning, like clockwork. Why don't you take advantage of the man's habit?"

"You worry about Kennedy. Leave Anastasia to me. I'm not worried about him."

A new voice said, "You should be."

It was Anastasia with men behind him.

"Vito," he said. "Wish I could say that it was nice to see you again, but I won't. And you, Lilo, make up your mind and light that damn cigar."

Anastasia came with armed escorts. Walker saw Steps. He saw Jimmy and then Johnny.

Anastasia ordered one of the men to cut Walker loose.

Walker was sore, dim in one eye, but his legs were good. He wanted more than a luxury ride in their Chrysler Imperial or the Cadillac Eldorado. He ached for some cold ice. He'd rather relive the Battle of the Bulge and sing "Die Wacht am Rhein" before he stayed one more minute in Jersey.

Chapter Thirty-Three

The Park-Sheraton's Mermaid Room offered enough flooring for a full dance troupe to do high kicks. In the middle of all that real estate was a circular island bar. Above the watering hole were four fishtails suspended from the gold ceiling that gave the place its name. These mermaids were topless, but either their long hair or strands of seaweed covered their assets.

The bar itself had plenty of steel stools, enough to surround and protect the barkeep on a busy night as he fed cocktails to Manhattan's attorneys, businessmen, and other sharks. The man behind the bar polished his onyx countertop, listening to Irving Fields and his Trio.

Kennedy sat with his back against the yellow leather in one of the booths, a white table in front of him, a black chair across from him, and papers spread out on the linen. He was sitting under one of the many scalloped mirrors that multiplied the back of his head and his profile around the empty room. The head forward and a pen in hand indicated an intent thinker. Kennedy's attire was nondescript as vanilla with a white shirt, and a striped necktie. The one sign of personality was a nervous wave of hair.

"Glad you could make it, Mr. Kennedy. Remember us from Philly?"

"I was told to meet you here and so I am here. Have a seat."

Jack carried a valise this time. Kennedy seemed to appreciate good leather because his eyes lingered on the briefcase in Jack's hand. He blinked twice at Walker's bruised face. He noticed that Johnny Mercury was standing guard at the entrance.

Jack had sent a Company man with the note about the time and place to the young Bostonian. Jack sat down, while Walker borrowed a chair from the neighboring table. Kennedy asked him, "Did that happen in Philadelphia?"

"No, this is what you get when you visit Jersey."

Kennedy caught a glimpse of Grable's dull heel when Walker unbuttoned his jacket. Kennedy asked if they wanted water or something stronger. Kennedy may have been Irish as clover, but he wasn't a day-drinker. Water would do. Niceties done and set aside, Kennedy's pen tapped a stack of paper. "Want to know what I'm reading?"

The young lawyer picked up a set of pages by their corners as if they were soiled laundry. "This is a crime scene report that includes two dead mobsters and an interesting car. There was evidence of a woman inside the house. I suppose you wouldn't know anything about those men or the woman?"

Neither Jack nor Walker responded. Kennedy put the papers down. He pointed to a single sheet of paper in another stack.

"This item concerns the vehicle I mentioned. Somehow the plates for the Buick at the mill earlier that day were found on the green Packard Super Eight at the scene. There's a passage in the report that's especially interesting." Kennedy's eyes searched and found the paragraph and paraphrased the text.

"Not a speck of dirt was found inside the Packard. No fingerprints either. The registration provides an interesting story. It says the Packard is a company vehicle. The company is here in the city. Now, one has to wonder how two dead men and a missing woman drove from Manhattan to Philadelphia without leaving a single trace of physical evidence in their vehicle."

Kennedy raised the piece of paper high and released it. Jack and Walker watched it fall sing-song in the air, back and forth until it landed on the crowded table.

"And there we have our triple, around the bases, gentlemen. Registration, New York. Company, mobbed-up and here, in Manhattan. Buick, green Packard and FBI plates."

Jack hoisted the handsome briefcase he had on the table. Kennedy leaned back and took a deep breath and released it. "Is there something you wish to share with me, Mr. Marshall?"

"More like an observation about your friend Roy Cohn."

"He's not a friend. Roy Cohn is a colleague."

"Your colleague has friends."

"You mean Senator McCarthy."

"No, I mean J. Edgar Hoover. Did you forget the men downstairs at the mill?"

"I was made aware they were Bureau agents when I arrived." Kennedy's fingers played with the pen. He kept rolling the cap between his fingertips. "Before you and Mr. Thompson left, you informed me that a young lady was missing. An actress in Mr. Thompson's play, if I recall. Correct?"

"That's correct," Walker said. "She plays Rosemary."

"How can I forget?" Kennedy said. "Without a statement from her, there's no crime. Kidnapping and crossing state lines is a felony and carries a sentence of twenty years. Now, Mr. Cohn might well point to those dead gangsters in that house and say they are casualties of some kind of dispute between mafia families."

"You had nothing to do with the girl's kidnapping?"

"I had no part in it, Mr. Marshall. I swear."

Kennedy's eyes maintained the gaze, his breathing was regular, and he didn't touch his nose. His answer, short of a hand on the Bible, was serious and honest as Robert Kennedy was Catholic. The man was telling the truth, and both Jack and Walker didn't doubt it.

"There'll be a statement from her. She's recovering from the unsavory ordeal."

Any holier-than-thou starch in Kennedy's birthright fell with his face. "You have to believe me when I say that I don't work that way."

"But Roy Cohn does," Walker said.

"How do you work, Mr. Kennedy?" Jack asked. He undid the brass flap on the valise.

"The two stiffs found in the house are connected to Vito Genovese. We both know that. I have but one question for you." Jack wagged his finger. "You're a man who likes results."

"Your question please."

"Indulge me for a moment." Jack leaned back in his chair. "Everyone looks the other way when it comes to Roy Cohn. Senator McCarthy, the Pepsi-Cola Kid himself, does. Now, we both know how Joe McCarthy works with shadows and innuendo. He suggests but never offers proof. And we both know J. Edgar Hoover will disavow Roy Cohn's methods, but will be first in line, hand out, to profit from the man's results. Roy Cohn did, after all, convict the Rosenbergs. My question is this, Mr. Kennedy: Do you look the other way when it comes to Roy Cohn, even if you were to profit from his misdeeds?"

There was the kind of silence heard after all the firecrackers had gone off. There was no smell of gunpowder, but something lingered in the air. A waiter approached and poured iced water. The ice cubes dropped, water sloshed. Walker reached over and moved Kennedy's glass closer to Kennedy.

"Let's talk about the subpoena for Vera Williams," Walker said.

"Cohn wants it both ways," Jack said. "He wants Miss Williams, either here in New York or when she returns to LA. Cohn also wants Judith Nussbaum, and that's where you have a problem."

Kennedy's hand brushed back the curl of hair on his forehead. Some might've found it a charming tic, but Jack understood it as a man thinking out his next move. He spoke, slow and cautious. "I take it you and Mr. Thompson here will create this problem for me."

"Not at all. Roy Cohn is doing that all by himself."

The Park-Sheraton promised a free reservation service, five restaurants, a combination of tub and shower, and free television in each room, but Robert Kennedy wasn't about to enjoy any of those luxuries; no, he was going to have to pay for it with a little sweat. Walker glanced over at Jack, who gave him the nod to lay it on Kennedy.

"You're a lawyer, Mr. Kennedy, which means you are a strategist, so I'll state the obvious first, before I move to the subtle nuances of Roy Cohn's game. If he wants to find Communists in the theatre community, his most obvious choice is to attack Adler, but he won't. Instead, he'll start with Vera Williams, who he thinks will cough up the names of West Coast Commies to save herself, but she won't. Cohn doesn't like women, does he, Mr. Kennedy?"

"Roy Cohn likes Roy Cohn."

Jack parted the top of the valise. "Cohn has his subpoena for Miss Williams, thanks to your father. You went to your father because The Prime Minister owns about every judge in Manhattan. You did Cohn's dirty work for him. He couldn't have moved forward on Vera until your friend of the family signed the subpoena, which puts you in an unfavorable light with The Prime Minister again. It's not the first time."

"You're alluding to Willie Moretti. That had a rather unfortunate outcome."

"Indeed, but a very Roy Cohn maneuver, on your part. You wanted results, you wanted Moretti, and you didn't care how you did it. The problem now is that you've given Cohn what he wanted: a second subpoena, and you did it by bypassing The Prime Minister. You found a judge and put yourself in the crosshairs of the Syndicate."

"Which J. Edgar Hoover says doesn't exist," Walker said.

"Anything else?" Kennedy said.

"Only the obvious," Jack said. "Cohn is ready to steal the spotlight from you. He'll claim something was missed the first time around at Fort Monmouth. He'll say McCarthy's claim to Commies in the military and defense contractors is true." Jack kept the valise open, as if to let it breathe like a good wine. "Vera will give him nothing and neither will Judith."

Walker said, "That's the wind-up before the setup and fall."

"What fall?"

"He'll hand you Judith for the cross-examination," Jack said. "Roy Cohn learned from his mistake with Ethel Rosenberg. He's aware of the perception around how he treated her on the stand, so he'll have you do the dirty work again. He'll ask you to break her as a witness."

Kennedy's face turned a shade of red that no number of freckles could hide.

"He knows you'll step up and do the cross-examination, like you helped him get the subpoena. You take the fall when you fail to make the case,"

Walker said.

"Why would I fail?"

"Because there's nothing to Mrs. Nussbaum."

"And do you have proof of that, Mr. Marshall?"

Jack's finger pointed to the valise. Kennedy was all stone and upper lip. Jack took out a bound volume from inside his leather carrier. He put the document on the table and placed the leather briefcase down on the floor. A faint breeze escaped the pages as Jack fanned the volume. He located the passage. "This isn't the entire file, but you will find this interesting."

"What is this document and where I can find a copy?" Kennedy asked.

"Venona file, and this is it," Walker said.

"The only copy?"

"Indeed, this hefty document is a sample of ongoing intelligence shared between our government and the British about the Soviets. Cohn knows about this document, and its contents. He's known about this paperwork since the Rosenberg trial. He also knows that nobody can use it in a court of law."

"Why not?"

"Because our government will never admit it records conversations in embassies, allies or otherwise." Jack tapped the page in front of him. "Please read the section."

Kennedy's eyes didn't look down. "And how did you come to have this document?"

"That's none of your concern."

Kennedy looked down and then back at Jack. "I suspect it'll say the Rosenbergs were innocent."

"Not at all."

"What does this have to do with Cohn or Mrs. Nussbaum?"

"Cohn made a deal with Ethel's brother and her sister-in-law," Walker said.

"I know about Harry Gold, Mr. Thompson."

"Not everything." Jack reached across the table. He picked up Kennedy's pen, admired the Shaeffer Touchdown, its burgundy casing. "You asked

Judith how well she typed in Philadelphia. You latched onto the discrepancy in typing speeds between the two women, Ethel and Judith. You asked because something in the original testimony at the Rosenberg trial bothered you, didn't it?"

Kennedy kept his finger on the open page. "Two witnesses bothered me, why?"

"You mean Mr. and Mrs. Greenglass, don't you?" Walker asked.

"When I reviewed the case files, Mrs. Greenglass never mentioned a meeting between her husband and a Soviet agent."

"A meeting Julius supposedly had arranged and attended," Jack said.

"In September 1945," Walker added.

"Correct," Kennedy said, now uncomfortable with the syncopation, between Jack and Walker. "The meeting Julius arranged should have been damning, but Mrs. Greenglass never mentioned it. In legal terms, it amounts to hearsay in any court of law, unless corroborated."

"But not hearsay to Roy Cohn," Jack said.

A bead of sweat ran down Kennedy's glass and pooled on the coaster. "Please make your point, Mr. Marshall."

"Mrs. Greenglass never mentioned any atomic sketches, any notes, or that Ethel had even been present at any of the meetings. Ethel had never typed up any notes and Cohn knew that. You suspected as much, which is why you interrogated Mrs. Nussbaum because you suspected that she had typed up the notes, but then you had an epiphany, didn't you? Say it out loud for us, Mr. Kennedy."

"I was abroad," Kennedy said.

"Indochina," Jack said.

"I spent a day at one of the embassies, and I noticed that Marines removed the ribbons from the typewriters at the end of the day and they lock them up."

"Here comes the epiphany," Walker said.

Kennedy explained what he had learned years ago. "The Marine detail collects the ribbons because anyone can unspool the ribbon and read whatever was typed up that day. It dawned on me, reading the trial transcripts that nobody examined any typewriters associated with the Rosenbergs."

Jack pointed to the volume in front of Kennedy. "Read the highlighted passage in front of you."

Kennedy's eyes searched the page. "Says here that all the notes had been handwritten."

"But in the trial Mrs. Greenglass said Ethel typed them up," Jack said.

Kennedy looked up Jack, and then over to Walker. "Cohn suborned perjury, but I can't use this because of what you said about recorded conversations in embassies."

"No, you can't," Walker said. "And you have proof that you can't use, that Cohn will do whatever it takes to win, even if it means a deal with Greenglass and perjury, and even if it means encouraging Judge Kaufman to sentence the Rosenbergs to death."

Silence. There was no mermaid song to be heard in the fog.

"So, when I cross-examine Mrs. Nussbaum for Cohn..." Kennedy's voice drifted.

Jack filled in the rest for him. "She'll say she is a good typist, but there was nothing to type up. Her testimony will reveal that both Mr. and Mrs. Greenglass had lied, and Cohn's courtroom victory is predicated on a plea deal."

The mirrors hadn't moved, and the reflections hadn't changed. Jack didn't stop.

"Nobody'll want to hear that Ethel Rosenberg was railroaded, Mr. Kennedy. Cohn may have done wrong, but they'll see you exposing the truth first. You say that to the American public at this point in time and your career is over, and Cohn knows it. Why? Because he understands history, and that when prophets tell the truth, people kill the prophet."

"The truth will always prevail, Mr. Marshall. I'll survive."

Jack grinned. Kennedy flinched, as if he had been ridiculed.

"Daddy can't protect you," Walker said.

"Read on," Jack said. "There's more to this story."

Kennedy's eyes skimmed the page. His finger went paragraph by paragraph.

"I must be missing something. I've read the page twice."

"What does it say about Judith?" Walker asked.

"Her sister was married to Adler and her husband was a traveling salesman. Her husband attended one meeting, but didn't care for the discussions, and never returned."

"And Adler's wife?" Jack asked.

"It says here that she attended meetings with Judith."

"It also says that Adler's wife spent time with David Greenglass. A lot of time. What was Adler doing at the time?" Walker asked.

"Working at CBS."

Jack took the document from Kennedy. With Kennedy's pen Jack made three short marks on the page and handed Kennedy the file. Kennedy searched for the three lines that Jack had made. Kennedy said, "The names Robert and Michael are underlined."

"And they are?" Walker asked.

"The Rosenberg children."

"And the third name?" Jack asked.

"David. David Greenglass, I presume. I still don't get it."

"It's not obvious, Mr. Kennedy," Jack said. "It took time for me to figure it out, too. Do the math. Look at how many times Adler's wife went to the meetings before she stopped."

Kennedy reread the intelligence. "She went four or five times."

"Look at the timeline. The meetings were when?" Jack asked.

"1944 into 1945."

"When did Judith's husband leave her?"

Kennedy's finger revisited the open page again. "1945."

"Adler's wife?"

"Same time in '45."

"The Rosenbergs were arrested in August 1950. Take a look at the third name again."

Kennedy's eyes returned to the page. His finger hadn't moved.

"David," he said.

"David Adler was born in 1945."

"Judith's sister and David Greenglass were having an affair?"

"Judith tells the truth in court about David, she destroys Adler and possibly the child the same way the Rosenberg children are damned for life with their last name."

"She could plead the Fifth, Mr. Marshall."

"Be realistic, Mr. Kennedy. Pleading the Fifth always makes you look guilty. You willing to take this that far, because Cohn is counting on it."

"You could stop Cohn, though," Walker said.

"How?"

Jack stood up. He reached over and closed the document and returned it to his carrier. Walker also rose. It was time to leave Kennedy to the tranquility of all that glass, all those reflections around the room. Time to leave him to order something stronger than iced water. Jack buttoned his jacket. "You'll figure something out, Mr. Kennedy. If I were you, I drop the matter with Judith and find yourself another distraction."

"What distraction?"

"Continue where Kefauver left off with organized crime. Hoover and Cohn won't like it. Start with Genovese, but don't push too hard. You were interested in the waterfront once. You should go there."

"Why would I want to do that?" Kennedy asked.

"Because Vito Genovese thinks Cohn can protect him."

"A fool's errand, don't you think, Mr. Marshall?"

"Not if The Prime Minister is out of prison early."

They left Kennedy as they had found him, sitting against the yellow leather, the white table in front of him. The black chair across from him was empty again, as if nobody had ever visited him, disturbed his thoughts, or his wave of hair.

Chapter Thirty-Four

The Ames Brothers and other top songs from *Hit Parade Magazine* played on a portable radio during the lunch hour. A crewmember had planted a one-speed fan near the cast. The artificial breeze lifted the heat up, softened the air, and dispersed cigarette ash elsewhere. Their rehearsals had reached a fevered pitch, but the results were palpable in the performance. The actors hit their marks, said their lines with both conviction and enthusiasm, even if they had repeated them for the hundredth time.

There was some muffled laughter and conversations. Wax paper crinkled as sandwiches were unwrapped. Potato chips snapped with each bite. And sometimes there came a crunch from a pickle. Vera sat apart from the other actors, at the edge of the stage, feet dangling off it as if she were on a pier. She tried to mingle, but the New York crowd seemed all hard edges and colder hearts.

She stabbed the straw into the mouth of the bottle of soda pop. She scanned the crowd for her Maggie. Jack Marshall and Walter Thompson appeared deep into a conversation and casual with each other, with the top button of their shirts and ties undone, and jackets flung over the seats in front of them. Walter used his hands when he talked. Jack Marshall stared ahead, always observant, always reserved, a quiet man who listened. When he did move, she would see the glint of his wedding band. Adler sat alone, sandwich in one hand, as if food were fuel and an afterthought. He held the script splayed open in his other hand.

Before lunch, they'd worked through the pages leading up to the intermission. Joseph's boss has learned about the social meetings. The fireplace had been lit, to symbolize the simmering tension between husband and wife. The couple were living paycheck to paycheck. Rose, the wife, argued that he would jeopardize what they had if he persisted with his damn meetings. His insecurity about no education didn't pay the mortgage, didn't pay the bills for their daughter Rosemary.

Joseph's boss owned the biggest business in town. His company had just lost a lucrative deal and the man suspected that someone within his company had sold company secrets to his rival. Rose reminded her husband that his boss owned the bank, like Mr. Potter in *It's a Wonderful Life*. The man owned the law, and there wasn't any chance of a fair trial. He owned the newspapers, like Charles Foster Kane in *Citizen Kane*. He could tap any judge, influence any jury, and write the verdict of his choice. Rose reminded Joseph that she'd be tried with him as an accomplice or convicted in the court of public opinion. As with every intermission, the audience needed a reason to return from the drinks and conversation in the lobby, so the cliffhanger was their daughter's medical treatment, and how he'd avoid the boss's net.

Vera bit into her chicken salad sandwich. Maggie, BLT and bottle of pop in hand, walked towards her. Vera smiled, pleased that Maggie was wearing the pink lipstick she had bought her at Schwab's Pharmacy on Sunset Boulevard. Vera brushed off the wood next to her, ready for her lunch date, but Maggie turned and started up the stairs.

Vera watched those long moonlight legs take the stairs in white nylons and blue Valentine heels. As Leslie's feet moved, Vera spotted the charm bracelet, a gift, trapped on the ankle. No jingle of the chain. No bouncing heart. Nothing at all to see but soft pounces up the stairs to the men, nothing but the curves of calves and the slight shake of hips. Her Maggie sat between Jack Marshall and Walter Thompson.

Jack Marshall spoke to her in one ear. Her eyes glanced down as if she heard a private joke. Walter Thompson tapped her shoulder, interested in sharing something with her. She moved her head closer to his so he could whisper that secret something into her other ear. She didn't blush but she was laughing that laugh Vera knew well. His hand lingered on her shoulder.

"What do you think of the play so far, Jack?" Leslie asked.

"It's *The Jungle* meets *Main Street* meets *Death of a Salesman*, and it'll cause quite the rumpus when Jack Warner reads it."

There was the sound of a door opening and closing behind them. Johnny Mercury emerged from the hallway holding a box with cups of hot coffee inside cardboard slots. Didn't matter if it was the hottest day of the summer outside because coffee, like cigarettes, was the poor man's digestif after a meal. Johnny Mercury stopped when he saw Leslie.

"I would've gotten you a coffee if I'd known."

"I'm good with my sandwich and soda."

Johnny glanced over at Jack. "I've got news."

Leslie surrendered her seat to Johnny and took the one next to Walker. Mercury handed a coffee each to Jack and Walker. He sat down between the men and held his cup with two hands, as if he were cold and had forgotten the oven outside, and spoke to Jack. "Kennedy is hopping from flower to flower like a bumblebee."

"Does our busy bee plan to sting anyone yet?"

Walker and Leslie listened. Jack sipped some coffee, as if it were the most perfect drink in the world. He'd never met a bad cup of coffee, thanks to the army. He could drink it hot or cold, whether it tasted like paint thinner or water with sock in it. "What did you find out?"

"He called Boston after the Mermaid Room."

"Advice from dad."

"Yeah, but get this. He also rang his brother."

Jack pulled his head back and stopped drinking his coffee. "He called John?"

"I'm waiting on the transcripts, but one of them, either old man Kennedy or our minted senator reached out to a judge with considerable pull with a certain parole board. Guess where?"

Jack didn't take long to answer. "Michigan."

"Looks like The Prime Minister might get sprung early."

"Which means everything will escalate with Genovese. This judge," Jack said, "he isn't the same one who signed the subpoena, is he?"

Mercury shook his head. "That's where I think brother John came into the picture. Old man Kennedy is savvy enough to know if he went hat in hand twice to the same judge, it'd draw flies to a stink. Like you said, things will escalate."

"Sooner than you think, and not in a way we expected." Jack blew on his coffee and asked, "Cohn found out about the Mermaid Room?"

"Not him. Anastasia."

Johnny Mercury explained that the day Jack and Walker met with Kennedy, Albert Anastasia ran late with his own appointment with the barbershop inside the Park-Sheraton. There, Albert received his hot towels and shave, followed by a maintenance manicure, while the bodyguard read the funnies. Albert Anastasia had the routine down, like the Royal Guards outside the royal palace, or the Swiss guards at the Vatican.

"The day you met with Kennedy; Anastasia noticed a car with Massachusetts plates. Imagine his peepers when the lot attendant gave him a description that matched Kennedy's. But it doesn't stop there," Mercury said. "Anastasia is not one for fast assumptions, so he greased the guy a twenty for the keys."

"He checked the registration?"

"Bingo."

"All that education and he's still not bright enough to stay out of sight."

Walker expected a crack about football games in mink coats, watching the Harvard Crimson try to restore their glory after inventing the forward pass in '06 and winning the Rose Bowl in '20, except there was no joke to be made since Kennedy attended UVA.

Mercury attempted to defend Kennedy. "He's young, Jack. We all started out a little stupid."

"Stupid gets you killed," Leslie said, and their heads turned.

"What's your take?" Jack asked her.

"The OK Corral at the house in Philly tells Anastasia that Genovese is up to no good."

"I can't have Anastasia attack Genovese," Jack said.

"He won't, at least not yet," Johnny Mercury answered.

"Because he needs approval from the Commission?" Jack asked.

"That, and he's patient because of Tania."

The bones in Jack's neck cracked when he turned his head. "Tania?"

Mercury reminded Jack that Steps had taken her to a doctor. Anastasia outranked Steps and Steps had to tell him what the doctor said. When a boss asked a question, he expected an honest answer. Anastasia had learned about Tania's ordeal.

"You know, people get it all wrong." Johnny shook his head. "They think the Sicilians invented the phrase 'revenge is a dish best served cold,' when it was a French diplomat who coined the expression. Anastasia is from Calabria, and people there have a better saying: 'Revenge has no statute of limitation.'"

"Ko-Ko has a heart," Jack said over his coffee. "Who knew?"

"The man might be a killer, but he has a soft spot for kids and he's strict about harm to civilians. What Genovese did won't sit well with Albert, but he'll bring the matter up with the Commission and soon. You still haven't said what you want to do, Jack."

"I've got an idea, but the friends you've made in your world might not like it."

Someone shouted, "In five," and everyone began to move. Leslie did a fast gallop down the steps in her Valentines. Vera brushed the crumbs off her lap. She hopped down, not quite the hangman's drop, but she twisted and turned. She grabbed her empty bottle behind her and when Vera spun around, she faced a radiant, gorgeous, and upbeat Maggie. "I'm sorry about lunch."

"You seemed to enjoy yourself."

"Oh, them," Leslie said, not looking up to where she sat with Jack and Walker. "I was just being social. Hope you didn't mind."

"Why would I?" Vera lied. "I know you knew Walter from LA, but you seemed quite at home with that Mr. Marshall."

"You mean Jack."

"On a first-name basis with him, are we? That was fast."

"You're cross with me."

"Not at all, dear. It just seems queer to me, though," Vera said.

"Queer, how?"

"All three of you chummy, up there in the rafters, as if you'd been friends for years."

"You're imagining things."

"Am I? Please don't patronize me, Maggie. I told you a long time ago that I know men."

She had. Vera was the one who'd offered Leslie advice on how to work Dr. Phillip Ernest. She was the one who'd pegged Walker's interest in her at one of her Mulholland socials. And it was Vera Williams who understood the ways and means of men, men such as Jack Warner and Lenny Moore.

"Walter Thompson looks at you like a dog, and he wants more than a treat."

"Don't be ridiculous."

"I still find it all peculiar."

"Find what peculiar?"

"All of a sudden Walter Thompson is in the room next to us at the hotel."

"What are you insinuating?"

"Nothing at all, dear. All you have to do now is swing that door between our rooms open and you and Walter can have yourselves a grand time with some of that Johnnie Walker you love so much."

"You're cruel, Vera."

"Honey, it's what actors do best."

Vera understood how to work words. There was no need to raise her voice. Delivery and tone did everything. She stood there, chin up in the air, shoulders back, and waited.

"I'll see you later," Maggie said, and walked away.

Not what she'd expected. Vera wanted to call Maggie back, but she couldn't bend her pride to say the words. She watched the white nylon, the navy skirt, the light blue shirt, and even the trapped charm bracelet walk away. She watched with every muscle in her body, every muscle, wanting to say she was sorry, but she couldn't. A light breeze from the portable fan smacked her face and messed up her hair.

Chapter Thirty-Five

Jack had learned one thing above all else in working intelligence, and that was to orient and redirect talent in the direction of the mission's target. The objective was to stop Roy Cohn, to end Senator Joseph McCarthy's quest for Communists within government and the defense industry. The Commie and Nazi of yesteryear were assets now, and his job was to protect former enemies in order to protect the country and Company today.

Robert Kennedy was born to money and power, wealth and prestige. His education had helped him understand the power of words, rhetoric as persuasion, but he had failed to understand what lawyers since the time of Cicero understood: the law is not about justice. The court room was about theater, about the story told, and how it was told. Roy Cohn had grasped this lesson early in his career, grasped it the way the baby Hercules strangled the snakes in his crib.

Kennedy did, however, have one strength that neither Jack nor Walker possessed.

Robert Kennedy understood water.

He understood the ways in which it could appear calm one minute, become enraged and destroy with impunity, the next. Water moved around things in its path, or it consumed them. Kennedy was like water, unforgiving.

Jack sent another message to Kennedy, this time to meet him at the waterfront.

Jack stood near the pier, his Hertz Rent-a-Car behind him, and the Hudson

River and New Jersey in front of him. Water made about as much sense to him as reading a biography on the ocean. The dark water reminded him why he had enlisted in the army instead of the navy. He preferred earth to sea, firm ground to shipwreck, the worms to the waves.

Nobody had warned Jack Marshall about summer in the city, or the stench between the states. A barge filled with garbage was crossing the ribbon of water right then. Seagulls as vultures careened, circled, and screeched overhead before they dove and feasted on mounds of refuse destined for the incinerators in Jersey. A summer's reluctant sun was setting and the oppressive humidity rising.

The swells brought with them the foul waste of factories, such as metals from the Anaconda Wire and Cable Company upstate; slick sheets of oil from Penn Central Railroad; pulp from the papermills, and Gotham's own raw sewage. Anaconda made Jack think of the Copper Kings and George Hearst, father of William Randolph Hearst, which, in turn, made him think of another father and son, Joseph P. Kennedy and Robert Francis Kennedy.

Jack had instructed Johnny Mercury to put the word out, starting with Steps, and Steps agreed to a time and to bring help. Kennedy would arrive last. Jack wanted all the pieces in place before the brash attorney showed up.

Water lapped against the piers, and the air introduced him to another odor, like the smell of a burned-out clutch. The tires of a car chewed the gravel. The driver of the Chrysler Imperial had toggled the headlights long before he parked the car. A door eased open and out stepped Jimmy Alabaster from the driver's side. Steps emerged from the passenger side, and behind him from the backseat, Johnny Mercury and Albert Anastasia.

Steps confirmed the time on his watch. A nervous Alabaster chewed his gum like a rabbit. Mercury acted the part and scanned the vicinity. Anastasia adjusted his jacket and buttoned the top button. His eyes lingered over the warehouses and all the broken windows. His suit wasn't a Botany 500 or some knockoff from the rack. Albert's tailor had let out enough material for his client to carry cold metal under both arms.

When the doors to the Imperial clapped shut, Walker and Sheldon emerged from Jack's rental car, a Buick Super Riviera. Sheldon walked towards Jack.

The other party paused in their stroll, surprised at the sight of Sheldon and Walker. If it had been a ruse, shots would've cracked the air and bodies would've dropped. That didn't happen. Walker stood behind Jack's left shoulder. "Are you sure about this?"

"It'll have to do. Sheldon?"

Jack reached down for the key in his jacket pocket and handed it to Sheldon, over his right shoulder. "You'll find what you need inside the trunk. If it looks like it's going south, now or later, take out Anastasia first and then Steps, so there's no war. Do your best to keep Mercury alive."

"Then what?"

"Get everyone the hell out of New York."

"No play then?"

Jack looked over his shoulder. "None of you will live to see opening night if you stay."

Sheldon walked away with the car keys. A breeze between the two warehouses delivered a fragrant veil of diesel, grease, and old sawdust. Jack and Walker began their walk to the mobsters.

Walker asked, "Think Sheldon can make the shot?"

"We shall see, won't we?"

Alabaster's unlit cigarette stuck to his lower lip. Mercury grinned. Steps kept a hand in his pocket. Within a few yards of each other, Jack said, "Let's talk there."

And they did.

Anastasia looked long and hard into Jack's eyes. "Hope this all adds up, Mr. Marshall."

"As if you didn't want the goods on Genovese."

"My feelings about the man don't matter. I'm here because of the Commission. I stake my reputation on whatever information I present to them, so this had better be true, or you and your friend the playwright here are in for a long night."

A car door slammed loud enough for Anastasia to reach into his jacket. The whites of his eyes glistened when he recognized the man at the car. "You invited the mick?"

"Keep your hat on, Umberto. None of this works without him."

"Explain yourself."

"You and the Commission take care of Genovese."

"And this mick does what?"

"He helps keep Cohn on the shelf where he belongs. The way I understand it, and do correct me if I have it wrong, but Cohn is a civilian, right? The Commission dislikes attention and they're hesitant to touch a public figure."

A tallish silhouette, wiry and in jeans, boatneck shirt, and sneakers, Kennedy moved towards them. Both Anastasia and Jack seemed to agree on one thing. They both found Kennedy's choice of footwear odd. Kennedy had detected their interest, looked down, and flashed them his toothy smile when their eyes met. Sneakers were not what they'd expected.

Kennedy pointed to all the shined shoes around him. "Saltwater and leather don't mix, gentlemen. You're better off with canvas on your feet. I learned as much on the Cape." He inhaled. "Smell that air?"

"All I smell is Jersey," Anastasia said.

Jimmy Alabaster was about to light his cigarette when Kennedy snatched it from the man's mouth. Jimmy said, "Hey, what's the idea?"

"Sun is going down."

"So what, you afraid of the dark?"

Kennedy tucked the cigarette into the breast pocket of Alabaster's suit. "If there's anyone out there on the water, they'll see you light up. A lit cigarette is as good as a flare. Something I learned in the navy."

For a New England kid with the silver spoon in his mouth, Kennedy had chutzpah and brass. Jack attributed it to all the bagels in Brookline and a strong Irish Catholic mother.

"Let's get straight to the point and not waste time. Heroin is moving from Jersey into New York tonight," Kennedy said. "We all know that Jersey is Genovese's territory, and narcotics violates the rules within Cosa Nostra. Isn't that right, Mr. Anastasia?"

"Cosa Nostra? I heard it doesn't exist."

"Then there's no truth to narcotics and to Vito Genovese's interest in them?"

Albert Anastasia didn't blink. "I'll tell you what's true. Your Jew friend Roy Cohn supports Genovese, like he condoned the kidnapping of that young lady."

"I've said it before to Mr. Marshall, and I'll say it again. Roy Cohn is no friend of mine. You must understand the feeling?"

"And what feeling is that?"

"Working with people you don't like," Kennedy said. "It's business until it isn't."

Kennedy and Anastasia squared off, like two prizefighters.

Johnny Mercury stepped up to referee before Anastasia took off the gloves. "Let's focus on why we are here," Mercury said. "Mr. Marshall says the shipment is in from France. Genovese's crew will send out a boat from Hoboken to pick it up. Then they ferry it to Brooklyn, where longshoremen unload it, and that's where we catch the proof. Understood?"

Kennedy asked Anastasia, "Isn't Brooklyn The Prime Minister's turf, and I thought he was against the drug trade?"

"It is, and he is," Anastasia answered. "If what you said is true, then this is Genovese's way of making everyone believe that The Prime Minister can't control his territory. And I can tell you that Vito doesn't move horse in Brooklyn, even if the longshoremen unload there. You want heroin, you go to Harlem."

"Didn't The Prime Minister grow up there?"

"He did. Why?" Anastasia said.

"Because heroin in Harlem is another way for Genovese to humiliate The Prime Minister. Nothing says embarrassment more than weeds in your own backyard. One question for you, Mr. Anastasia?" Kennedy said. "Doesn't your brother control the piers in Brooklyn?"

"You saying my brother is mixed up in this?"

"There's a sugar factory in Brooklyn."

"A Domino's, why?" Anastasia shot back.

"Heroin is white. Sugar is white."

"I don't like what you're implying." Anastasia was within an inch of

Kennedy's face. "My brother isn't into smack. The stuff is poison to kids. If he plied the garbage, he'd answer to me. Rules are rules and the Commission said, no narcotics."

Steps worked his arm between the men and wedged a shoulder in to create space between Anastasia and Kennedy. "Good to hear, Albert, because there's a change of plans. Sorry, Mr. Marshall, but we're not going to Brooklyn or Harlem," Kennedy announced. He looked out to the water. "I have a boat waiting."

"A boat?" Jack asked.

"We go out to where the ship is and wait for Genovese's ferry to pick up the dope."

Kennedy stepped away from the crowd. He contemplated the darkening sky. His abrupt departure surprised them. They looked around at each other and waited. Kennedy returned lit up, with more wattage than Sardi's neon sign. Anastasia asked him, "What's got you all chipper?"

"Because it's a good night to be on the water."

"And who pilots this boat?"

"Me," Kennedy answered, and pointed to where he had his boat docked.

While the others headed to it, Jack approached Kennedy and said, "I don't know what's going on inside that head of yours but promise me one thing with your boat. If we're not going to Brooklyn for the heroin, then we need to seize the shipment and not allow that boat to return to Jersey. You understand me?"

Chapter Thirty-Six

Jack exchanged an uneasy look with Walker. Their dislike for water dated back to the time both of them had slept and puked their way to Europe inside the belly of a troopship.

As the others boarded, someone asked the skipper about his course. Kennedy explained that international waters started at three miles out. They would intercept the boat there and, at some point, seize the shipment the minute they could board the ferry.

Alabaster joked, "Like taking a taxi to the SS Rex from Long Beach is what this is."

Anastasia told Jimmy to shut up. Alabaster had worked operations on the West Coast and came east to duck a criminal charge. As for the boat Jimmy had mentioned, Anthony "Tony the Hat" Stralla first ran rum and then a series of offshore gambling boats in Southern California and Alabaster provided muscle.

Their transport was a forty-foot cruiser that could accommodate twenty-plus people. Kennedy had untied the boat and assumed the helm. Moonlight illuminated amber glass, shiny hardware, and the mixed wood of mahogany and spruce. Everyone sat stone still in the cabin while Kennedy eased the boat away from the dock. Even at low throttle, vibrations from the engine cut to the bone and stirred the gut. Kennedy recited Shakespeare.

"We few, we happy few, we band of brothers."

He boosted the speed and New York disappeared into the darkness. Their ride was no slow chug up the Congo to meet Mistah Kurtz. Kennedy handled the boat's speed with skill. Waves slapped the sides of the boat, and everyone rose and fell in their seats. A mist spritzed the glass in front of their pilot.

They sailed into the outer Hudson and a breeze blasted them with the sulfurous bad breath of New Jersey. Jimmy Alabaster retched and heaved. Kennedy inhaled the rotten-egg scent the way a lumberjack found pine tar refreshing. Sailor Kennedy was oblivious to their discomfort. Eyes ahead, both hands on the wheel, he entertained them with nautical chitchat. The river, he explained, originated in the Adirondack Mountains upstate, and emptied into the Atlantic at New York Harbor. Hoboken was inside a tidal strait, and he droned on about estuaries.

Anastasia looked as if he wanted to shoot Kennedy, but realized the lawyer was his ride back to civilization. Walker was one shade away from pea soup. Johnny Mercury, a navy man, stood tall on tested sea legs. He retained his natural color and touched the brim of his hat when Jack looked his way.

"There she is," Johnny announced, pointing out the French ship to Kennedy. The ship sat there, waiting for the rendezvous with Genovese's boat. Kennedy pulled back on the throttle so their signature in the waves would lessen and the boat bobbed with the water's natural rhythm.

"I'll cut the engine when we're closer. That way, any sound we hear will be the boat from Hoboken. Now we hurry up and wait."

They floated like a cork, creaked to-and-fro like a pendulum, and time crawled. Jack's mouth tasted like a tarnished penny. Alabaster stopped chewing. "Listen. Hear that?"

They heard the put-put of a sick lawnmower in the distance. The volume increased as it came nearer to them and the big foreign boat. "Here comes Hoboken," Kennedy said.

Anastasia rose from his seat and stood next to Kennedy. "Where? I don't see a thing."

"You're not supposed to. We keep our distance, and we wait."

"Wait for what?"

The put-put turned into a low growl, as a motorboat approached its destination. Jack and Walker shared the same look, the same exchange moments before an ambush or skirmish. Kennedy was their captain and he had sized up the enemy for them.

"I doubt they'll go aboard a ship that size," Kennedy said. "All depends how much heroin there is." He glanced over his shoulder to Johnny Mercury for an answer.

"Twenty-three kilos."

"Fifty pounds," Kennedy said. "We'll watch for the drop then."

Their boat rose and dipped with the swell from the other boat passing them. Then came the diesel mist, which passed over them like perfume. The Hoboken ferry was yards away from them since sound on water travels like an echo.

They heard a voice, an exchange. Something metallic.

"What the hell is that noise?" Anastasia whispered to Kennedy.

"The French are pulling up anchor. Sit and wait."

"Sit and wait for what?" Anastasia said, on unsteady and uneasy legs.

"Until we hear the big ship's engine. When she leaves, Hoboken should bolt for Brooklyn." Kennedy's eyes evaluated Anastasia. "You don't look so good. Sit down, before your dinner comes up."

"Any chance of a better look?" Mercury asked.

Kennedy indicated a button on the panel in front of him. "We use the light on deck once we confirm the smaller boat has the cargo."

Kennedy explained that someone had to direct the beam on top. Sit and wait, he advised again, but Steps would have none of it. "Any volunteers?"

Jack stood up. "I'll work the light and Walter will shoot, if he must."

Kennedy advocated patience. Steps said, "Nuts to that."

"We don't know what kind of firepower they have on the larger boat," Kennedy said, and read potential mutiny in their eyes. "I'll give Jack and Walter a few minutes to put on life vests before I turn the light on. And you two," meaning Jack and Walker, "lash yourself to whatever you can up there as I bring the boat up to speed."

Anastasia, the unlikeliest stewardess of all, disappeared and reappeared with two vests. He dished out a jacket, first to Walker, and then to Jack. "Be careful out there. They'll aim for the light."

They climbed up to the deck holding on to the railing. Walker used a small section of rope there to tie a loop around Jack's foot to the deck and then himself. Jack stood behind the light and Walker assumed a lower position on his knees.

The light went on and Kennedy surged his cruiser forward. Jack swept the searchlight and focused it on the foam behind the smaller boat from Hoboken. The French ship sounded its horn, loud enough for hands to cup ears and protect eardrums. Jack found a lever to keep the light fixed in place. There were two seamen on the motorboat in front of them. Jack hoped the glare would blind them from shooting Kennedy or their boat.

"Mind if I join the party, boys." It was Johnny Mercury without a life jacket.

"Are you crazy?" Walker asked.

"I can swim."

The shooting started. Anastasia had been right. They went for the light but not with any success. Walker wielded Grable. Jack fired his Mauser. Johnny contributed shots from a revolver. The exchange of bullets didn't change the skunk smell in the air. Whenever the other boat tried to break free of Kennedy, he gunned the engine and forced them to take a course he wanted them to take. In the last mile, Jack and Walker looked at each other. Kennedy was forcing them to where they had left Manhattan. They had expected a chase towards Brooklyn.

The pier loomed into view. It wasn't much for a silhouette, but Jack welcomed it like a convict swimming from Alcatraz. The men in the other boat stopped shooting.

Jack worried as he reloaded.

Kennedy angled his boat so Jimmy Alabaster, Anastasia, and Steps could jump onto the other boat, then sped up and blocked it in front so there would be no escape. Steps worked his way to the helm to relieve the skipper. Mercury hopped off and joined the takeover. Jack and Walker untied themselves and ditched the lifejackets and jumped onto the boat, as if they were pirates.

Alabaster and Mercury held the crew at gunpoint while Anastasia rutted through the hold to verify the cargo. His nod confirmed it.

CHAPTER THIRTY-SIX

Heroin.

Chapter Thirty-Seven

It seemed that before he met with Jack and Walker earlier, Anastasia had instructed his crew in Murder Incorporated to assemble on the pier. They were there waiting for their boss. Whether it was insurance on his safe return or not, these men had rounded up the boat crew and lined them up, their backs against the warehouse wall. While the Lord High Executioner reviewed the captive crew, two of Anastasia's men ransacked the rest of the cargo hold. In addition to the fifty pounds of French heroin, they discovered a small arsenal of pistols, revolvers, and some rifles.

Jack witnessed similar situations during the war. Civilians liked to believe POWs were marched off, handed a blanket from the Red Cross, and locked up in a shanty with a wood-burning stove. Facts ran contrary to reality. Germans shot Russians, Russians shot Germans, Germans executed Americans, and GI Joe executed Fritz and Hans.

Jack and Walker had seen as much at the liberation of Dachau. Outraged and enraged, the boys, some of his men, killed every German they could find. They didn't keep it simple and efficient either, like a bullet to the head. None of that reckoning compared to what the half-dead camp prisoners did to their former captors. There's nothing like watching a skeleton in striped pajamas beat a man to death with a rake.

Anastasia ripped into the jacket of the man in front of him, in search of identification. He thumbed through the expected driver's license, odds and ends such as coupons, until he found something he could work with. A union card. "Longshoreman. You're not from either local, Hoboken or Brooklyn. Explain yourself."

"What can I say? The ILA and ILB are at war with each other, and a man has to make a living."

The small and thick fire hydrant of a man might've spent his last ounce of living talking to Anastasia like that, but he figured this was his last show and he'd make it count for something. He was right, though. The International Longshoremen's Association and the International Brotherhood of Longshoremen were at each other's throats over membership and territory. A day didn't pass in either Brooklyn or Hoboken where violence wasn't in the papers. Most days, the piers had to be washed down, the blood hosed off. The men fought with ax-handles and chains. It was not unheard of to find a body in the Gowanus Canal.

Anastasia thrust the card into the man's chest. "Zero loyalty."

"You don't look like you're hurting any."

"What did you say to me?" Anastasia stepped back, reached into his jacket, and pulled out a .45.

Steps rushed and whispered into Albert's ear, "Off this guy, and we'll have to waste the whole bunch. It's too much work, between them and the boat's score here."

"Don't tell me what to do," Albert said to Steps, through clenched teeth.

"Wouldn't dream of it but look around and reconsider."

Albert had the muzzle pressed to the man's forehead. The man stared and didn't blink. Anastasia said, "Give me one good reason why I don't blow your brains out."

"Don't expect me to apologize or beg. What do you expect us to do? You guys in your fancy suits hold all the jobs in your hand. The bosses beneath you expect a kickback, and we have to borrow money from stooges so we can support our families."

"Be grateful you have a job at all, you crumb." Anastasia cocked the hammer, for effect.

"Some job. I'll have my wife write you a thank-you note when she comes home from the hospital in Boston after visiting our kid."

"Boston?" Anastasia blinked, thrown off center. "Why is your kid in Boston?"

"Polio. What world are you living in, mister? Don't you read the papers? There's an epidemic in this country. My son is in Children's Hospital in Boston. The March of Dimes helped him some with hydrotherapy, but my boy needs leg braces now."

Anastasia was speechless, but he didn't have time to respond. Two cars pulled up, headlights on, and Anastasia lowered his gun. The automobiles stopped. One car unloaded longshoremen, hungry for a fight and it looked as if they'd been paid in advance to bust heads. Nobody had time to figure out who had notified them. Out of the other vehicle stepped Lilo Galante, Genovese's friend, and another bruiser.

"Who are they?" Kennedy asked Walker.

"The lead guy with the stogie is a chum of Genovese's. The rest is the goon squad."

Lilo chewed on an unlit cigar as if he were Edward G. Robinson. His bodyguard stood there like a statue. The cigar came out of Lilo's mouth, and he spat on the ground. "Thought we'd have a talk, Albert. You're gumming up the works."

"Your batteries always did run low, Lilo. If you haven't noticed I have more juice here. My men outnumber yours, and I'm not one for conversations."

"Have it your way." Lilo snapped his fingers. All eyes looked to the car behind him. Out came the shoe, then the leg, a hand on the door, and then the first of two men. The Bureau agents from the mill in Philadelphia.

"Convinced Cohn and Genovese are together now, Counselor?" Walker whispered to Kennedy.

Lilo stuck the weed for a pacifier into the side of his craw and spoke. "These boys have to make a living, too. Government don't pay them enough, so they supplement."

The first agent came over to Jack. "Remember me?"

"Yeah, I do. You're coffee breath and your partner over there is mustard stain."

The Agent showed some teeth and demonstrated fast reflexes. He clocked Jack with an uppercut that could've jacked a car. Walker caught Jack as he reeled backward.

CHAPTER THIRTY-SEVEN

"That's for that little trick with the license plates."

Jack straightened and wiped his mouth. "Not bad, since your boss Hoover recruits his men from the lingerie department these days."

"What did you say?"

"Come over here and I'll whisper it in your ear."

Kennedy stepped in. "Robert Kennedy, Counsel to Senator McCarthy."

"Like I give a shit." The man put his hands on his hips. The parted suit jacket revealed a badge, a gun, and a leather belt. He stepped close enough that his nose almost touched Kennedy's. "You best step aside. No luck of the Irish here. Get in my way and I'll break your shamrock and then I'll work my way down to your knees." His arm winged and his finger pointed at the cargo on the pier. "That is all part of an ongoing investigation. Step aside or I'll take you in for obstructing justice."

"Let it go," Jack said to Kennedy.

"Listen to your friend," the agent said.

"Do you know who I am?"

Jack grabbed hold of Kennedy's arm and pulled him back. "I said, let it go."

"These men are federal agents. They took an oath."

"These men will kill you," Jack said. "Now is not the time to be idealistic. See those men, next to the car."

Kennedy looked to the rough crew. "Yeah."

"They'll cut out your heart and send it to your mother in a box, postage due. This isn't Agincourt, and you're not Prince Harry."

Kennedy said softly, "But the narcotics."

Lilo joined the agent in reviewing the packaged heroin. Each man shook his head, as if they were looking at a flock of dead seagulls. The agent flipped a packaged brick on the ground over with his foot.

"Lab will need to verify all of this. We'll have to inventory it. Then there's the tedium of researching ship manifests, and paperwork with the harbormaster." His toe tapped a package. "For all I know this could be sugar for or from that Domino factory in Brooklyn. The world is a funny place, isn't it?"

Anastasia walked over. "About as funny as how you licked a stamp and someone mailed that badge of yours to you."

The agent turned to Lilo who was nursing his cigar. It was a look seeking permission, which Lilo gave by taking his cigar out of his mouth again and nodding his head.

The agent stood eye-to-eye with Anastasia. "What's funny is I have a mick lawyer here whose old man made his bread bootlegging Scotch and banging Hollywood dames while your dago brother drops a vowel at the end of his name, thinking the world won't catch on that he's related to you. Got anything to say to that?"

Albert moved but Walker's hand gripped Anastasia's arm.

"I didn't think so." The agent buttoned his jacket. "The shipment is in my custody."

Jack put his foot on one of the bags when the second agent leaned over to pick it up. Lilo stormed over to Jack. For a teapot dictator, Lilo knew how to blow off a head of steam. He screamed at Jack, "What the hell do you think you're doing?"

"Thinking you better light up that cigar and enjoy it while you can because when Genovese's connection finds out operations didn't run so smooth, it'll be the last of you."

"What the hell are you talking about?"

Jack pointed to the heroin. "Heroin came off a French ship. I'll bet good money that Vito believes his merchandise is from Marseilles. It's not."

Lilo Galante searched the ground, as if he'd missed a clue, and turned his fat face to Jack. "What are you saying?"

"The heroin is from the Unione Corse, Corsican mafia."

"And how would you know that?" the agent asked.

"My business is international affairs."

Anastasia started laughing. Kennedy looked around, confused. Each longshoreman acted nervous as if his nails were being filed with sandpaper. Lilo about chomped through his cigar. "What's so damn funny?"

Jack answered. "You think Don Vitone has problems with the Commission. Wait until the Corsicans learn the feds seized their heroin and think that Vito claimed it as his own."

"You were never bright, Lilo," Anastasia said. "When they find out these lowlife G-runts Cohn has leased out have confiscated their heroin, Vito will need to make out his will."

Lilo turned china white. Anastasia poured the rest. "If an ounce of this garbage touches any New York borough, you tell Don Vitone to expect a visit. You tell him the Commission said so, The Prime Minister said so, and I said so."

The two agents ordered some longshoremen to move the heroin to the trunk of Lilo's car. The strongman next to Lilo stepped forward, gun drawn and pointed at Jack's head.

Lilo panicked. "Put that thing down."

"I want to know who the hell this guy is, and how the hell he knew the junk was from Corsica? I'm not putting this gun down until I get some answers." Lilo's bodyguard kept his arm up, his gun drawn. "This guy comes out of nowhere, shows up on our territory, with these two over there," he said, meaning Walker and Kennedy, "and nobody asks what crew he belongs to?" The man maintained his stand. "Who the hell are you? I want—"

A bullet shattered the man's skull.

Everyone hit the ground or scattered like pigeons. Anastasia grabbed ahold of the longshoremen's shirt, the man with the kid in Boston.

Anastasia called out to his men while he held onto his captive, who started crying and begging for his life, calling upon every saint he knew in the liturgy. "Shut up and stop crying. I'm not going to hurt you."

"You're not?"

Anastasia shoved his hand into one of his pockets. The dockworker flinched. "Relax." Kennedy came over. Anastasia worked through a thick roll of bills.

Kennedy asked, "What are you going to do with this man?"

"Nothing. How much money do you have on you?"

Kennedy dug into his pocket and came out with some tired bills and counted them. "Two hundred, why?"

Anastasia took a hundred of Kennedy's money and told him to keep the rest. He turned to the dockworker. "Show the man here your driver's license, so he knows your name." The dockworker fumbled and handed his ID to Kennedy. Albert explained to the scared man, "His brother is Senator John Kennedy in Massachusetts. If you need something, or your wife and kid need something, you call the Senator and let him know your name. Understand?"

"Yes."

Anastasia held up the thick wad and said, "There's five grand here. That's more than a year's salary. You found it, you hear me, and you take it for your kid under one condition and that is I never see your face on the docks on either side of the river. No more ILA and ILB for you. I don't want to see your face on the docks again. Ever. You find yourself some other line of work so you can be around that kid of yours. Here, take the money."

The squat plug of a man pocketed the cash. Kennedy returned the man's identification. He'd used his Sheaffer pen and wrote something on the back of his business card. "My brother's phone number. Call that number next time you're in Boston."

They watched the man run to the edge of the piers and board the small boat. They looked at the dead man on the ground as the warehouse door opened and a car came out. All Kennedy saw was the profile of the driver. Sheldon.

"I should be going," Jack said.

"What about the dead man?" Kennedy asked.

"My men will take care of it," Anastasia said. "You didn't see a thing. You have amnesia, remember." Anastasia walked away and whistled at some of his men and pointed to the corpse.

Jack ambled over to Kennedy, asked him if he was okay. "You know the dead man had a legitimate question," Kennedy said.

"Night, Mr. Kennedy, and don't forget."

"Yeah, I have amnesia."

"Not that." Jack gave the address, date, and time of Walker's play before he stepped away. Kennedy watched Anastasia's men carry the dead man away. Another anonymous death in the big city.

Chapter Thirty-Eight

Outside Leslie's hotel window, car horns blared, traffic moved, and neon signs blinked advertisements on and off like Christmas lights. She watched the world below from her window, like a god from Olympus.

The pavement was full of silent couples and single people. She imagined the couples, each with a story. There were the adulterers and the faithful, bosses and secretaries, men with diplomas and women with correspondence-school certificates. Everyone was shuttling from one part of the city to another, ending the day with a small key in a door to shut out the world for another night, until it started all over again in the morning.

She had nicked the bottle of whiskey from Walker's room next door and poured herself a splash. She did censure herself for drinking alone. If men could do it, so could she, but the voice in her head reminded her that this is what alcoholics do, and she answered that voice, saying that she was not one of them.

Another cascade of amber liquid fell into the glass. Not disorderly drunk but rather encouraged by the whiskey's warmth to confront the coldness, the reflection in the mirror, she started brushing her hair. The bristles raked her scalp and her hair passed through the spaces between them. The occasional tangle made her wince. If life were only as easy and comforting as the ritual of brushing one's own hair. The communicating door to Walker's room creaked with an unexpected breeze.

She lifted the short crystal glass again and drank. Her other half in the mirror wasn't giving her answers. She could squeeze her eyes shut all she wanted, close them hard and open them again. The world hadn't changed.

The play was in two days. Leslie thought of the morning after the premiere, after all the newspapers said what they had to say about Walker's play. People who read reviews fell into two groups: those who measured words by the ink left on their fingertips or the size of the column on the page.

New York would still be New York outside her window. Unlike downtown Los Angeles, unlike her home with Vera in the hills, New York was stabs of steel in concrete, hard and crowded life pushed tight together, mugging and pawing for answers. It never slept. It never rested. Times Square was an insomniac's nightmare of lights and brightness, walkers and hawkers, from the cheery bum wanting your last dime to the ticket taker at the Lyric Theater behind curved glass, in her booth, behind her dark sunglasses hiding answers to questions. Her reply to everything is to point to a sign: Adults are fifty cents; children, thirty-five.

She heard a knock.

She walked across the cool carpet, forgetting to close the other door. She was in decent enough shape that she voyaged across the room without incident. She opened the door, used the frame as post to lean on when she held it open. She expected that it would be Vera telling her that she had forgotten her key.

"Tania?"

"Hello. Is this a bad time?"

"Not at all. This is a surprise," Leslie said, closing the door once Tania entered the room.

"Vera must still be at rehearsal. Uncle Sheldon hasn't returned either."

So, she didn't know that Sheldon had gone with Jack and Walker.

"Have a seat, please," Leslie said, amazed at how unexpected company seemed to sober her up. No black coffee or splash of cold water needed. She framed her words with clarity in her head but hoped that they didn't come out of her mouth slurred. Tania had already seen the bottle and the crystal glass. Leslie returned to the vanity, while Tania took another chair in the room and moved it closer to Leslie. They sat. Leslie tried to think of something that could pass for polite conversation.

"I'm certain it won't be a late night for them. Premiere night is around the corner."

"I doubt anyone will sleep."

"All part of nerves," Leslie said, holding the brush but doing nothing with it.

Tania eyed the small crystal glass and licked her lips. Their eyes met in the mirror. Leslie gave a weak smile but not an embarrassed one. Tania saw the open door to Walker's room. She looked down. "That's a pretty anklet," she said.

"Charm bracelet."

"From Vera?"

Leslie nodded and pressed the bristles into her other hand. The flesh had to remember something. There was an awkward lull, like in the movies.

"May I?" Tania asked.

"Drink? I don't think that would be a good idea."

"I meant, let me brush your hair."

Tania stood up and Leslie found herself surrendering the hairbrush. Tania stood behind her, fingertips pulling her hair softly and running the brush through it. It was a different hand, a different pressure and strength that Leslie felt, and was enjoying. She steadied her eyes on her reflection, then on Tania, who was smiling.

"You have beautiful hair."

"Thank you."

Tania returned the brush to Leslie's hair for the next sweep. One long brush stroke, the bristles dug in deeply. Tania's hand brushed over the top of Leslie's combed hair the way a beautician does at the salon. "How come you're not at rehearsal?"

"Mister Adler thinks I've done my lines perfect. It's such a short scene and not difficult."

Tania continued brushing Leslie's hair, working the brush this time with a stronger rhythm. She smiled into the mirror for Leslie. The pull of the brush left behind calmness in its wake, in her muscles, in her breathing, and in her bones. Touch the skin and she'd tremble.

"Aren't you afraid of the stage?"

"Not at all. I've been acting all my life. I'd like a drink If you don't mind."

"I can get another glass."

"We can share yours."

Tania was a tall girl with long arms. She was thin but not fragile, her hair almost white. And those eyes, deep, dark, and blue. Leslie admired Tania's firm and toned back and shoulders as Tania pulled the cork from the bottle and poured some whiskey.

Tania nodded to the door. "I'm sorry about Walker."

"Sorry about what?" Leslie asked, realizing that instant how stupid she sounded.

"You've always loved him, haven't you?"

"I'm fond of him, yes."

"Fond?" Tania smirked. "Why can't you admit you love him? It was obvious to me when I visited him in California."

"That was years ago. What could you possibly know about love?"

It was a callous remark and Leslie knew it. Words can hurt, maim and wound, and leave scars. Mother had taught her that lesson. Tania absorbed it politely. "You don't have to understand everything you see."

"Don't be in a hurry to grow up, Tania. Love will happen to you."

"Enough has already happened, thank you."

Leslie felt flush. "I'm sorry. I shouldn't have said what I did."

Tania sipped half her whiskey and handed the glass to Leslie.

"Know why I can play the daughter Rosemary well?"

"Why?"

"Because I'm just as broken as she is."

Leslie shot back the whiskey and poured herself another. Walker's bottle was down to a quarter full. She handed the glass to Tania and then corked the bottle.

"You're not broken, Tania. Damaged and scarred, yes, but fixable. You can play Rose the daughter because you have empathy. If you didn't have that, you'd be a complete monster. A harsh truth, I know, but I think you'd agree. So, you've experienced more than your share of misfortune, but I hate to tell you, life won't get better. That's the godawful truth, unfortunately. Everybody knows pain, but some are better at hiding it from others."

"Or themselves. What prevents you from loving Walker?" Tania paused to savor a taste of whiskey. "Is that why you're with Vera?"

"It's more complicated than that," Leslie said, taking the glass back.

"Is it?" Tania reached for the bottle. "You care for Vera, but it's not love. You feel safe with her, is that it? You feel safe from the world with her."

Tania's remark had disoriented her and made Leslie feel nasty. "If you're just going to stand there with the bottle, then pour another drink."

Tania placed the bottle on the vanity. "The thought of being with him terrifies me more than anything else in the world and that's also what draws me to him."

"Same here, I suppose. Loving him does terrify me."

"The difference," Tania said, "is he loves you and not me. Deep down, I frighten him. I frighten most men."

"Hate to break it you kid, but most men are afraid of women."

The conversation she was having with this young woman whom she had met six years before in Vienna unnerved her. Her lips tried to give shape to words, but Tania uncorked the bottle, and poured herself a drink. Leslie was light-headed but sober. "We should stop."

"Should we? You should know that he said no."

"I think you've had enough." Leslie tried to take the glass from her, but Tania's hand held it tight. The more Leslie pulled, the more Tania resisted, the more she stepped closer to her.

Tania had the look. "He might not say no the second time."

"You can't go around behaving that way."

"Why not? You do. You do what you please with Vera and him, so why can't I? You should make up your mind about Walker. It isn't fair."

"You mean, unfair to you," Leslie said.

"Unfair to him."

Leslie blinked. Tania let go of her glass.

There was a click. The light in the next room went on.

"I should go," Tania said. Leslie's hand dropped, Tania caught it, interlaced her fingers with Leslie's, and squeezed. It surprised Leslie to feel a surge of strength travel up her arm.

"Go to him."

"Why?"

"You know why," Tania said, releasing Leslie's hand.

Before Leslie could say another word, Tania had left. The front door closed and clicked shut. Leslie crossed the carpet in a fast, determined stride, the charm galloping on her ankle.

Chapter Thirty-Nine

Between the curtains, Walker had a glimpse of the crowd. Full house. He wondered how many of those seats were a result of a community-outreach campaign on the part of Steps and the Prime Minister. A sweep of the crowd showed plenty of suits and narrow ties, plenty of shawls on shoulders, kid gloves, and pearls roped around numerous necks. He had found his critic in the crowd. The lone pinstriped suit, high collar, and tight bowtie belonged to the dull face of a man ready to walk into the propeller of a plane.

Sheldon had the carpenters remove every armrest in the theatre. His motivation was subtle and psychological, to force the audience into a sense of community, complicit and without boundaries. Implicate, involve, and indict. Tania was onstage now, doing her scene. As Rosemary, the afflicted and troublesome daughter of Joseph and her namesake mother Rose.

[In a hospital bed Rosemary clutches her Vogue doll. The nurse has just exited, leaving Joseph and Rose with their daughter.]

ROSEMARY: Will you take care of Jill for me, Mommy? You know she must sit next to her sister Ginny.

ROSE: I know, sweetheart. I'll take care of her. [Accepts the doll from her daughter]

ROSEMARY: I'm afraid, Daddy.

JOSEPH: You'll be fine.

ROSEMARY: I promise I'll be good. I can try harder to be just like everyone else. I know I'm slow in school, but I can do better, I promise.

[He pats her hand.]

JOSEPH: I know you try, but this procedure is for the best. The doctor said so. Mother and I will be waiting for you. The doctors and nurses will be with you the entire time; there's nothing to fear, nothing at all. Be a brave, good little girl.

ROSEMARY: And I'll be different afterwards? Better for you and Mommy?

[Rosemary sees her mother start to cry. Joseph seems annoyed with his wife.]

ROSEMARY [softly to her mother]: Why are you crying? Daddy says it'll be all right.

ROSE [holds a handkerchief to her nose]: I don't know why. You'll be all right, sweetheart. Listen to Daddy.

[A nurse comes in and nods to indicate that it is time. She holds the door open and two male orderlies enter the room.]

JOSEPH: Be a good girl for the both of us. Don't give them any trouble.

ROSEMARY: They'll put me to sleep?

JOSEPH: You won't remember a thing.

ROSEMARY: Like a dream? And you'll both be there?

JOSEPH: Like a dream, and we'll be waiting for you.

ROSEMARY: I can try harder, you know. I can be a good girl.

JOSEPH: It's okay. I know. You'll be fine. You won't remember a thing.

[Rose sniffles.]

JOSEPH: Will you stop that, please? You're not helping.

ROSE: I'm sorry. I'm doing my best.

[An orderly places his hand on Joseph's shoulder.]

FIRST ORDERLY: We need to proceed and take her, sir.

JOSEPH: I understand, thank you.

[The other orderly leans down and offers Rosemary a big smile.]

SECOND ORDERLY: It's time, Miss.

ROSEMARY [hesitant but determined]: I'll go. I'll be a good girl.

[Orderlies wheel the bed out of the room. Rosemary holds her hand out to her mother.]

ROSEMARY [voice trailing as she is wheeled offstage]: Take care of Jill for me. You'll be proud of me, Daddy.

[Inside the hospital room, Rose's head is buried into Joseph's shoulder. She clutches the doll tight.]

JOSEPH: Nurse?

NURSE: Yes, sir?

JOSEPH: How long…how long is the procedure?

NURSE: Each surgical procedure is an individual case, sir. An electroconvulsive shock will sedate her, and the doctor will move quickly to perform the operation. Don't worry, your daughter is in good hands. The doctor studied with Dr. Freeman. We'll keep you informed.

[The nurse touches the sobbing Rose's arm before she departs.]

JOSEPH: See, she'll be fine.

[The curtain closes as Rose continues sobbing.]

Hushed, the audience were intent on every word. They were surprised that Joseph had gone through with his plan and stunned that his dutiful wife had acquiesced to it. Their daughter Rosemary had been a difficult and troublesome child, and the doctor had recommended the procedure.

A lobotomy.

Before the curtain closed for the intermission, the audience learned that the doctor had botched it. The prefrontal lobotomy had rendered Rosemary unable to speak and, it would turn out, permanently incapacitated. A speechless Joseph listened to the doctor, the same man who'd reduced his daughter to a mumbling and incontinent vegetable, explain that she would need around-the-clock care, and that he could recommend a facility, although he emphasized that continuous care was costly.

The play resumed; the curtains parted. The audience observed the couple onstage.

In writing the play, Walker had thought of what Jack had said about the fifth when he had met Costello in prison. Not the fifth as in the legal right, but the musical term. *Diabolus in musica.* The devil in music. Jack had explained it all as a matter of listening to the music, waiting for the dissonant note because it signaled downfall and the devil's presence. Walker was not a religious man, but he agreed with Jack. The devil existed.

For the audience in the theatre, the discordant note had come from the doctor. "There's been a complication." Impossible to resolve, their daughter destroyed, the unhappy couple was in motion, to their mutually assured destruction.

Walker understood what other writers had not. The "work" was not divine nor inspired; it was a defense. He had realized one hard truth in this dark and dangerous new world. It was not that harmony did not prevail or that all endings were not sweet and just. It was not that there existed a new wilderness and frontier, a cold war. No. The one thing he knew, that he had heard, had discerned, of which he was certain was that the infernal music played on, in boardrooms and courtrooms. In his pages, in all that he'd written, a response had emerged, as an answer to when the devil asked his question and made the music stop.

Rose, numb and stoical at first, who had always been the good wife, turned on her husband. The audience listened to her soliloquy, mesmerized if not hypnotized. Walker, inspired by the aggrieved and scorned women of literature, starting with Medea and then Queen Dido, wrote a speech that railed against the medical deities that dismissed women as extensions of their fathers and husbands.

Rose raged against every injustice to her sex. A wife couldn't open a bank account without her husband's permission. A woman needed her father's consent to rent an apartment. Her greatest contempt she reserved for doctors whom she said discussed every appointment, every confidence, and every test result with the "man in her life."

The nerve touched, the audience fidgeted in their seats when men, hired by Joseph's employer, applied pressure to the couple. The bank moved the date on their mortgage payments. The company instituted a spending freeze and threatened a furlough. The company's stores ratcheted up their rate of interest. The financial constraints tightened and constricted around the couple's resources. Their credit line at the limit, the bills mounting, and then the flicker of hope, offered to Rose, and not her husband.

Investigators approached her one afternoon, while her husband was at the office. They offered her assurances that her daughter's bills would be paid in perpetuity, if and only if she'd reveal the names of her husband's social club. List names, and she secured a future for herself and her daughter.

The audience watched the exhausted and paranoid Joseph confront his wife, accuse her of infidelity and other crimes. In a moment of marital combat, she revealed to her husband that she had been approached by his employer. She spelled out the terms and conditions. At first horrified, Joseph began to laugh, and Rose was taken aback, convinced that her husband had lost his mind. When his laughter ceased, the audience heard the man utter his fatal mistake.

He said a wife could not testify against her husband.

And then he asked her when dinner would be ready.

She gave him the time and told him that she was done with him. She said she'd serve him dinner and then leave because she wanted a life that she could call her own. She left him in the living room and went into the kitchen.

The audience watched Joseph remove the shotgun from above the mantle. He verified both barrels and loaded them. They saw him walk towards the kitchen. He pushed the door open. The audience heard her scream. He pulled one trigger, entered the room and the audience heard him sob, confess what he was about to do, and then a long silence before he pulled the second trigger.

The fire in the fireplace burned red. The curtains closed.

Walker watched. He checked the critic's face.

"How did I do?" Tania asked from behind.

"You were wonderful."

"Honest?"

"Honest."

Walker searched for another member of the audience.

Robert Kennedy's eyelids fluttered, as if he'd just been gut-punched and thrown out of a moving car into the street. He stood up, only to realize the oncoming foot traffic was upon him. He couldn't run fast or far enough from the audience and theater.

Tania, still behind Walker, pressed against him. Members of the crew filed past them. She turned this way and that, frustrated, until Walker pulled her into his arms.

"Thank you," she said.

"For what?"

Her fingers curled around his tie. "I never got to thank you. What I did was terrible."

"He had it coming to him."

"I wasn't talking about him."

He tried not to think of that day at his apartment, with her in his arms and the touch of her lips, the way her eyes read his face for a reaction.

"You could have…" she said.

"But I didn't."

"There's something I need to tell you."

He avoided her eyes. "I need to go," he said, and walked away.

Chapter Forty

The stewardess locked the door. Jack had booked Mercury Service, the flight from New York to Los Angeles in under eight hours on American Airlines.

Two days after the play's last performance and they were aboard a DC-7. The Flash Gordon lightning bolts down the sides of the plane and the plane's metal interior didn't offer Walker the same kind of assurance Grable did. No matter how many times he'd strapped himself into a bucket seat inside airborne transport during the war, the nerves frayed the same.

He joined every Ozzie and Harriet who could pay for the pleasure of flying at four-hundred miles per hour in an engineered tube of toothpaste. Jack forked over $300 for his own ticket, roundtrip, to visit Jack Warner in LA, and then back to New York for the drive home to family in Virginia. The girls, as Jack called Leslie and Vera, decided to stay behind for another day of sightseeing before they left for LA. Sheldon and Tania were well on their way back to Boston.

Walker's one-way ticket cost $160. Jack expensed it to his Company front, an insurance company, and reserved two car services for when they landed in LA. One car would return Walker to Malibu, while another car would take Jack to Burbank. As for the other expenditures—the rent in Hell's Kitchen and other expenses guaranteed Jack a visit from a government accountant, who'd wave the receipts at him and scream that the taxpayer had been mugged.

Walker considered the décor American Airlines had installed for the forty modern and sophisticated travelers onboard. No amount of dark carpeting could hide all the vomit from turbulence and a bad air pocket. Window shades may have blocked out the sunlight but not the fact that travelers were four miles above the earth. Walker read somewhere that, to pass the time, passengers wrote postcards about their trip and holiday plans. That's a lot of postcards for an eight-hour trip, he thought. He looked around and confirmed a darker truth. One hour into the flight, most of the men started the coordinated hand-to-mouth reflex of booze or cigarettes to their lips.

There were three stewardesses, one more than the advertisement promised. The same advert proclaimed that each stewardess was a registered nurse. One of them, the extra he guessed, handed Jack a thick envelope. Walker recognized the Company clasp and ribbon. He resigned himself to the dailies he had carried onboard with him.

Another stewardess, this one in a navy dress past the knees, a short and styled cut of brunette hair tucked under a beret, and her makeup neat and natural as a Barbie doll, asked him if he wanted a drink.

He capitulated and ordered a bourbon. She handed him the lunch menu, which the airline served on actual china and with real silverware. She left him to fill his bar order.

Jack grinned when he heard the choice in refreshment. "Need to fortify yourself against those reviews?"

"I don't expect accolades."

"I would hope not," Jack said. "You ended the play with a failed lobotomy, as if there's a reason to celebrate the success of one, and you ended a marriage with a murder-suicide. Not what I would call *Make Room for Daddy*."

Walker parted one of the papers in his lap. He had opted not to respond. Jack Marshall didn't understand or care for art. Jack appreciated the skill behind a Remington rifle more than the anxiety behind a Remington typewriter. He was a practical man, born and bred in Montana, and preferred horseback riding and fly-fishing. Jack planned for contingencies, like an actuary at the insurance company calculated risks and premiums.

Which is why the night at the pier with Kennedy, he had Sheldon inside the warehouse, armed with an M3 Carbine and an infrared Sniperscope.

They had been over it before they rode out to LaGuardia Airport. Walker had asked about the Corsicans. Jack grayed his answer within the lines when it came to details. Genovese's heroin was due to arrive on a French ship, out of Marseilles. The bit about the Unione Corse was pure Jack. Vito Genovese would have to dig himself out of a hole with the Corsicans. Jack elaborated on the history, on the favors owed and paid with interest.

"While De Gaulle was preoccupied with Algeria, the Corsican mafia helped the Company keep the Reds from controlling the docks in Marseille, not unlike how we asked Lucky Luciano to secure the New York waterfront for us. I called in a favor, and they wrote the heroin off as goodwill among friends."

Jack worked his way through his paperwork. Jack could've sat across from Walker. The seat there was free. He chose to sit next to Walker and Walker saw the photos.

Aerial reconnaissance. Eight-by-ten photographs. Originals.

The Air Force used color-blind men to conduct surveillance. Their inability to see color allowed them to identify camouflaged installations. The planes flew at high altitude like a lawnmower across the sky, doing one strip of land one way and another the other way. The color-blind snoops would look through their scopes and click pictures.

"Vietnam," Jack said.

"We don't have commitments there, do we?"

"Not yet, but we will, thanks to the French losing ground to Ho Chi Minh. If we don't step in, the French won't join NATO, or so I was told. Want to hear a remarkable coincidence?"

"Sure, why not."

"A British writer started his next novel in '51, while working for MI6 in Saigon. At the same time, on the other side of the city, a young Congressman was on a fact-finding mission. He told his brother, who was with him, that we would lose in Vietnam, if we perpetuated the colonial adventures of our British and French allies. Curious as to who the three men were?"

"No idea, but I assume we're not on the Truth or Consequences radio show."

"The writer was Graham Greene and the politician and his brother? John and Robert Kennedy."

"I think I should read my reviews."

"Self-pity never did anyone any good."

Walker straightened out the newspaper and read, "Diminished Fifth is a powerful and disturbing play." That was the best line from the critic in attendance on premiere night. The rest of the newsprint was about as charitable as the ghosts with Scrooge. Walker read three different reviews, because writers flogged themselves with bad reviews. He started with one and plowed through the toxic ink.

> *The climax of the play is cruel, unrealistic, and a malicious attack on parents, and tears at the fabric of the American family. This is excrement of the highest pretense, since it aspires to instigate discussion of serious matters but fails, and the stench is made worse by the unseasonably hot weather.*

And:

> *An otherwise talented cast including the enjoyable Vera Williams was wasted on angry polemics. In light of Mr. Miller's play at the Martin Beck, your money is better spent on The Crucible than on this meat-pie of melodrama. Save your money for Bromo-Seltzer because the only promise here is a case of indigestion.*

And for the coup de grâce:

> *In response to their stultifying existence, a couple form a discussion group. One thing leads to another until their parlor talk threatens the town's main employer's security and competitive edge in business. When their consequences inconvenience them, the couple lack the fortitude and gray matter to board a bus or train out of town. The couple wring their hands over a loving and simplistic daughter. It is a tale of a eunuch*

and his brainless wife signifying a veiled and pinko screed against the American way of life. Skip.

The bourbon arrived. Except for one page, Walker surrendered his stack of newspapers to the lady, apologizing if the ink stained her gloves. She thanked him for his generosity on behalf of his fellow passengers. Jack and Walker chose their lunch selections from the menu. Walker nursed his drink and thought of Malibu, seagulls, and a cold glass of milk.

When they were over or past Chicago, they'd receive a full meal of chicken soup, Salisbury steak, peas and carrots, a garden salad, and dessert of apple pie, with a choice of coffee or tea. Unsure of airline food, they both agreed anything was better than what the US Army passed off as food in the field. MRE were not Meals Ready to Eat but Meals Rarely Edible.

"I'm glad you ditched the masochistic exercise of reading the reviews."

"Kennedy was in the audience after all."

"He was," Jack said. "Johnny Mercury said he bolted to a booth and called his father."

"Old man Kennedy put the kibosh on the play?"

"I'm sorry about your play, Walker, but we accomplished what we'd set out to do."

The mission seemed to stall McCarthy's rutting through the fields of clover for Commies at government installations. It seemed like ancient history now.

"Adler, Judith, and the kid?" Walker said.

"New identities."

That made sense. It wasn't an area of expertise for the Company, but the Company was learning new skills with each passing week and month. Walker watched Jack read the brief before him. The color of the paper betrayed its importance. Something was in the works and Allen Dulles had copied Jack.

"Something important?" Walker asked.

"It's always important."

"Not Vietnam, I presume."

"The desert, this time," Jack said. "Iran."

"If not the French, then our British friends?"

"For someone who claims to have no interest in foreign policy, you have an acute understanding of cause and effect, Walker."

"It's called plot. Same thing. What's the hook?"

"Oil and money. I've had enough for one day," Jack said. He straightened the edges of the report on his lap and inserted the stack inside an oversized envelope. "Any other questions?"

"What ever happened to Hoover's men at the pier and the heroin?"

"What heroin?" Jack shifted in his seat to find a comfortable spot. "As for the bent agents, they were found shot to death in a car. Some place called Cook Road."

"New Jersey?"

"Where else," Jack said.

"Anastasia or Genovese or Cohn?"

"Does it matter? They were loose ends and somebody had to tie their shoe." Jack leaned back as if he wanted shut-eye. Walker reached down and pulled up the part of the newspaper he had saved. He put it on Jack's leg. His eyes opened and he looked down and pulled the paper off himself. "What's this?"

"You were wrong about Kennedy."

"Was I? What did Robert do?"

"He tendered his resignation to McCarthy, but read the rest yourself."

Jack turned the page around, in search of meaningful text. He found it. Walker let him savor it, mull it over, and then acknowledge it. "You're right. I was wrong."

The column on the social page announced that John Francis Kennedy was engaged to Jacqueline Bouvier. Their marriage was set for September 12th. John, of the bad back, the sickly one, was in motion, guided by his father's hand. First, the pedigree, and then the political profile, from House of Representatives to the Senate.

Jack had been as wrong as wearing white after Labor Day. The marriage brokered respectability, a flagstone on the ambitious path. Joseph Kennedy was the kingmaker.

John not Robert Kennedy was being groomed for the presidency.

Chapter Forty-One

The New York behind them was a hard, fast, and immortal city, while Los Angeles was soft, seductive, and immoral. One hundred degrees of dry heat ironed every wrinkle out of Jack's face as he walked off the plane with Walker. Palm trees waved in the lazy air, ready to catch fire, and there wasn't a drop of rain anywhere.

Two drivers with signs waited for them at the bottom of the stairs. A skycap worked the belly of the plane like an obstetrician. He delivered one set of luggage after another onto the hot tarmac. The Negro whistled a chirpy tune, filled with staccatos and trills. His short-sleeved shirt revealed muscled arms and a military tattoo. Jack folded a Lincoln and stuffed it into the man's shirt pocket. Walker foraged for his bag, found it, shook hands with Jack, and they parted until the next phone call, the next mission, brought them together again.

The car Jack had hired drove the Sherman Way to the studio in Burbank. He gave his name to the guard, who ticked it off on a clipboard and raised the mechanical arm and waved them in.

Miss Elkins greeted Jack on the steps outside the main building. Jack remembered her from his last visit. Elkins advertised a nice figure, good taste in dresses, and a penchant for one flower behind the ear. Her heels clicked on all the polished flooring as Jack followed her. He liked what he had read in the report on her. Born and raised in Utica, her father was a lifer at Savage Arms, which produced rifles, shotguns, and the Thompson submachine gun.

As they passed the door to the Writers' Pool, the racket of typewriters could be heard from behind pebbled glass. Two years ago, Walker worked there for him and JL. The Pool was Warner's talent farm of cheap Steinbecks, sober Faulkners, and wannabe Thalbergs. Walker had perfected his keystrokes there. Miss Elkins said "Hello, Mr. Wald" to a gentleman who had passed them in the opposite lane. Jerry Wald was departing. Jack Marshall was arriving.

Miss Elkins knocked on a door to *the* office, heard nothing, so she opened Jack Warner's door halfway and found to her surprise another gentleman inside. Not Jack Warner. She apologized, proceeded to close the door slowly, embarrassed. The man inside yelled out to her to come in. She asked whether he was sure. He was. She eased the door open for Jack, and said she'd return with Earl Grey tea.

The blinds were drawn, the room was dark. The man before Jack sat in a chair, a captain's hat, white with nautical gold rope and all, on his head. Dark sunglasses covered his eyes while he chomped on the end of a linen handkerchief. A smoker's pipe sat in his jacket pocket like a neglected toy. It'd been years since they'd seen each other.

"How are the eyes?" Jack asked.

"I'm due for cataract surgery on 'em."

"Still the tough New Englander."

"And you look about as comfortable here as an ironing board."

The two men embraced, did the ritual of two slaps on the back as old friends reunited. Jack set down his valise, took the chair in front of JL's desk.

"Still with the insurance company, Jack?"

"It treats me well."

The director gnawed on more linen. John Ford had been working as a photographer for the navy when Wild Bill Donovan, Jack's boss at the OSS, recommended him for a project. John Ford would film the Battle of Midway and then work with Gregg Toland and Budd Schulberg on a prop piece about Pearl Harbor. Both projects earned Ford Oscars.

They were laughing when the door opened again. Both men stood up. Miss Elkins came in through the door with a tea tray that chattered as she walked. She seemed flattered by their manners in the darkness. The room filled with the scent of bergamot and citrus from the tea.

"I apologize for not introducing you earlier. Mr. Marshall, this is Mister John Ford, Director." Miss Elkins turned to John Ford and introduced Jack as Mister Jack Marshall.

She excused herself and Ford poured his tea and offered Jack some. Jack watched the steam fog Ford's glasses. Ford may have had a captain's hat on his head, but he separated from the Navy Reserve as a Rear Admiral. They reminisced about their boss Wild Bill, and both agreed that Hoover gave William Donovan grief at every opportunity. Jack thought about Joe Kennedy for a flash of a second. Churchill had lobbied for Donovan as Kennedy's replacement as British Ambassador. Hoover, of course, snarled at the nomination and at the thought of a spy agency after the war. He dismissed the Company as "Roosevelt's folly" and planted the idea that Bill, as its head, wanted to establish an "American Gestapo."

When Jack asked Ford about his latest project, the director said that he now headed Argosy Productions with his old pal Merian Cooper.

"Bill loved two things about you, John. The first is that you were ornery. Wild Bill always did like a non-conformist."

"I'm still ornery. You can ask JL yourself." Ford's eyes narrowed to black beads above the china near his mouth. "Second thing he loved about me?"

"You're prudent with your resources and leave little to the editors."

Ford started with a laugh and ended with a cough. "Not prudent at all. There's hell to pay before I'd allow a committee of moneymen to profane my work." He pointed to the far wall. "Tell me what you see in that picture."

Jack stood up and reviewed the landscape picture on the wall. Ford rose slowly from his chair and walked over to the picture and stood next to Jack. "Point to the horizon," he said to Jack, and Jack did. "Now, imagine yourself looking in the camera, at that horizon. Think with your eye now and ask yourself whether the horizon is at the top or the bottom of the frame."

"Are you trying to make me a director?"

Ford put his hand on Jack's shoulder and said, "Hell no, I need my day job. I'm trying to keep you alive in Hollywood, my friend. Knowing the horizon is knowing your target and never forgetting your perspective. That keeps you alive in this town."

"And elsewhere."

The door opened and in came Jack Warner, surprised to see John Ford and Jack Marshall together. He closed the door, and they did the obligatory handshakes. Warner appeared in starched shirt, black knit tie, short hair, and his Warren William moustache.

Warner looked at the wall. "Did he use the Remington on my wall to give you advice?"

"He was telling me how to stay alive in Hollywood."

Warner smiled. "America lives in Hollywood, Mr. Marshall. Survival requires knowing what is real and what is not."

Ford said to Jack, "Remember the horizon, my boy," and then to Warner, "I think I should go and leave you two to business."

"But your tea is still warm, and I wanted to talk to you about doing a comedy, a naval film. I'm sure Mr. Marshall wouldn't mind."

"Some other time, JL. I'm tired and my brother is ill."

"I didn't know. Is it serious?" Warner asked.

Ford shook his head and went slowly to the door. Warner, seeing that he couldn't persuade Ford to stay, insisted that Ford call him if he needed anything for his brother Francis.

"Goodbye, Mr. Marshall," Ford said.

Warner met Ford at the door. "If you can make John Wayne cry, then I'm certain you'll make Cagney sob in this film I want you to direct for me. Don't forget to call me. I'll have you over the house and we can play golf." Ford grumbled a few words about golf and the door closed again. Warner turned his attention to Jack. "Where's Mr. Thompson?"

"In Malibu, licking his wounds over the criticism in the papers."

"Most critics are idiots. Tell him I said that. Today's newspaper is tomorrow's toilet paper is what I say. I've advised him in the past not to cut the cloth too close to home."

Walker had written a drama for Warner, on the liberation of Dachau. JL loved it, but experienced cold feet at the last minute, knowing the American audience was not prepared for wartime atrocities.

"Ah, yes. Audiences can't have an allegory," Jack said.

"Just because it worked for Dante doesn't mean you still can't get burned at the stake."

"Since you funded Vera's adventure, I thought I'd deliver the script." Jack pulled out the play and placed *Diminished Fifth* on Warner's desk. "I'm sure it's worth every penny Joe Kennedy paid you to squash it."

"You know about that?" Warner asked.

"'Course I do. The play is poisonous to the Kennedy cause. Skeletons in the closet, and all that. You're a Republican, you understand the game."

Warner's moustache twitched. He gave Jack a serious look. "You do understand the difficult situation I was put in. I dislike Roy Cohn, and Vera is like family."

"I understand," Jack said. "I also understand the power of Joe Kennedy's money in this town. The man ran three studios at once while the lot of you moguls were still learning English." Jack showed his hands. "Save your breath, JL. I'm well aware that you're Canadian. My point is that it's quite the accomplishment for an Irish lad from the brokerage firm of Hayden, Stone, and Company."

Warner blinked when he lied. "It wasn't just him buying the rights to *Diminished Fifth*."

Jack walked about the room now. "He flipped you a pretty penny for your silence. No need to fret, Mr. Warner. I live in the real world, too, and it's always about the penny."

"Kennedy can make my life miserable, and I'm not talking about McCarthy."

Jack relaxed. He enjoyed this. "Hoover?"

Warner waved a hand through the air. "You know damn well the same as I do that Hoover can't stand the Kennedys. Now, is there something I can do to make this right between us?"

"Funny you should ask." Jack walked over to the window and talked while he twirled the rod to let in the light. "Give Irwin Adler a job. He's changed his name, like your blacklisted writers, which should make it easier for you.

He's here in California with his family. I can provide you with details on how to contact him. What do you say?"

"I can do that."

Jack pushed a slat down and viewed the building, Columbia Pictures. "Which one is Harry Cohn's office?"

Warner came from around his desk and pointed it out. Harry Cohn was the man Jack Warner hated most in this life and in the afterlife. He referred to the Columbia icon—the lady with a torch—as the bitch with a light.

"I've been hearing a rumor," Jack said, "that Columbia wants to do a film about longshoremen and corruption. You ought to beat Harry Cohn to it." Jack let the slat spring up from his finger. "You've heard, I presume."

"I have. Elia Kazan and Budd Schulberg are writing the script. It's not an upbeat story, Mr. Marshall. Malcolm Johnson might've earned a Pulitzer for the article, but as a poet once said, people can't bear too much reality. Besides, it's not a good time for Kazan."

"Because of his testimony before HUAC?"

Kazan had named names the year before, and the stench stuck to him.

"Give Kazan an alias then," Jack said. "It's been done before."

"Budd says they don't have a clue as to who to cast."

"I have an idea," Jack said. He pointed to the window again, to the studio across the way. "*From Here to Eternity* is out next month. There's an actor in it named Frank Sinatra. Have him do a screen test."

"The man can't act."

"But he's from Hoboken, and I'll bet he'd fit what Kazan and Schulberg have on the page to the letter." Jack watched Warner's face. No sale. He continued. "I wouldn't be surprised if filming in Hoboken went smoothly if Sinatra played the lead."

"I don't know. Filming on the East Coast brings up a whole set of problems. Logistics."

Jack appreciated Warner's euphemism for the mob.

"Which is why I suggested Sinatra."

"I don't understand you, Mr. Marshall. Not to use the actor's lingo, but what is your motivation? Give me something."

"Strategy, plain and simple."

Jack didn't need adjectives to make it exciting or enticing to Warner, only the angle.

"Robert Kennedy is severing ties with McCarthy. You can say he can't stand Roy Cohn."

"About time he smelled the soap," Warner said. "And how does that buy me peace? Cohn has already taken a swipe at me. Are you saying he'll do it again?"

Jack had an idea. He had studied Warner's films and noticed the trend from film noir to explicit Right or Wrong in his latest films. "You like social pieces."

"I like what sells seats. What do you suggest?"

"Do a film as a preemptive strike against Cohn."

"Tell me more."

"Do Kazan's film about corruption on the docks. It'll appeal to Mr. Kennedy, and it'll make you an ally. Don't do the film, then you'll be under the microscope, like the studio outside your window."

"You're suggesting that I pander to Mr. Kennedy."

"Better Harry Cohn pinned like a butterfly to the board than you, right?"

"An alliance alters perception."

"No, this is about maintaining perspective." Jack pointed at the landscape on the wall. "Remember the Remington on the wall?"

"Ah, Mr. Ford's advice. He's a good man behind the camera, Mr. Marshall, but I run a studio and I have other concerns."

"There's your mistake, JL. You quoted T.S. Eliot saying people can't bear too much reality. Talk to Schulberg and consider the crooner. Sinatra knows the right people, who can make most of your concerns disappear."

"I don't know, Mr. Marshall." Warner shook his head. "A bobbysoxer?"

"Might I suggest a strategy?" Warner said he'd listen. Jack explained. "Put pieces of paper and notes into the script you send him. He'll read it."

Warner's eyebrows peaked. "I'm not sure I understand."

"Old trick from the OSS that Mr. Ford and I used with committeemen. It's a matter of psychology and persuasion. If bits of paper fall out, the reader thinks they mark something important in the text. They'll read the material, already convinced of its importance. Try it. You won't regret it. I should get going."

Jack walked out of the building after he'd said goodbye to Miss Elkins. It was still hot, still bright. Warner might have been watching from the window. Jack didn't care. He found his car and driver. Warner could cold-shoulder the riverfront script he had recommended, and the actor for the lead part. John Leonard Warner could call the story grim and depressing, but Jack Marshall kept his eye on the horizon and what was above and below the frame. He tried to help Jack Warner with Roy Cohn and Harry Cohn. He had given Jack Warner an umbrella for when the rain came to Southern California. A storm was on the horizon. It was coming.

Chapter Forty-Two

Walker staggered into his bathroom and turned the dial to the shower, heard it squeak, then the pipes shudder before the water fell. He stepped under the cold water. He disliked hot showers. The move from a warm bed to warmer shower delayed the reality that came with each new day.

He ambled into his kitchen, undecided about breakfast. An omelet with vegetables would be nice, but that meant he'd have to raid his neglected garden. Toast with butter, eggs easy, and a side of bacon meant cooking. The easiest solution would be to thrust his hand into a cereal box, find the toy first, cereal second, and end the expedition with some milk. Bachelor's prerogative.

Coffee was mandatory. No cream or sugar. The war years and army rations had taught him to keep it simple, black and strong.

He opened a window and leaned into a lungful of fresh air while the joe dripped away. A salted breeze from the ocean slapped his face. He pulled his head in and located a mug. He poured himself some coffee. His bare feet enjoyed the familiar floorboards.

He was home.

He had solitude. There were no neighbors. There was no assignment from Jack Marshall—nothing but the stretch of hours to himself, to write whatever he wanted. He nosed the dark coffee, let it touch his lips for the next taste. He looked out another window. He ought to tame some of that brown scrub and wild grass. He could mow it or let it go to hell for a few more days before it bothered him. He could do a lot of things. He could do whatever he wanted. He could do everything in reverse, like dessert first, then the main meal, salad, and end it all with an aperitif.

Walker scanned the trees and didn't hear or see his friend the woodpecker. A morning choir of mixed chirpers serenaded him. Grable rested on the table next to the typewriter.

Before he'd left for New York, he'd written Elmo a note and left an envelope with a generous amount of money to make sure the place would be stocked with eggs, milk, Bulldog beer, and newspapers on his return. He left a key under the doormat because he trusted the man. He decided on breakfast.

He cracked a couple of eggs. He watched the collar of white around the egg yolk. Cooking an egg right was as hard as writing a good sentence. Proust would have described egg and toast in a sentence that would have run for five whole pages. He'd remember the egg as forgetting, as birth and rebirth; the shell as sanctuary and the yolk as a fluid of creation, whereas the toast was an intrusion, the inevitable reality of collusion and corruption. Fitzgerald would rhapsodize on the egg as the crack-up. Hemingway would just let the yolk run.

Bacon sizzled and fluttered in a separate skillet.

The toaster hiccupped and he buttered his toast.

He stared at the green Remington while he ate. He'd taken the punches, fought in the war, and earned himself medals and ribbons. None of it mattered now as much as the typewriter in front of him. He was a writer.

Blessing or curse, he was a scribbler, a farmer of words, sweat on his brow and calluses on his fingers from the keys of his preferred weapon. He was an idea man, a word man. Jack Marshall, his boss, was sympathetic and tried to understand the affliction.

Dachau for Warner and *Diminished Fifth*, also with Warner, were ticketed for the tombs. They were somebody else's property now. He didn't have the originals, hadn't been allowed to keep the carbons.

Roy Cohn had been exposed and, like his play *Diminished Fifth* and his screenplay about Dachau for Jack Warner, the country wasn't ready to hear and confront the reality that their own government courted the enemy for secrets. It was a new war, with new idealists. There will be deterrence men and policy men with Harvard degrees and Fifth Avenue suits. They'll make decisions, and the decisions will in turn make them. There will be optimists, most of them misguided. There will be opportunists, men like Roy Cohn and Joseph McCarthy.

Ethel Rosenberg might have been guilty of something, but she had not deserved the electric chair on a hot June night. The Kennedys, unlike the husband and wife in his play, had the means to care for their daughter. Rosemary Kennedy didn't deserve a lobotomy.

The Prime Minister probably didn't deserve the contempt-of-court charges, or the time in prison. He'd been made an example of the price paid for defiance, despite his legal right not to incriminate himself.

Genovese was the future of crime in America, and it made Walker ill, but it would be hypocritical of him to criticize since the Company had done its share of shady things, such as manipulate the outcome the election in Italy in '48. The Company was ready to destroy yet another election in Iran, possibly reduce a country to subsistence and religious extremists.

Anastasia was an enforcer, and such men live as long as their benefactor does. If The Prime Minister retired or Don Vitone struck first, with the blessing of those who succumbed to the lure of money from narcotics, Albert Anastasia's name in the book of life would end.

Jack Marshall had a career, and Walker freelanced for Jack Warner. He had his house, Grable, and his typewriter. He had steady money. He worked when Jack called him.

After he'd finished his meal, he washed the one dish, the utensils, and the skillet, and cleaned the stove. He poured out the last of the coffee. He dawdled another hour away. He would write later. For now, he would read.

He read until he wanted Bulldog beer. He opened the refrigerator again. Within the white square of cold light, among the bottles of beer, he picked the coldest one when he heard a sound.

Somebody was at the door.

The first rap was light. The second set was insistent, demanding.

He pulled on the wood and opened the door to a face with soft worried eyes. She was wearing a dress, all cotton and dazzling floral print. Her smile was pained but polite, and she held down her skirt so the wind would not lift it. Red and pink roses breathed and settled down on her skin.

"Leslie?"

"May I come in?"

He held the door open and stepped aside. A white Saratoga Club Coupe was in his driveway. She came in and ungloved.

"I wasn't expecting you."

The screen door closed with a slap. He had left the main door ajar.

"I should've called first. I'm sorry."

"I was about to have a beer. Want something to drink?"

"Beer? It's not even noon." She looked for a place to set down her small purse. He pointed to the nook and told her to have a seat. She put her handbag on the counter and sat down. He sensed nervous energy. Her eyes wouldn't focus on anything.

"You look like you could use something stronger than beer."

"A beer would be nice, but it won't solve a thing."

"Tell you what. I'll get you one and I'll listen."

"Sure. On second thought, no. A whiskey instead, please."

"But it's not even noon."

"Just pour, and please don't judge."

Walker put down his beer. He identified all the good citizens in his cabinet and fished out the correct type of glass. Her handbag faced him. He could bet good money on what was sleeping inside. She noticed and said, "Beretta 950."

"Twenty-two, accurate up close but painful to shoot."

"Not if you use a light grip. Twenty-five caliber. Nine rounds. How about that drink."

He hoisted up a bottle of the good stuff. "As the lady wishes."

"And double for you if you want to sit at the adult table. Beer is for kids."

She knocked hers back, squinted, and shook her head in response to the mule's kick.

"That was good," she said.

"Another?"

She tapped the table, like she was playing blackjack.

He tipped the bottle again. "Care to talk now?"

She slammed it back and scowled.

"You take your medicine like a good girl."

"Knock off the hardboiled chatter."

"You said you wanted to talk. I said I was willing to listen. Talk."

Walker took her glass. Her hand went over his. He let the glass and bottle stay.

"Vera knows."

"Vera knows what?"

"About us."

"What us? How?"

She swiveled the purse around. She took out the gun. He went to examine it. "Don't," she said while she rummaged, "and don't call it a mouse gun. Here it is."

The envelope was simple, plain, and white. Leslie's name Maggie was written on the outside. A graphologist would describe the cursive as neat and unpretentious. "Read it."

"Why don't you just tell me what it says?"

Leslie took back the envelope. He sipped some of his beer. He waited for an answer.

"But the letter says it all."

"I'm not reading it, Leslie. It was written to you."

"The night I came into your room. Remember it?"

Walker put down the beer. This is what had made him swear off women at different times in his life. The rhetorical question killed off half of Shakespeare's characters.

"I remember."

Leslie held up the envelope.

"Vera found the bracelet, the one I wore around my ankle, in your room."

"What was she doing in my room?"

The beer, though nice and cold, had lost its appeal.

"She must've gone in after she'd come home from the last rehearsal."

"I know when. I want to know why she was in my room," he said.

She flinched at the tone in his answer.

"I was in bed," she said.

"You were in your bed, and I was in mine."

Her mouth opened when she heard the distinction in his voice.

"She must've seen the whiskey bottle on the vanity. She wrote that when she was returning the bottle to your room. You were asleep. She stepped on the bracelet on the carpet."

"You left the door between our rooms open?"

"I must have. It's all a blur."

"I bet it was. I hope you at least remember me."

"Of course I do, and don't be cruel. I was drinking."

"So, I was a lapse in judgement?"

"Stop it," she said. "You know that's not true."

"You were saying…a blur."

"Tania had visited that night. I was drinking your whiskey when she'd arrived."

"Busy night…first Tania; then me; and then Vera."

"Vera never said a word about the charm. I found the letter this morning. She was upset."

"I bet. She'll be more upset when she finds one of her cars is missing."

"She was devastated when I told her that I'd lost the bracelet."

"We both know she's upset about more than a lost trinket, Leslie."

There was a coldness to his words and behind his eyes. Here he was the good guy, the decent guy, and the kind of guy a woman called in the middle of the night to discuss headaches and heartaches. The fixer. The sap. He had to get one cheap shot in since there was no dignity left.

"And you're not upset that the entire time the play ran she had your charm bracelet tucked away in her pocket? Not upset that you said it was lost and that she probably watched you crawl around the room on your hands and knees?"

He couldn't resist laying on the spite.

"You're mean but yes, she watched me retrace my steps for the charm."

"You could've just said that you were in my room for a conversation or to borrow the bottle, but you didn't."

"She was suspicious the moment she'd seen the whiskey bottle on the vanity and the communicating door open."

"I don't want to hear more of this. Vera is your affair, not mine."

"What about you and Tania?" Leslie's eyes glinted, a poor attempt at expressing outrage.

"If you talked to Tania that night, then you know damn well nothing happened."

He felt more tired than when he'd come home from the flight.

"May I stay?" she asked.

"What…here?"

"Yes, here."

"You know you have to deal with Vera at some point. You have the woman's car."

Leslie looked over her shoulder. The car was still there.

"Are you asking me to make a choice?" she asked.

"If I have to ask, it isn't a decision, is it?"

The drumming started up. Walker went across the room and looked for his friend the woodpecker among the trees. Leslie had come up behind Walker. Together they watched him thump on the tree until the bird seemed aware that he was being watched. He turned his head and the eye blinked.

"Is he new?" she asked.

"He's my writing partner. It's like he uses Morse code when he talks to me."

The bird blinked once more and returned to drumming on his tree.

"What do you think he's saying?" she asked.

"He offers the best advice when it comes to writing."

"What advice is that?" Leslie said as she looked at the woodpecker, who stopped long enough to stare at her again. The bird blinked before he resumed his knocking sound.

Walker let go of the curtain. "Fewer words, bigger impact."

Leslie walked to the sink and washed her glass. She then went to the refrigerator and helped herself to a bottle of milk and other things. She sought out two glasses from the cupboard. She moved about the kitchen as if she had known it for a decade.

"What are you doing?" he asked as he came over to the nook, the customer at the counter in his own home.

"I'm making you lunch."

"You're making me lunch?" he asked, and sat down where she'd been sitting before.

"I'm making us lunch."

"Us?"

The corners of her mouth lifted into a vague smile as she peeled some cold cuts. She asked whether he wanted another beer.

The bird outside continued to peck away at the bark of the tree, thumping and drumming an insistent rhythm, a possible distress call or a reminder that there was writing to be done.

He watched her. He remembered their meal together in Vienna, five years before. They'd shared a meal, a bed, and she'd handed him a box of pastries and called it breakfast before she closed the door in his face.

As a writer, he never believed in fairy tales, disliked cheap romances, but he understood from the war how a love letter could have been lost or delayed. As the bird outside hammered the tree, the question Walker had forgotten the answer to was how to read a love letter that had walked in, delayed but now delivered.

The Devil in the Details, An Afterword

We've all seen it in a movie or on television. A man or a woman is on the witness stand. The attorney bombards the person with an unrelenting barrage of questions, perhaps to make the person cave and confess, or to undermine their previous testimony. Suddenly, the individual invokes the Fifth Amendment and says the iconic words, "I refuse to answer on the grounds that it may incriminate me."

It makes for good drama but it's not realistic.

Rather than say it's suspension of disbelief, call it deliberate avoidance of procedure. Lillian Hellman, whom I mentioned in the conversation between Jack and Frank Costello, learned about the subtleties of the Fifth Amendment from her lawyer, Joseph Rauh, when she was subpoenaed in 1952.

The Fifth Amendment, as part of the Bill of Rights from 1791, is connected and linked to nine amendments, all of which were created to establish essential rights and liberties; more importantly, they are safeguards to protect citizens from governmental overreach. In spirit, the Fifth Amendment protects both the accused and the innocent. In practice, pleading the Fifth prompts an adverse inference. The jury and those in the courtroom are likely to conclude that the witness is guilty or hiding something.

Why is that? The answer is psychology, a matter of perception.

The American legal system, which we inherited from the British, is adversarial, meaning that the judge is neutral, and both precedent and procedure determine the rules of engagement for the attorneys. The jury is, in effect, an audience; lawyers, like writers, argue the most compelling narrative to achieve a desired verdict.

In Griffin Fariello's *Red Scare: Memories of the American Inquisition*, he discussed strategy. Lillian Hellman's attorney, Joseph Rauh, explained to her that her amendment right was waived the minute she discussed *anything* about herself. In essence, don't talk. The perception is that of an uncooperative witness; and, given the era, Hellman's gender amplified animosity.

Rauh's solution was to have Hellman compose a letter to the committee that had subpoenaed her. She asked them—knowing their answer—not to ask her about other people. She then held a press conference, saying that she'd plead the Fifth because she didn't want to lose her amendment right. The strategy was preemptive, and the perception was, I daresay, patriotic.

On the day of her testimony, Rauh's associate circulated a copy of the letter to the press in the courtroom, much to the chagrin of the committee. Freedom of speech and press are First Amendment rights.

At the end of the meeting between Frank Costello and Jack, I had Frank duplicate the questions and answers Rauh and Hellman practiced, the exchange that would've created a "diminished Fifth." In theory, the witness answers questions, appears cooperative, the protection inherent within the Fifth Amendment isn't waived, and the lawyer is forced to move on to another line of questioning. In reality, the circulation of Hellman's letter on her day in court resulted in the committee dismissing Hellman.

As the saying goes, do not attempt this on your own. Hellmann won, on a sleight-of-hand technicality, but her companion Dashiell Hammett did not.

The conversation between Frank and Jack also discusses the diminished fifth, the musical term, or what Frank's lawyer and scholars call the "devil's music."

Humans are hardwired for structure. We hunger for all the parts to come together in a cohesive and coherent manner, especially in the arts. We seek resolution, symmetry and unity, a way to form our own narrative out of what the artist has created and what we experience, either intellectually or emotionally, or both.

In literature and music, we want Good to triumph over Evil, or glimpse some form of justice. We'd like to see all the threads tucked and all the buttons buttoned. We've learned to accept open endings, but only with some reluctance. With music, our ears discern patterns, like our eyes and mind do in reading. Music excels at creating tension, and we take pleasure in resolution.

The Devil's Music is based on the appearance of the tritone, specifically a sound that won't resolve itself, a sound that splits an octave exactly in half. Like the devil, who is known by many names, the diminished fifth has also been called the flattened fifth, or the augmented fourth. This discordant note is dark and upsets us, disturbs our innate sense of right or wrong when we hear it. The diminished fifth unnerves us because it inverts harmony and falls a half-tone short of being a perfect fifth.

I could try and write pages explaining musical theory and blunder why and how consonance pleases us and dissonance jars us. I could write about pitch and intervals, vibration, octaves, and scales, but I'd rather have your ears do the work. The tritone is scattered throughout classical, pop and rock music, and movie scores. It always signals a restless and sinister theme. When we look for examples of the devil's music or the diminished fifth, you'll notice that the devil seems to prefer entrances.

The opening of Jimi Hendrix's "Purple Haze."

Black Sabbath's intro to their song "Black Sabbath."

The first stanza of "The Star-Spangled Banner" has—wait for it—five instances of a fifth. The truth is, as "The Star-Spangled Banner" proves, their presence makes it difficult to sing in key.

This last example brings up another interesting point. There is a myth that the Church had banned the diminished fifth, or threatened composers. Not true. The tritone was not banned in medieval music because it does indeed occur in several compositions.

Satan's predilection for entrances suggests that evil is ever-present in our lives, that the Devil is in the room, and he asks us a question. We choose to answer him or not. Free will, like the Fifth Amendment, is our right.

The inclusion of Robert Kennedy may seem an audacious choice since he is in our national pantheon of martyrs. The truth is I presented a much softer version of RFK than how the man acted in life, at this point in his career. The RFK of the 1950s, when he acted in a professional capacity, was arrogant, headstrong, and tenacious, though he paled in comparison to the ruthless and relentless Roy Cohn.

The two men knew each other and worked together for Senator Joseph McCarthy. I resurrect this forgotten detail, just like I remind readers of *The Devil's Music* that McCarthy was godfather to Robert's daughter Kathleen, and that Robert's father, Joseph Kennedy, called him the runt of the family and subjected Robert's sister Rosemary to a botched lobotomy.

Contrary to popular belief, John F. Kennedy was not the likely choice to fulfill his father's political ambitions. Bedridden for long stretches in his childhood, treated for ulcers and other intestinal maladies, the young John Kennedy was no stranger to chronic pain and to pharmacopoeia. Like FDR, the Kennedy family hid his numerous health problems throughout his life. Chronic back pain plagued him in college and a wartime injury exacerbated it. I should note that it was his father's political clout that got JFK into the navy.

In 1954, he underwent a spinal surgery—one of many—that almost killed him. He'd write *Profiles of Courage* that year while convalescing, though I think the title should've been *A Portrait in Pain*. He would become dependent on opioid injections and a back brace, which his wife called "his Linus blanket."

The brothers Kennedy, John and Robert, could not have been more different, the inverse of each other. John's public persona exuded charisma, while behind closed doors he was moody, likely because of his ailments and pain. Robert was warm and affectionate in private; ferocious, if not unwavering in public. Ted Sorenson, advisor and speechwriter to JFK, described Robert as "militant, aggressive, intolerant, opinionated, somewhat shallow in his convictions…more like his father than his brother."

While beset with tragedies and flaws of Shakespearian proportions, the irony of the Kennedy legacy is that death compelled each brother to find his own way. Joe Kennedy Jr.'s death made JFK possible, and John's death transformed Robert's character, in public and private. His chances for the presidency obliterated, Ted Kennedy would become a legislative force, The Lion in the Senate. The metamorphosis of Robert Kennedy, from the Attorney General with a Teddy Roosevelt stick in hand, to a man who saw poverty and racism as the great social ills is no less mesmerizing. The arc of this transformation became visible only after his brother's assassination in 1963. The growth in Robert's world view is palpable in his own letters and speeches, and I recommend reading *RFK: His Words for Our Times*.

If Robert Kennedy had one fatal flaw, it was that he suffered from dichotomous thinking, seeing only black and white, and no shades of gray. This is a fault that's not conducive to a political career, and we'll never know what kind of politician Robert Kennedy would have made, but we do know that his inability to accept gray created enemies for him and, by extension, his brother. In 1957, with John at his side, initially, Robert tackled organized crime. Like J. Edgar Hoover, Kennedy was not above extralegal measures in his pursuit of organized crime figures. He ordered wiretaps and surveillance. In the public arena, he sparred with numerous mafiosi, but he is forever associated with one opponent, Teamster Jimmy Hoffa.

RFK's assault on organized crime in the labor unions became an obsession after he had distanced himself from Senator McCarthy. The precedent for Kennedy's investigatory committee is with Senator Estes Kefauver's United States Senate Special Committee to Investigate Crime in Interstate Commerce in 1950 and 1951. In a barnburner of a tour that included hearings in fourteen cities and testimony from more than 600 witnesses, Americans learned about the mafia from their television sets. They would meet Frank Costello, a man who did his best to avoid public scrutiny.

Historians say that the inspiration for Vito Corleone in Francis Ford Coppola's *The Godfather* is an amalgam of different mafiosi, namely Joe Bonnano and Joe Profaci, and Carlo Gambino. Like Bonnano, Vito did not want his son to enter the "family business," and, like Profaci, Corleone used an olive oil company as a front to his criminal enterprise. While Carlo Gambino had wanted his "family" to become completely legitimate, the intent for organized crime to be legal was the brainchild of Arnold Rothstein, Meyer Lansky, and Charles Luciano. The Jewish Rothstein and Lansky are the true architects of organized crime. Luciano created the organizational schema of Five Families, a hierarchy and reporting structure, territories, and a Commission, in order to avoid the descent into chaos and violence that came with feuds.

As for who was most like Vito Corleone, my money is on Frank Costello. Marlon Brando's Vito and the real Costello spoke with a raspy voice and they both used their hands when speaking. Both Vito and Frank were against narcotics, and both men trace their power to their connections to politicians and the legal system. Costello sought to fulfill Rothstein's vision of a legal empire. Vito Genovese wanted Costello's power and prestige, and he was attracted to the money that narcotics promised.

The coda not written in this novel is how that struggle between Costello and Genovese ended. In May of 1957, Vito had tried to have Frank Costello assassinated but the bullet had grazed Frank's head. Costello took the hint and retired.

With Costello out of the frame, Genovese ordered a contract on Albert Anastasia. Anastasia was shot and killed in his barber's chair at the Park-Sheraton on October 25, 1957. Genovese's success would be short-lived. He convened a meeting to discuss the organization and territories and promote Carlo Gambino as the replacement to Anastasia. However, the onslaught of luxury cars converging on a house in upstate New York triggered a raid and ruined Genovese's reputation. He had escaped arrest. The dragnet would result in a who's-who in the mafia, which Hoover could no longer deny the existence of.

The US government tried to deport Frank but failed on a technicality. Costello would die of heart attack in 1973. Vito Genovese assumed power of what had been Luciano's family. He was called to testify before the McClellan hearings, which I'm certain Robert Kennedy watched. Genovese invoked his Fifth Amendment over a hundred times. In a dubious case, Genovese was convicted in 1959 of personally buying and trying to import heroin from a Puerto Rican drug dealer. The idea that a mob boss would be directly involved in a narcotics deal seems too on the nose. Sentenced to fifteen years, Genovese tried to run his empire from a cell. He died in prison in 1969.

Acknowledgments

This book, first written in 2012 and revised more times than I care to count, owes a debt of gratitude to my first editor, Dave King, a frequent contributor to Writer Unboxed, who read the novel and offered both suggestions and praise. I encourage writers to consult his *Self-Editing for Fiction Writers* for advice and strategies.

I'm grateful to my publisher, Level Best Books, and my editor, Shawn Reilly Simmons, for their continued faith in my work. Thank you, Dames of Detection.

I'm thankful for the kindness and consideration of my proofreaders and editors, Dean Hunt and Deb Well, and to Tina deBellegarde, author of the Batavia-on-Hudson Mystery Series, for reading a draft of this novel, and for her comments and continued friendship.

As always, nothing but gratitude to my fellow Level Best authors, and to friends of the pen and keyboard in crime fiction, the best and most supportive community around for a writer.

GV

About the Author

Gabriel Valjan is a member of ITW, MWA, and a lifetime member of Sisters in Crime. He is the author of The Company Files and the Shane Cleary Mysteries with Level Best Books. His work has been nominated for the Agatha, Anthony, and the Silver Falchion awards. Gabriel received the 2021 Macavity Award for Best Short Story and the Shamus Award for Best PI Novel in 2024. He is a regular contributor to the blog *Criminal Minds* and an active supporter of writers on social media. Gabriel lives in Boston, and answers to a tuxedo cat named Munchkin.

AUTHOR WEBSITE:
  gabrielvaljan.com

SOCIAL MEDIA HANDLES:
  Bluesky: @gvaljan.bsky.social
  IG: @gabrielvaljan

Also by Gabriel Valjan

THE COMPANY FILES
The Naming Game
The Good Man

SHANE CLEARY MYSTERIES
The Big Lie
Liar's Dice
Hush Hush
Symphony Road
Dirty Old Town